The Villa Violetta

By the same author

The Heart of the Rose
Rooks Nest
Kindred Spirits
A Time to Love
Generations
Ghosts at Cockrow
Portrait of Maud
Time Will Tell
Familiar Acts
Swifter Wings than Time
Daughter of Haworth
Family Snapshots
No Time Like the Present

The Villa Violetta

JUNE BARRACLOUGH

ROBERT HALE · LONDON

© June Barraclough 1997
First published in Great Britain 1997

ISBN 0 7090 6155 2

Robert Hale Limited
Clerkenwell House
Clerkenwell Green
London EC1R 0HT

2 4 6 8 10 9 7 5 3 1

Photoset in North Wales by
Derek Doyle & Associates, Mold, Flintshire.
Printed in Great Britain by
St Edmundsbury Press, Bury St Edmunds, Suffolk.
Bound by WBC Book Manufacturers Limited,
Bridgend, Mid-Glamorgan.

Contents

. . . Il giardino abbandonato
Serba ancora per noi qualche sentiero
Ti dirò come sia dolce il mistero
Che vela certe cose del passato. . . .
                    Gabriele D'Annunzio

PROLOGUE

Milan
1957

. . .'but when from a long-distant past nothing subsists,
after people are dead, after things are broken and scat-
tered, taste and smell alone, more fragile but more endur-
ing, more insubstantial, more persistent, more faithful,
remain for a long time poised, like souls remembering,
waiting, hoping, amid the ruins of all the rest; and bear
unflinchingly, in the tiny and almost impalpable drop of
their essence, the vast structure of recollection. . .'
Proust: *A La Recherche du Temps Perdu*

She opened her eyes.

Everything was dark, so she held up her arm to look at her luminous watch, which she always kept on in bed. For some reason it was not on her wrist and she felt too tired to look for it.

She must have fallen asleep again, for the next time she opened her eyes there was a blurry line of light seeping through a crack at the top of the curtain. Sometimes when you wake in a strange place you don't know where you are and need a few moments to get your bearings. It was like that for her then. But things did *not* fall into place. She had a recollection of a sort of dream she'd been having between looking for her watch and then waking again, but all she could remember of it was the image of a church, and then the sound of water lapping near a little boathouse. How did she know that church? Why had she dreamed of it – and what

---

9

had it to do with the sound of water?

As the room grew lighter, she knew she had never woken there before. She lay now wide awake, wondering where she was. Where did she usually wake up? She could not remember. Panic seized her as she realized that not only did she not know where she was but could not remember *who* she was.

She sat up in bed and tried to calm herself. If she knew that she didn't know who or where she was, at least that was knowing *something*!

Which must mean that she knew other things?

Her mind stuck on this thought as she tried to get out of bed. Her limbs felt heavy and it was only with a big effort that she finally heaved herself out. There was a white rug under her feet and she saw that the curtains were red and that the sun shining through them was now casting red splashes on to it, like blood.

She sat on the edge of the bed and, with an even greater effort that caused a dull pain in her mind, went over what she did know.

One: She did not think she was in a room that was familiar to her.

Two: She had remembered that she usually wore a watch in bed, otherwise she would not have lifted up her arm to look at her wrist. She did remember doing that, had expected that the time would be telling itself on that small round dial.

Three: She felt sure she was a woman.

She put her feet on the ground. They met something soft – a pair of feathery mules. She looked over the room and saw a neatly folded dress on a chair under the window. She had been right that she was a female: that was something encouraging. . . .

Just for a tiny pinpoint of time a whole life was in her head before flashing away again.

She went over to the window. The outer shutters were only

half closed so she leaned out and saw a small balcony with a wrought iron balustrade.

Feeling just a little less weary, she went back for the mules, put them on, and then ventured out on to the balcony. Outside, the light looked like that of a bright early autumn morning. The view was of a long descending avenue, pave-mented, and with tall houses of five or six storeys on each side. Where had she seen houses like this before? She searched her memory and all that came up was a kind of shape – she could not call it a memory – the shape of a wide straight boulevard that seemed to end in the church she had dreamed of, before continuing into the distance at a slight angle. 'The real avenue ended at the church,' she said aloud.

She heard her own voice and it sounded croaky and faint. She sat down at the head of the bed and for the first time noticed a telephone. She knew it was a telephone. Her memory was serving her perfectly well for *things*, if not for *facts* about herself. Dare she pick it up? There was only one number on it: 39.

Was she in a hotel? What day of the week was it? What time was it?

She'd get dressed and then pick up the telephone and ask the time. Yes, that's what she'd do.

She wavered a moment, then walked over to the chair and looked at the clothes to see if they gave her a clue. There were a pair of navy blue cotton knickers and a petticoat folded under the dress, which was also blue. Under the chair lay a pair of blue sandals. They must belong to her. Only one thing for it, get dressed. Slowly she pulled on the clothes. They fitted perfectly. So did the sandals.

She saw a door in the far corner of the room so she opened it and switched on the light she found on the wall. On the left, a towel rail; on the right, a bath and bidet; facing her, a wash basin. Above the basin, a mirror. Dare she look in it? No. She would leave that until she'd tried the telephone.

She beat a retreat but left the bathroom light on. She'd count back from ten before picking up the 'phone. . . . Nine, eight, seven . . . three, two – one!

She took the instrument off its cradle and put it to her ear. It crackled for a moment and then a woman's voice said

'*Pronto?*'

Without thinking, without even being aware, she replied:

'*Chè hora è, per favore?*'

'*Undice, signora. Le prende una colazione en la camera?*'

'*Si – si, per favore – caffè e panini,*' she replied.

'*Numero trenta-nove?*'

'*Si, grazie.*'

'*Aspette cinque minuti,*' said the voice.

The line went dead and she put down the phone. She was trembling. This conversation had been in a language that was familiar to her, but was not, she knew, her native tongue. So she was abroad! She was making some progress!

Before she returned to the bathroom to look in the mirror she went to the cavernous wardrobe opposite the bed. There was a suitcase at the bottom, but nothing hanging up above.

How had she got here? How was she to get home? This room was not home.

She dragged the case out and on to the bed and then opened it. There were a few books on top, and a sponge bag and some clothes underneath, some summer dresses, and at the bottom a soft silk scarf, apparently wrapped around something solid – another book perhaps? For the moment, she couldn't have said why, she would leave it undisturbed. She opened one of the other books: *Guide to Piedmont and Lombardy* it said on the jacket above the picture of a lake. There was no name on the fly-leaf of the book.

The picture affected her strangely. She didn't want to look at it and yet it held her gaze. There was a kind of pain in her mind. If the brain could feel sick, this was what it would feel like.

She took out the sponge-bag, closed the case, and went into the bathroom. She bent her head down and half closed her eyes as she walked towards the basin with the bag. Then she opened them just a little and raised her head. In the mirror she saw the pale face of a young woman with rings under her eyes and greasy hair.

Horrible!

She must wash her hair. She found some shampoo on the bathroom shelf, so she washed and rinsed her hair and rubbed it with a towel hanging on the rail.

A chambermaid knocked and brought in her breakfast on a tray as she was drying her hair.

She sat down to drink her coffee. She was not hungry, even though she felt empty.

Had she any money to pay this hotel? She looked again in the suitcase and found no purse. No purse either in the jacket she found hanging on the door.

She was alone and she didn't know who she was.

Ought she to go to a police station? She must be English, for a voice inside her said: 'Go to the British Consulate,' as if the thoughts were thinking her, rather than she them. She washed her hands and face and went back to combing her hair. There was another knock at the door. She froze.

'Flora, it's me. How are you this morning?' said a man's voice in Italian.

Flora. Was that her name?

She would have to dissemble. Somehow she didn't want whoever was at the door to know she had lost her memory. Even if she were Flora, it would not help.

'I'm just washing my hair,' she replied, also in Italian.

'I'll come again in half an hour then. I've checked and your plane goes at three. It's an hour to the airport.'

She said, as though she knew everything about herself: 'I can't find my purse.'

'It's all right. I took your handbag up with me by mistake last night and didn't want to wake you when I discovered it. Your passport's in it. Sorry, I forgot to bring it back just now. Don't worry, you shall have them both back as soon as you are ready. Have you eaten?'

'I had some coffee – I wasn't hungry.'

'I'll be back in half an hour,' the voice said again.

Who was he? He had sounded quite friendly.

Why had he been carrying her passport and handbag? Why hadn't she had them with her?

She felt very shaky, left half the bread on the breakfast tray. She'd have to open the door in half an hour to whoever he was and confront him. Would she give herself away? Would the sight of him bring everything back, including herself?

More important, as she sat drying her hair, was why she had forgotten everything. Had she been in an accident? As she sat there she began to try to remember other things – not personal ones but things she might know that were not connected with herself. If she approached her memory sideways, perhaps something would come back?

She let her mind drift, pretending she was quite normal. It must be the same old brain inside her head, mustn't it? The one that had been there for however many years her self had been there. How many years was that?

She thought: in the mirror I looked about thirty – but maybe I am ill, and that would make me look older than I really am. I feel a hundred!

She banished thoughts of herself and her age and her face, breathed in deeply and waited to see what her mind came up with. Nothing happened for a time, no mental picture drifted into her head.

Then a line of words provided by whatever was 'I', began

to go round her brain.

English words, English poetry: *The days of our youth are the days of our glory. . . . Whither have fled the glory and the dream. . . . Fare thee well! And if for ever, still for ever, fare thee well. . . .*

Those and other remembered lines were unbearably sad.

She stood up and began to prowl round the room. She needed something. What was it? She was looking for something that she usually had in her hand when she read these poems that she knew so well by heart.

She needed a cigarette! That was it. Her body was telling her that she smoked.

Her cigarettes would be in her handbag, wouldn't they? and the man who had come for her had that.

There was a knock at the door again. Had half an hour passed whilst she recited romantic poetry to herself?

This time she could not avoid opening the door. She needed that cigarette.

'Flora?'

She went to the door and opened it.

A tall elderly man with a slight stoop and a worried look on his face was standing at the door, a handbag on his arm.

'Come in,' she said, and thought her voice sounded husky. She had absolutely no idea who he was. She said, 'I was just remembering my favourite poems and reciting them to myself.'

He came in: 'Are you sure you are all right? It's better for you to leave today – but if you are still too tired I dare say I could get them to change your ticket to tomorrow.'

She supposed she must sound a bit odd talking straight away to him about poems. 'I'm all right,' she answered, thinking that must have been the biggest lie she had ever told in her life.

'We can eat at the airport,' he said.

She plunged in. 'Is anyone meeting me when I land?'

'I told you last night what I'd do and I've done it already. I got your friend's name from the address book in your bag, and wired him – Signor Thornton. He'll be there, I'm sure. Then you will be all right. From what you've told me I'm sure he'll look after you—'

'Thank you,' she said feebly. 'You are very kind.' She was at a loss.

'You can go home and forget all about everything,' he said.

'I think I already have!' she said, and he looked at her quizzically. She added: 'I need a cigarette.'

'I'm sorry. I remembered too late they were in your bag. Here.'

She took the handbag. The passport in it would reveal her full name, and the address book might tell her who *he* was. He seemed to know her quite well but she was sure he had never been more than a friend to her. How could she be so sure? She supposed you must just have a sixth sense that operated even when you had lost your memory.

'I forgot to give you your watch,' he said. 'You dropped it in the lift last night.'

She thought, I seem to have been *non compos mentis* last night as well! She thanked him and put a sensible-looking watch on to her left wrist, knowing as she did so that she must be right-handed.

She couldn't immediately look in her bag for the passport – he'd have thought it a bit odd – but she opened it, found some Italian cigarettes and then scrabbled about for some matches. 'Here,' said the man and brought a lighter out of his pocket. So he too was a smoker.

'You agree to a snack at the airport?' he asked. 'I've settled your bill.'

'Oh, can you just give me another fifteen minutes, to – to get my hair dry?' she asked him.

Why should he pay her bill? Had she any money in her

bag? Had she even a purse? She must look at the passport and the address book.

'Very well. I'll be down in the foyer – I can take your case for you now if you like?'

'No, I can manage – I expect there's a lift, isn't there?'

'We came up in it last night.'

'Oh, yes.'

He went away. She shut the door, sat on the bed and opened the blue handbag. She seemed to like the colour blue. She found the passport and opened it with trepidation. There was a photograph, and the name: Flora Mary Russell, who was apparently born in Lancashire. But that did not help! There was a purse too, and a handkerchief and a bottle of scent. She opened the purse first. There were several thousand-lira notes in it.

Then she opened the address-book at the first page on the right where people write their own names. **F.M. Russell** it said, but she knew that already. Who was the man who had brought her things? Perhaps she might find him in the book, but how would she know it was him?

She hadn't much time – her hair had dried and she must go down to the foyer. She riffled through the pages as though she were shuffling cards. Where should she begin? Look up other Russells perhaps? She did so. Nothing – but probably she would know her parents' address if she had parents still alive, hadn't needed to write it down. Then she had another thought. The man had said: 'your friend Signor Thornton.' She looked up Thornton and there it was: John Thornton, 37d Belsize Park Square London NW3.

She tried and tried to imagine number 37d Belsize Park Square but nothing came into her head. She felt panicky. She took a deep breath. She had to trust the man who had brought her here – wherever she was – and so she just had to believe that she would arrive in London and be met by this John

Thornton who would recognize her at the other end even if she didn't know him from Adam.

There were two pages in the little book for each name, and at the end just one page for X, Y and Z.

Perhaps she knew a Mr Zweig or a Mr Zuckerman, names that came unbidden into her head. She turned to the last page and saw only one name: Bruno Xavier Leopardi, with, underneath: Villa Violetta, Lago di Como.

It was as though something, some obscure muscle, suddenly moved inside her. It wasn't that she suddenly knew who she was – Flora Russell was still as mysterious as she had been before – but she knew that the name Xavier had been important to her.

Was it the man downstairs? She did not think so. She was sure this man would know who Xavier was. She would try to introduce the name into their conversation if she could.

She put her address-book away and went downstairs. A taxi was waiting for them. The hotel receptionist smiled and said '*Arrivederci*' as though nothing had happened. To her and the rest of the world Flora didn't suppose anything had. Nothing happened either on the way to the airport. The man was silent and she didn't know how to start asking him questions. It was a drive of only about half an hour and then she saw it, saw the airport from the taxi window and it said: MILANO – MALPENSA.

She thought: the address in the book had said Como. She would ask him a geographical question.

'How far is Como from Milan?' she asked, trying to sound as innocent as possible.

'Oh, about 75 kilometres,' he said.

What else could she ask him: Why couldn't she say: 'By the way, I think I've lost my memory. Could you please inform me who I am and what I am doing here?'

She wasn't hungry but he made her eat half a pizza at the

snack bar. She drank a glass of Chianti and that made her feel
a bit better. She was just about to say something like: My
memory's rather hazy about the past week, when he turned
to her and said: 'Don't blame yourself, Flora, nothing is your
fault.'

'Oh,' she said. 'Isn't it?'

He looked at her, nonplussed.

'Please write to say you've arrived safely,' he said. Here
was her opportunity.

'Where shall I write?' she asked him.

'Yes, that is a point,' he said. 'I shall most likely be at the
Como flat.'

'I can't remember its address,' she said. 'Will you write it
down for me?'

'It'll be in your address-book,' he said.

'Write it down for me again – I feel like starting a new
address-book when I get home. Here on this paper napkin.
It'll remind me of Milan and of you!'

Obediently he took out a biro, wrote something very carefully and handed it to her.

'Ludovico Leopardi,' she read, and an address in Como
which she certainly did not remember.

'Thanks, Ludovico,' she said, and pocketed it.

'You needn't be so formal,' he said. 'What Xavier does is his
business. He's a grown man. But I do object when outsiders
are made to suffer.'

Obviously she ought to have called him by a pet name.

'Sorry, Ludo,' she said. 'I'm just not up to thinking straight
today.'

'You seem to have made a good recovery after yesterday,'
he said. 'But you must have had a difficult time and you need
to rest. Keep in touch with me, won't you?'

'Thank you – you have been very kind,' she said. 'I'll write
to you, I promise – but perhaps not straightaway.'

He looked gratified but still very worried as they got up and found the check-in point and then the place to send off her luggage.

She was ready to go to the departure lounge. She felt sad. What exactly was she leaving? They said goodbye, and shook hands, and he walked away. Then he turned back and came up to her again as she stood there, and said in a low urgent voice:

'Don't come back, Flora! Be happy! Don't come back!'

At last she was sitting in the plane, and soon they were flying over the Alps. She felt grubby and sweaty but remembered you could get little sachets of cologne from the toilette at the back of aeroplanes. But she felt too exhausted to bother to get up. Instead, she took out a scent bottle she found in her hand-bag. It was then, as she sniffed the perfume before tipping the bottle – it was called *Belladgio*, and it smelled of carnations – then that, all at once, with a painful mental jolt, she knew who Flora was, knew why she had found herself in Milan with Ludo Leopardi, and remembered, with a terrible sense of loss and anguish and anxiety, everything and everyone she had left behind her.

She remembered also that it was her journal that was wrapped in the silk scarf at the bottom of her suitcase, the suitcase which was at present in the hold of the aircraft.

As soon as she got back she must read over what she had just remembered having written two nights ago.

There was however nothing she could do at present but sail along in the sky.

Until London she would have to wait.

ONE

The Violet Rooms

1939

'. . . a scent can recall to us more immediately than any other sense the specific impression of an event or a place, however distant in time . . .'
Schopenhauer: *The World as Will and Idea.*

In summer, the deep lake usually lay dark blue, calm and unruffled. This was deceptive, for sudden thunderstorms could start up and crackle like gunfire in its valley, tear the branches off trees and rip up the lake waters, turning them in a trice into heaving grey sheets. Less often, colder, unseasonable weather would arrive when rain might fall for several days. The tourists would sit dispiritedly then in the covered arcades of the little towns that littered its shores, waiting for their holiday paradise to return.

Fortunately, summers were more often warm and bright, though by the lakeside the sun was rarely too hot or too glaring. The lake would at such times thank the weather, its benevolent despot, and return a reflection of its calm blue skies. In autumn, the season most loved by the local inhabitants, the lake was green and grey, matching the gentle conifer-clad slopes that fell like long skirts to its waters, under misty skies. Behind the lower hills that encircled the lake was a land of small mountains, none much above four thousand feet and most only a thousand feet high.

The Villa Carolina had been built at the beginning of the previous century on the western edge of the lake, only half a mile or so from one of the spots where, a little later on, English artists, writers, and retired gentlefolk began to settle. The Villa's gardens sloped down almost to the shore in terraces with many fountains, gravel paths, and high box or privet hedges that screened walkers in the gardens from prying eyes.

The square white Empire-style building was a landmark for the people sailing boats on the lake. It had three floors; on each floor there were five windows on either side of a large central window. Those in the middle of the top storey boasted a wide pillared balcony commanding a magnificent view of the whole lake. Over the central window of the top floor a large golden clock had been fixed, surmounted by three finials resembling ravens.

By the time Ferdinando Leopardi had begun to rent the Villa from his first wife's family, ten years or so before the Great War, the neglect of years had diminished its grandeur. It had lost its wash of pink stucco, and its gardens had become untidy. Each spring still produced magnificent if dishevelled magnolias, camellias and azaleas which hid the house.

In 1910 Ferdinando changed the Villa's name to *Paulina*, but later, after his American wife of that name ran off home without him, it became once more *Carolina*.

Ferdinando's grandson, little Xavier Leopardi, was born at the Villa at the beginning of the year 1930, and for a time it was his principal childhood home. He was later to name it – at first privately and then, when he was grown up, publicly – the Villa Violetta.

During Xavier's childhood the window shutters were more often than not closed, except for a few on the ground floor where pale curtains moved slightly if there were a breeze from the lake. Butterflies haunted the gardens; they fascinated Xavier. By the time the second war was declared his grandfather had bought the Villa, and painters and decorators had made it look very grand once more.

'Butterflies communicate through their smell,' his Aunt Guiseppina said to Xavier once when he was about five years old.

'But they don't smell of anything!' he had replied.

'Not to you,' she said. 'To other butterflies, they do. Their scent carries for miles.'

He puzzled a long time over this. If there were things you could not smell but that butterflies could, there were perhaps other things you could never know? Birds might know things, and flowers. He knew that dogs were very clever in smelling things out. The Villa and its gardens were full of smells – jasmine blossom in the garden, thyme when his aunt took him for walks on the hill behind, and warm fruit ripening in the kitchen gardens at the back. There were smells inside the villa too: hot smells in the kitchen, wet smells in the corridors downstairs if someone had hung up a damp coat, and a funny metal smell in the hydraulic lift that was one of the first lifts to be fitted inside a villa – so his grandfather said – which went slowly up from the terrace end of the ground floor, past the first, or 'middle', floor, where Madame Edwige, the housekeeper, had her rooms, and on up to the top floor where was Xavier's own bedroom at the other end from the lift.

Xavier did not often use the lift; usually he went up the back stairs that led from the kitchens to the attics. He would pause on the middle floor before going up to his room on the next, and sniff the air as though he were himself a dog, like Carlo, Aunt Guiseppina's spaniel. He had always been told not to linger on the middle floor because there were offices there, as well as Madame Edwige, who didn't like her apartments to be invaded by children or dogs. But almost always, if he did stop for a moment to look down the long corridor with its many doors on the side facing the lake, he would smell the most pleasant scent of all, one to which at first he could not put a name.

One Easter however, when he was seven years old, around the time he was preparing for his First Communion, he recognized the same smell on his chocolate egg, not the smell of the chocolate but a sugary sweet smell almost like the scent of a flower. He could smell it as soon as he opened the box after lunch on Easter Sunday with only Aunt Jo and Uncle Ludo at the table with him. He sniffed the golden paper the egg was wrapped in. It was not that. But when he carefully opened the paper he knew where it came from. There was a cluster of beautiful purple flowers on the egg for decoration. It also reminded him of something long, long ago, something nice and happy that was to do with the flowers pinned on his mamma's jacket. He knew it was his mamma – he did remember her, he did! She had gone away and he did not think of her so much now; it was only the scent of the crystallized violets that had made him think of her.

'That's my smell!' he said without thinking, and sniffed the egg rapturously.

'What, dear?' Josephine asked absent-mindedly. She was reading a letter from an envelope with a French stamp on it.

'It's like the smell of the corridor upstairs,' he said. 'It smells just like that.'

'Xavier, you know you have been told often enough not to bother anyone on that floor. Your grandpapa has important business meetings up there.'

'And political friends,' added Ludo, 'who don't want little boys sniffing around.'

'I only stop there sometimes for a minute,' said Xavier, thinking, *they* can't smell it, then. I'm like a butterfly.

Ludo said: 'Let me,' and smelled the egg flowers with his long pale nose. 'Crystallized violets,' he said. 'Violets from Parma. It must be violets.' He looked at the boy thoughtfully.

'Perhaps Edwige has some in her room?' said Josephine.

'But she never smells of them,' said Xavier. 'She smells of yellow soap – and on Sundays of eau-de-cologne.'

'Well, don't go up there,' said Uncle Ludo. 'There's enough space for a boy in all the rest of the house, not to mention the garden. Take the lift and save your feet.'

They must have gone back soon after that to the flat in Como, because Grandfather wanted peace and quiet at the Villa to discuss his business. They often had to leave the Villa to go to the flat at weekends. Xavier did not have a chance to smell the violets again till much later, by which time he had made his First Communion, and it was winter, and during the week he was attending a little school in the town where Grandfather had his silk factory.

By then his aunt had received another letter from Paris, this time from her half-brother, Xavier's father, Paul Leopardi. He sent his love, she said, but he hoped soon to go to America to stay with his mother, Xavier's grandmother. Xavier could remember his father, and could also just remember his own mother, who, he thought, was called Victoire. She never wrote letters to his aunt. Xavier still thought a lot about his mother: she had gone away a long time ago, they said. He knew that she had not gone with his father.

One day Aunt Guiseppina said that she was going to marry Monsieur Edouard, whom Xavier had once met at the Villa. They had not decided whether to live in Italy or France. She did not say whether they would take him with them but he did not bother about that. He loved the Villa more than he loved his aunt. She was quite kind though, and really he liked her better than Uncle Ludo. He would not want to go away with Uncle Ludo, but it would be all right to stay on at the Villa with him, he supposed. He hardly ever saw his grandfather the businessman either, unless he was in Como, when Grandpapa would be working at his office at the silk factory. When Grandpapa was at the Villa he took his meals alone.

One night when they were back at the Villa, somebody somewhere was singing a beautiful song that woke Xavier. He got out of bed and crept down to the middle floor, from where he felt sure the music was coming. He stopped in front of a heavy panelled door in the middle of the corridor and waited a long time, not daring to knock. It did not open and nobody came, and the music had stopped.

His aunt was away in Paris, so in the morning he asked his uncle if he had heard the music. He did not mention that he had got up in the night to look around. Uncle Ludo said it must have been the maids – or perhaps Madame Edwige had a phonograph in her room and listened to music when she had insomnia.

'What is insomnia?' asked Xavier.

When this had been explained, he decided that he must suffer from the same complaint. He scarcely knew Madame Edwige, had always sensed that his aunt did not like his grandfather's housekeeper who was always busy and had no time for Xavier now, though they told him she had helped bring him up when he was a baby.

Nothing happened after that for ages and it was all a bit of a muddle in his memory, but he did remember later that it had been after Aunt Guiseppina had returned from Paris with her new husband, and they had gone away again to Stresa on what his grandfather, with a great guffaw, called an 'extended honeymoon', that something strange happened. This time though there was no music.

Since everyone was away, a little maid, Delphine, had been giving him his meals. Grandfather had gone to Como the day before and so the house was quiet. As his grandfather was a very noisy person it could not have been him Xavier saw the night he could not sleep. It was very hot, so he decided to get up and explore.

The moon was shining through the open casement at the end of the top corridor as he came out of his bedroom. Moonlight illuminated the iron staircase rail. He crept down the back stairs to the middle corridor. He sniffed the air: there was that smell of violets again. He walked along towards the middle of the corridor, passing several doors. One door was not quite shut so he pushed it gently and looked in.

There was a dim light in the room from a lamp near a sofa upon which two dressed-up ladies were sitting with their backs to him. They did not appear to have heard him, so he decided to go further. He tiptoed past them to the far end of the room where an inner door stood half open.

For a moment he stood there looking in. Moonlight was coming through an uncurtained window. A man stood there, looking out. At the back of the room was a bed. On top of the bed lay a lady with no clothes on, her legs were spread out. Standing at one side of the bed looking down on her there was another man, a big man. Suddenly he fell right on top of her and began to murder her. She started to kick her legs up and down and then to moan and scream. . . .

Xavier didn't know why he called out, but he did: 'Mamma!' he cried.

His heart was thumping like a drum as he turned and ran back to the outer door. One of the ladies on the sofa jumped up and ran up to the inside door and shut it. The other lady got up as well, yanked his arm and pulled and pushed him outside into the corridor.

He was gasping. 'He's murdering her, he's murdering her!'

She said: 'Shut up – it's only a game! You wicked boy, I'll take you back to bed – you've been sleep-walking.'

She gripped his hand. He was trembling as she marched him upstairs. The man had frightened him, and so had those screams.

The lady said again: 'It was a game, a secret game,' but he knew she was frightened too. Then she said: 'You'll have forgotten all about it in the morning – you were sleep-walking, weren't you?'

This seemed puzzling to Xavier, who was a clever boy even if he was only eight years old.

'If you remember your dreams you have to keep them secret,' the lady said as she tucked him up in bed.

'He was hurting her,' he said.

'No, no he wasn't. . . .'

'I shall tell Madame Edwige,' he said then. 'It's her apartment – she'll be angry!'

'Oh, I wouldn't tell her if I were you,' said the lady.

Now he came to look at her in the dim light coming into his bedroom from the corridor he saw she was quite young.

'What is your name?' he asked her as she turned to leave.

She said again: 'It was all a dream – forget it.'

'Tell me,' he said.

'Cécile if you want to know.'

'Cécile – was Grandpapa there?'

'Your grandfather? Oh! No!'

'He'd be cross with me. Don't tell him I was there. Uncle Ludo said I wasn't to go to the Violet Rooms.'

'The what?'

'You know – the rooms that smell of Parma violets.'

'Well I never! Of course I won't tell him,' she said hurriedly. 'Though there isn't anything to tell – since you dreamed it all.

You mustn't get up at night again – I expect they'll give you some medicine to stop you sleep-walking if you do,' she added.

'Don't tell Madame Edwige, will you?'

'Certainly not,' she said and gave him what she intended to be a definitive goodnight kiss.

It made him remember suddenly that he had shouted for his mother and he said in a whisper as the lady went to the door: 'Cécile – do you know my Mamma? She is young like you. Was it her I saw? She's not dead, is she?'

Cécile stopped as if she had suddenly been shot and turned back to look at him.

'Your mother? Who is *she*? Why should you think I know her? Did they tell you she was dead?'

'No – but I thought she might be, or else she'd come for me, wouldn't she?'

The lady paused, and then she said: 'I'm sorry, I don't know her – but I'm sure she wouldn't want you sleep-walking. Go to sleep now and it will all be a dream in the morning.'

'If I don't go down there again, do you think she might come back?'

'I don't know, I'm sure. Ask your aunt where she is. I have to go now. Go to sleep.'

He did feel drowsy after she had gone, and he soon fell asleep. He had a dream, he supposed it was about his mother – perhaps she was wearing a black jacket with a bunch of violets pinned to its lapel, perhaps she was staring at him . . . just staring. . . .

When he woke in the morning he had forgotten whatever it was that he had seen, forgotten everything but Cécile. He said nothing to anyone then, but when his aunt came back, looking more anxious than usual, he did venture to ask her if they had a maid called Cécile at the villa.

'I don't think so,' was her answer. Then: 'Madame Edwige

tells me you have been sleep-walking – she saw you one night outside your bedroom.'

'She saw me! But I didn't see her!'

'Well, of course if you were asleep you wouldn't have done, Xavier, would you? I do hope you'll grow out of the habit – it can't be good for you.'

He would have liked to have asked Aunt Jo then and there about his mother but something stopped him. Perhaps he didn't really want to know?

He asked Delphine one day if she had ever seen a lady at the villa called Cécile, but she replied: 'Who? No, I never.'

The strange thing was that he never sleep-walked at the flat in Como where that autumn he and Aunt Jo were to return. They stayed at the Villa for only three weeks that summer.

One August morning a year later he was told by his grandfather that there might soon be a war between France and Italy. His aunt, who since her marriage signed herself Josephine, wanted to go to France with her husband.

'Your father is said to be going back to Paris,' the old man said. 'You had better go there too. *She* wants to look after you. I'm too busy.'

Xavier knew that his grandfather was having a lot of meetings with men who wore black shirts, because he had seen them walking in the gardens of the Villa. He supposed they were connected with the factory in Como that spun and wove silk.

Uncle Ludo, though, was staying put in Italy. Xavier shook hands with him when he left for Rome. It seemed that the army wanted him for a soldier.

Before Xavier had decided what he thought about Ludo leaving them, and about this war that everybody – even Delphine – was talking about, he was swept away in a large car one night with Aunt Josephine and her husband and

Carlo the spaniel, and many suitcases, to Milan.

There had been no time even to say goodbye to the Villa nor to Grandfather either, who was not at the Villa that evening.

In Milan they took the train to Genoa and then to the Italian-French border near Ventimiglia where his Uncle Edouard got them a taxi to Menton.

War was declared between Italy, the ally of Germany, and France.

Xavier's Violet Rooms remained shuttered on the middle floor of the Villa Paulina but were not at first empty or abandoned. The scent of violets possibly remained too, even after those who had brought it there had gone away, but there were other stronger odours and other nostrils to sniff them. Pleasure was for a year or two no stranger here, nor were the faces all new ones, though some were. Officers danced to music downstairs, but not to the songs that Xavier had once overheard.

Little Delphine Domani went to work at a munitions factory in Lombardy, and the war parted other employees. Ferdinando Leopardi carried on his business in Como and Madame Edwige stayed on at the Villa for a time. But she was not there at the end of the war, at the time her employer was disgraced.

Madame Edwige was however not disgraced: had she perhaps always known how to look after herself?

Ludovic Leopardi was wounded in Sicily in 1943.

Elsewhere in Italy a woman still wept for her lost child and the young man she had loved. But they were both far away, and the young man would disappear for ever sometime during that terrible war.

Parigi O Cara. . . .

1949

Flora met Xavier Leopardi for the first time in Paris. She was eighteen years old, and Paris at the very end of the 1940s was for her a wonderful place. Although less than four years had passed since the war ended, its food, its buildings, its boulevards and its chattering cafés were a revelation to a child from the Puritan north of England.

In later years those days were to return to her in their original freshness only in dreams or if, for one piercing yet evanescent moment, she smelled a certain scent that she had smelled for the first time then. A whiff of mimosa from a street barrow, a waft of *L'Air du Temps* and she was back walking along the twilit boulevards.

Dreams and memories: the two well-springs of the imagination. Whenever she returned in dreams to the Paris of long ago, the feel of that time of her life was like that of a beloved's skin recognized in the dark, a remembrance that could still infuse her adult existence with a kind of magic, too poignant a magic even to be expressed in words.

Her place at Cambridge being secure, she had nine months to spend improving her French. A kind businessman on the board of governors of her grammar school had endowed a scholarship for people like Flora, and she went to Paris for six months as the only English pupil of a girls' lycée. Later she might have to take some lowly employment whilst waiting to take up her university studies. The scholarship paid for her board and lodging; the school was free, since anyone of school age living in Paris could attend a lycée, provided he or she was up to the intensive academic work.

Flora did not board at the school but lived in a small pension called the *Foyer Accueil* run by Marist nuns, where she was the only non-Catholic and the youngest student. The Foyer was on a narrow street between the streets of Cherche-Midi and Vaugirard and most of her fellow pensionnaires were studying at the Sorbonne. Like them, Flora had a room of her own in the old house which overlooked a courtyard where grew an ancient tree.

Four times a day Flora had a twenty-minute walk to and from the lycée. She was extremely happy, for she had more freedom than she had ever had before, and could spend time by herself if there were a lesson she need not attend. Sometimes she was invited to spend the week-ends with the families of some of her co-pensionnaires at St Germain-en-Laye or Bougival. Then she savoured the strange formality of their *surprise parties* when there would sometimes be dancing, and always a lot of Gauloise-smoking and much talk. The Métro smelled of Gauloises too – as well as of strong eau-de-cologne, diesel oil, and garlic.

Coming face to face for the first time at the Foyer, with the theology of the Catholic Church and with philosophy at the lycée, neither of which had been on offer at home in England, Flora began to broaden her knowledge of both, more particularly of Catholic theology, since at home she had been brought up as a Protestant. A Monsieur Cordonnier, a Jesuit seminarian – she learned he was not a fully-fledged priest – arrived at the Foyer punctually after supper every Thursday evening to provide an antidote to the university teaching on evolution which the science students were required to study for their examinations. Flora was instructed that it was permissible to reproduce what you had been taught, so long as you did not really believe it! She came to the conclusion that if the Catholic God existed, then he must be all-knowing – so why should he want to put the wrong ideas in the heads of clever people like Darwin? She supposed Monsieur Cordonnier would call these ideas the work of the Devil.

Mother St Agatha told her Catholic boarders that there was only one truth and that was the Catholic variety, whereas the philosophy lessons at the lycée led the girls to ask questions about matters they might previously have taken for granted. Flora found these lessons wonderfully intoxicating, even the *cours de morale*, delivered in a rapid monotone by a lecturer from the Sorbonne whose hair was always escaping her pins, and whose utterances were taken down word for word by the less intellectually endowed. She found some of the girls quite brilliant. They asked complicated questions, and were revered, not teased, as they might have been in England. One student in that class was even married! This impressed Flora.

She also found that living in France, and having to speak French developed her conversational powers. She found it the ideal language for long discussions about art and life and love. It fertilized the top soil of her mind, the conscious part and she tuned in to a new part of herself that had never been quite acceptable in England.

Flora's walks along the Boulevard du Montparnasse and the Boulevard des Invalides, before spring arrived, were what she was later to remember best of her time in Paris. The very name of Montparnasse spoke to her of Poetry and Romance;

she realized that the gods had once lived on Mount Parnassus. Even though Paris was sometimes colder than she'd bargained for, the days were often bright until evening, when a mist might fall. There were few cars – mostly pre-war Citroëns with long chassis and square bodies, headlamps looking as if they had strayed from a Marcel Carné film. On cold January mornings during her first weeks in Paris, as she walked to school on cobbled streets and grey pavements, passing by shops and cafés, she would always look into the café on the corner by the Duroc Métro station where work-men stood at the counter drinking their first cup of coffee or swallowing a brandy before beginning work. She felt they were privileged, and that she also was privileged: she too now belonged to Paris and had her work there, free of home and parents and England. She was warmed by the bowl of hot coffee she had gulped down in the Foyer's *salle à manger* and could still taste on her palate the delicious bread plastered with pale butter and greengage jam which was her daily breakfast and which she dunked in the bowl of coffee as did everyone else. She was always first for breakfast since her classes started at half past eight and she would walk quickly in the cold dry air, wrapped up in her heavy, brown, belted, English coat.

It was in the afternoon though – at noon, at two o'clock, and at half past five that she felt the boulevard was even more interesting. When the morning lessons were over she would come out of the tall black double doors that were unlocked for pupils only at certain times of the day, and walk back to the Foyer, often in wintry sun. She loved that sun. She always looked across the wide boulevard, which had here been given another name – Les Invalides – at an enormous church where sometimes a black velvet pall would hang over the main entrance to signify that a funeral mass would soon be taking place. She discovered the name of that church: St

François Xavier. A Basque girl at the Foyer told her that Xavier was a Basque word: *Etchaberri*, meaning New House. The French pronounced the name differently from the English who rhymed it with 'saviour', but the French said 'zav-I-ay'.

Until about the beginning of March she would walk home in the dusk, since the school often did not finish before half past five, and it was on foggy late afternoons or early evenings before spring arrived that she most felt the charm of this particular part of Paris – and of life itself, dark as the streets behind the boulevards were, especially on misty evenings with the sun setting behind tall buildings, fog swirling around Métro entrances, tall street lamps, and lines of leafless trees. Women wore either very short or very long 'New Look' skirts and wedge-heeled shoes. Their legs were thin even if their coats were bulky, and many wore head-scarves. Perhaps people were thin because they had not yet recovered from being hungry during the war. But she was thin then herself, and young – and always hungry – so hungry that she'd go to the baker's on her way home from school on the rue du Cherche-Midi to buy a freshly-baked *petit pain* for five old francs, and sometimes devour her bread on the street. As she sat in the Luxembourg Gardens on the warm Saturday afternoons of spring, she would sometimes think of Katherine Mansfield, who had lived at one time on the nearby rue de Tournon which led down from the Luxembourg.

She too wished to grab greedily at life. She applied herself to admire all that was before her; she was ready to fall in love with Paris and fall in love with it she did. She did not imagine she would meet anyone who might fall in love with *her*, and therefore did not waste her time thinking about it. Until she met Xavier Leopardi, Paris seemed quite enough to be going on with.

*

The Foyer was well placed for visits to the theatre and art galleries. Flora went with some other students to the theatre to see *Partage de Midi* with the actress Edwige Feuillère, a play about holy and human love, but she was not sure she had understood it properly. As one of the nuns had accompanied them there, she imagined that it must be because its author, Paul Claudel, was a Catholic, and that they therefore approved of him.

Only a short walk away was the headquarters of the Alliance Française where actors and writers would address meetings open to anyone who was interested and where you did not have to pay to be a member of the audience. It was there one cold day in February that she saw a famous film star – and met Xavier for the first time.

At first Flora did not take all that much to Xavier Leopardi when Colette Rocque, one of her fellow pupils, introduced him to her. Xavier was at the Lycée Pasteur, along with Colette's cousin Michel, whom Flora found at first more approachable than Xavier. Michel was fairer, stockier, more talkative than his friend, who had nut brown wavy hair and deep-set pale hazel eyes. The look in those eyes was challenging. Flora imagined they were saying: 'I am just as intelligent as you – probably more intelligent,' an impression she had sometimes gained from clever young men, not that she had met all that many.

The four of them were sitting in a row at the back of the lecture hall. She supposed that Colette would prefer her to concentrate on Michel rather than his friend. After all, Michel was Colette's cousin, so Colette couldn't flirt with him. Flora thought that Colette might want to get to know, even get off with this Xavier, whose surname she hadn't caught at first. Colette was sitting between Xavier and Michel, with Flora on Michel's other side. Xavier seemed to be listening to Colette, or at least he had his head turned in her direction, when Flora leaned back to observe how things were going.

Michel announced to her that his friend – *mon camarade* – he called him – was 'a quarter American'.

'Oh? Does he speak English then?'

Flora was not especially keen to speak English since it was more of an effort to speak one's own language to a foreigner than to speak French.

'I suppose so – but his first language is Italian.'

'His father's Italian?'

'I'm not sure. He lives with his aunt, who seems to be Italian.' After a pause, he added: 'You might like to come to my "surprise partie" next week? I live in the *quinzième*. So does Xavier.'

That was the *arrondissement* next to the *sixième*, where the Foyer was, but on the other side of the big Montparnasse station.

'Are you in the same class then?'

'Same year – but Xavier's in the philo section and I'm in math elem.'

'I'm in philo too,' replied Flora. 'I love it – it's all so interesting. English schools don't teach philosophy.'

Colette leaned behind Michel and poked Flora in the shoulder. 'Shh – *he's* here!' she whispered.

They all turned their heads round to the door, and there he was, the famous actor, the star, in a Sloppy Joe top and blue jeans, ambling down the hall to the platform at the other end, followed by a woman and man.

'That'll be his girl-friend and his agent,' said Michel sagely. 'Xavier says he's a Communist.'

Gérard Philippe, tall, thin, romantic looking, with a cloud

of soft hair, was chewing gum like an American. That disappointed Flora, though she had realized that many of the French had acquired more American habits than had the English.

Everyone was clapping, and the famous film star sat down behind the table on the platform.

'Sh-h- Shhh!' went the audience, which as far as Flora could see was mostly composed of students like themselves.

'He'll answer questions,' said his agent, bobbing up beside him. A man in the audience stood up, gave the name of his magazine, which Flora knew to be extremely left wing, and asked about the future of the French cinema. In Paris she had soon realized that the French regarded *le cinéma* as an art form – which was not the way she'd been brought up to think of it. But she certainly liked French and Italian films best.

Gérard Philippe was good-looking in a romantic way, and was taller than she had imagined but, like many actors, he was rather shy and had very little to say for himself. He spoke of his last film in a quiet voice, seemed rather modest. Then Xavier stood up to ask a question:

'Xavier Leopardi,' he said with a flourish in his voice: 'I'd like to know what you think of the Italian neo-Realists.'

Flora knew what he was talking about because before she had come to France she and some friends had gone several times to the Arts Cinema in their nearest city and seen *Roma, Citta Aperta* and *Paisa* with the magnificent Anna Magnani. People raved over these films because they were so natural, often had to do with the lives of the poor, in stark contrast to the Hollywood films they were used to. Xavier didn't seem keen on them though, and Flora felt that the famous actor, in spite of enthusing over 'the lives of ordinary folk,' was not a lover of naïve spontaneous life in the raw, however much he rooted for Picasso's *Dove of Peace*.

Flora liked French films even more than Italian ones. They

were down to earth, more stylized, more melancholy, more *literary*, than the Italian offerings.

She sensed some drive, some strongly held conviction behind Xavier's words. He spoke in faultless French, with no trace of an Italian accent. She had thought he might have an Italian accent, but he didn't, seemed as French as anyone in the room. He said something about aesthetic appeal before he sat down and the actor smiled and mumbled something. She could not see Xavier's face unless she leaned forwards.

Another young man got up then with a comment on costume drama. No young women spoke. The meeting petered out soon after but Flora decided to join Colette in the queue for the actor's autograph.

Xavier looked haughtily condescending when the girls returned with their trophies but Michel smiled and said: 'Au café alors?'

It was a Thursday afternoon, and Thursdays were always free. Pupils either went to their *curés* for religious instruction, or took part in *le sport*. Neither Colette nor Flora was interested in either activity. So, whilst the men drank their cold light-coloured beer and Colette her *citron pressé* she was free to observe Xavier Leopardi.

'Bit of a waste of time,' he said when he had drained his glass. 'He hadn't much to say for himself, had he?'

Flora replied: 'Actors aren't very often intellectuals, are they? In England they're not, anyway.' She felt quite bold. He looked at her, then:

'You like these post-war Italian Realist films?'

'Well, they are a change from Hollywood,' she answered.

'How long can they go on producing them though? The war's been over for nearly four years and there are still things left undone since before '39 – lots to write about. Not just about the poor in Naples and Rome – slum dwellers, but about the Church, the Mafia, the political system, the people who went along with Hitler and Mussolini. People will soon want their films to be more sophisticated.'

'De Sica's films are very well-directed,' offered Michel, chipping into the conversation.

Xavier moved on to another tack: 'There's been no actress to hold a candle to Garbo,' he said. He had a disconcerting habit of changing the subject of a conversation in mid-track when he'd thought of a new viewpoint.

Flora had seen *Queen Christina* and *Anna Karenina* at home at the Arts Cinema but neither film had impressed her more than *Les Enfants du Paradis*. That was by far her favourite film and one she had seen over and over again. Jean-Louis Barrault was at present her favourite actor, but tactfully, thinking women would interest Xavier more, she said: 'What about Arletty?'

Xavier looked at her searchingly.

'She is beautiful,' persisted Flora.

'Not much of an actress though – *and* she collaborated with the Boches.' Flora hadn't known that.

'Are you a Communist, Xavier?' Colette asked him.

'All parties stink. If I voted Communist it'd be because I thought they were the only party to put Italy right, never mind this country. Answer to your question: No, I'm a Marxist.' *What's the little English girl thinking?* wondered Xavier Leopardi. Michel, apparently reading her thoughts answered for her, saying: 'I expect Flora thinks Marxists are misguided?'

'I suppose Marxists need not espouse the Communist party?' Flora asked hesitantly.

'Quite right,' said Xavier.

She had nothing against politically-minded people so long as they did not claim that their doctrine took in everything in the world – including the things she cared about most – art and love and nature and personal relations. The meaning of life, she supposed. She wanted to say to Xavier Leopardi that he didn't look to her like the sort of man who would believe in any dogma, religious or political.

'I'm a Liberal,' she said. He laughed. 'Are you a Catholic?' she asked. She could talk about *that*.

'I was baptized a Catholic,' he replied. 'Most Italians are – like most of the French.'

'But are you a believer?' Flora persisted. 'I only meet believers in special places – like my convent. That's run by Marists, not Marxists!' They all laughed.

'Oh, that's quite normal,' said Xavier.

'But some of the girls there – the Catholic girls I live with – say they are Marxists as well!' she went on. She was thinking of Anna and Maria, sisters who came from what was called Indo-China.

Xavier perked up at this and said: 'Bourgeois offspring like to rebel against their parents by calling themselves Marxists.'

Flora didn't think that Anna and her sister were exactly bourgeois but she let it pass. She really wanted him to talk about himself. 'Oh, is that what *you* are doing then?' she answered rather daringly. Michel laughed but Colette looked at her in surprise.

Then suddenly Xavier laughed too and said: 'Too right – except my family were worse than bourgeois.'

She wondered what he meant. She was to discover later.

'I refer only to the men in my family,' he added. 'They don't believe in any case that politics or political discussion is for women.'

'It's true, your aunt doesn't look like a Marxist,' teased Michel.

'Aunt Josephine is a good Catholic, I believe. *I* don't think one can be both a Catholic and a Marxist – in spite of the worker priest movement.'

Flora had not heard of the worker priests at the time, and

so she asked him: 'Why not?' thinking she'd have something to talk to Anna about.

He raised his very clear hazel eyes to hers. 'You're not a Catholic then?' he asked.

'No – I'm a Protestant.'

'The worst of both worlds,' he said, and Michel smiled.

'I suppose that's true,' Flora agreed, for she had already come to feel that Protestants were in a half-way house, though she was no longer a believer.

To her own ears Flora had sounded argumentative. She thought Xavier would definitely not approve of her. But before they said *au revoir* that afternoon, Xavier said to her: 'You must come and visit me and my aunt one day. I could practise my English with you perhaps?' He looked quite serious.

'Thank you,' she said.

'I shall see you all at my *surprise partie*,' said Michel. 'Xavier's coming too, aren't you, *mon brave*?'

Xavier smiled. She thought he looked extraordinarily attractive when he did.

When the men had gone in another direction and they were walking back along the rue de Rennes, Colette said to her: 'Xavier's cousin Solange is at our *petit lycée*. She's only eight – my sister knows her. The family is very odd.'

Flora wondered what she meant.

Later, Colette said to Flora: 'Xavier thinks you are not very English.'

Flora supposed Michel had been talking to her. 'Is that a compliment?' she asked, knowing full well it was meant to be. The French were always very critical of the English. But of course Xavier wasn't really French, was he, only French-educated?

Colette teased her: 'You know the general opinion of the English!'

'Yes, I've heard it often enough: "cold, boring, badly-dressed, but gentlemanly!"'

'You are not a gentleman though, Flora! We do make the distinction between English men and English women. Nevertheless—'

'Teeth like horses and always dressed in tweeds?'

'There you are – but I don't think he was referring to either your clothes or your teeth.' They both giggled. Colette was very nice, and strangely enough adored everything English. They complemented each other nicely.

Lying in bed that night Flora thought, I don't dress well – not as well as most of the girls here anyway – but my teeth are not large. Perhaps he just meant that? But she knew that Colette had meant to convey something else. People here liked lively women; what had been regarded as talkativeness, even argumentativeness, at home, was seen here as a social asset. Yet that was not the real Flora, not her true self. She had thought Xavier Leopardi interesting but she was finding it hard to distinguish between surface attractions and the deeper layer of personality.

Men must have the same problem when they thought about women. A pretty face helped one along, just as men who were tall and dark and handsome had all the girls after them. Xavier was neither especially tall nor very dark, but on thinking it over Flora found him quite handsome.

The next time they met was at Michel's party. Flora wore her Moygashel blue-and-white-patterned skirt and a pale blue blouse and hoped she did not look too English. Her hair was down, for once. When he saw her, Michel said: '*Que tes cheveux sont longs!*'

Xavier said nothing. Perhaps he would appreciate her conversation: He was talking to a tall girl in red and the expression on his face was slightly cynical. She determined to find out more about him that evening.

Who knows when a general curiosity turns into an obsessive desire to know everything about another person? Flora had always been subject to passionate phases. At that party she was not obsessed with Xavier, but she supposed she might already have some of the feelings that are often said to be a prelude to falling in love. She wanted to know about his childhood, his antecedents, his tastes in books and music; she wanted to understand *him*. She did not imagine that anybody would really want to understand *her*. She thought there was nothing mysterious about herself, even if living in a foreign country made her possibly less of an open book for others to read.

When Xavier Leopardi finally came over to talk to her that evening she was not intimidated by him; he was after all only a few months older than herself, though she might have been in awe of a much older man, even an older student. He was a good conversationalist and Flora found him a good listener too. She made up stories to amuse him and practise her French at the same time, embroidered on the imaginary life of the Foyer orphan skivvy, and the rich young woman who had introduced Flora to a friend of hers, an artist who slept in a hammock hung from the high ceiling of a studio in Montparnasse.

It had been her *anniversaire* that very week and some of the girls at the Foyer had presented her with a bottle of scent, a recently launched fragrance which they thought would suit her. She'd been touched, pleased they liked her enough to give her a present, and she had doused her wrists and neck liberally with *L'Air du Temps*. Xavier sniffed the air around her and remarked: 'Carnation – with a hint of lemon, I think? It smells like the Villa garden.'

There were only about sixteen of them in all in the high-ceilinged room next to an equally large *salle à manger*, and they were all seated by then in little clusters. Michel had put on a record – Leo Ferré singing a sad song. The party was not quite like an English party but was less formal than the two or three others Flora had so far enjoyed in Paris. Most people were smoking Gauloises as they talked about their *bac* studies and Flora felt privileged to be among them – and smoked Gauloises too.

Two of Xavier's other friends, Pierre and Marc-Henri, grabbed girls with whom to dance. Flora didn't consider it was real dancing – they just swayed along with their eyes closed. Xavier began to talk to her then about the subject of that week's philosophy *devoirs* and in no time at all she was telling him about some of the questions they had discussed in her classes, questions more to do with psychology than philosophy. 'Philo' covered a multitude of sins.

One question had been: *Men write more than women since it is easier for them to sublimate their sexual instincts.*

'I disagree with both parts of the question,' said Flora, 'unless they mean paternal or maternal instincts?' She had no idea whether she possessed such instincts herself.

'Men do write more than women,' said Xavier. 'And when women' – he called them *créatures féminines* – 'do write, it's usually of their emotions.'

'I enjoy reading about feelings,' said Flora. 'And men write about those too.' She wanted to argue, even to disagree with him, but he seemed amused.

'Can one by changing oneself change the world?' he asked. 'That was our subject this week.'

'Oh well, I suppose you wrote of politics?'

'No – it goes deeper than that,' he said, and for a moment a veil of sorrow seemed to pass over his face that she was sure she did not imagine.

Michel and some other young men came up and Xavier became cynical again, joining in and speaking at length. They teased him, telling him he was not yet before the examiners. She enjoyed listening to them all with their theories of pleasure and pain, their serious appraisal of drug-induced states, their dismissal of a life of fantasy and their reiteration of something called the reality principle. Heady stuff.

She deduced that morality here was something you discussed in theory, just as you discussed Eros, or the cause of feeling, or the fear of death, and much more. They were clever, serious minded, not so moralistic as their counterparts in England would have been. She found it all refreshing.

The Gauloises were extinguished and they all trooped into the dining room to sit down for a long and delicious meal prepared by Michel's mother. She must have spent days in preparation, but there was a maid hovering in the kitchen so perhaps it had not been too much for her. After the supper and the glasses of Burgundy, they all went back to smoke and talk and dance.

Marc-Henri asked her for *un slow*, and Pierre for one of those dances the French seemed to specialise in – a lot of jigging up and down of shoulders and hips. She enjoyed it, though she had never been regarded as a good dancer in England, had never mastered the fox-trot or the quickstep.

'You ought to learn the *paso doble*,' said Xavier when the music stopped and Pierre and Flora ended up in a group at the far end of the room, where Xavier was sitting in a large armchair smoking the inevitable Gauloise. 'I mean – you have a lot of nervous energy,' he added.

Flora wished *he* would ask her to dance, even if it were just jigging up and down, but he did not. He danced with nobody.

Soeur Marie Claire was waiting up for her when she arrived back at the Foyer at midnight as arranged in Colette's father's car.

'Enjoyed yourself?' she asked.

'Oh yes,' Flora answered fervently – and she had.

*

Young people in Paris went round a good deal in groups and she was soon to see Xavier and his friends again. They met at weekends, usually in favourite cafés. Naturally, she spent most of her time in lessons or at the Foyer but was free to wander round on Saturdays and Sundays when she would hint to the good sisters that she was with Colette.

It was always Xavier who interested her most. She still didn't think she actually *liked* him any more than she liked Pierre or Michel but he fascinated her more and more. He still seemed to regard her as a challenge. She wasn't sure why, though he was certainly one himself for an English girl from a conventional background.

Many times, as they sat for hours over a coffee or a cold blond French beer, he would say: 'I have to get back to Italy as soon as I've finished my studies.' She felt he was lonely in spite of his several friends. She thought they regarded him as something of an outsider, perhaps even more so than herself.

One Saturday afternoon they were sitting in a café on the Boulevard du Montparnasse. Colette and Michel had been sitting along with them but had left for a family get-together. Xavier then began to speak of the Villa Carolina on Lake Como, which had once belonged to his disgraced grandfather.

'Is that your father's father or your mother's father?' asked Flora.

He stopped for a moment, disconcerted. Then: 'Oh, I don't know anything about my mother – Victoire's – family. My grandfather was a Fascist – that's why our Villa was requisitioned in '45. It isn't just that I want to go back home, Flora, it's that I feel – compelled – to return. It's a beautiful place . . . but that's not it either.'

'You want to rediscover your childhood?' Which was torn apart by war, she thought.

He told her then of some of the rifts in his family and she listened to him as though she were reading one of those long complicated nineteenth century novels like *The Woman in White*. She had the impression his mother was dead but did not like to ask. He was telling her enough to be going on with.

'You really must meet my Tante Jo,' he said. 'She likes English people. Of course *she* believes in leaving things well alone. But my Uncle Ludo – that's her brother – knows more than he lets on. I'm sure he's holding things up at the Villa so we don't go back.'

Knows what? Flora wondered. Was Xavier looking for a lost paradise?

Later, he was to hint at other things. She was not sure, to tell the truth, what he was talking about. There was a woman called Edwige, he said, who had helped to bring him up and who had stayed in Italy throughout the war. She was a sort of general factotum, and had her own rooms at the Villa.

'I dream about the house such a lot,' he said. 'It's strange, I'm always a child in my dreams. Children have strange fancies, don't they?'

She wanted him to tell her more about the disgraced grandfather, so she said nothing.

'Even before the war we didn't live in the whole of the place – it's very big. I had my favourite corridor – there were rooms there I used to call my *chambres violettes* because of the scent they had. . . .' He stopped for a moment. Then: 'Parma violets,' he said. 'Women don't wear that scent any more now, do they?'

Flora said she wasn't sure and, without thinking, sniffed her own wrist.

'Nothing like yours,' he said. 'I told you, yours smells more like our garden. There were lemon trees and orange trees and masses of flowers and butterflies. . . .'

'Yes, you were right about the carnation,' she said. 'I

couldn't place it at first.'

She had the strong impression that something – somebody
– perhaps a dead mother? – haunted Xavier Leopardi. How
different his childhood had been from hers in an Edwardian
suburb – though they had had a garden too.

'I love those names,' she said, 'Carolina and Violetta – and
Joséphine.'

'Carolina was the original name of the Villa,' he went on.
'Then my grandfather changed it to Paulina when he married
my father's mother – but he changed it back when she left
him!'

She waited but he said again: 'You really must meet Tante
Jo.'

In the beginning she did not ask herself why Xavier Leopardi
was telling her these things. She was content just to listen to
him. Slowly she pieced together what, in the course of many
conversations, he told her about himself and his childhood
and family background. Some pieces did not seem quite to fit
but she dared not ask him too many questions for she sensed
that he was still trying to understand himself and was at an
age where he needed a passive listener. In these early days of
their acquaintance he never spoke of his mother though grad-
ually he told her more about his father, Paul Leopardi, who
had apparently gone to America in 1938, then returned to
Paris and eventually joined the French Resistance. He had
been killed in 1944.

Just before war was declared in the summer of 1939, Xavier
had fled to France with his aunt and her French husband,
Italy being on the side of Germany. Flora gathered that Aunt
Joséphine no longer lived with her husband, but that Xavier's
cousin, the eight-year-old Solange, whom she was also to
meet one afternoon, was their daughter.

Italian bureaucracy was a legend, said Xavier. The family

had waited four years for the necessary papers to be produced to enable them to return to their Villa. The Villa had been requisitioned after the war, because his grandfather, Ferdinando Leopardi, had been a Fascist, an ardent follower of Mussolini. Ferdinando was dead now, but he had left the Villa to Xavier. Whether Xavier would ever be able to afford to live in it was another matter. Whenever he spoke of the Villa Carolina he always added: 'It was so beautiful, you know, as though she could not possibly know how beautiful.

Flora sensed more and more that there was something that troubled him about his childhood. Eventually, he showed her a photograph of his grandfather, taken in the early years of the century, a man with a big nose and hooded eyes and side-whiskers, looking older than the twenty-five years Xavier said he had been at the time. He was wearing a large overcoat with a velvet collar over a black frock coat and a large cravat. 'It was taken in Paris,' Xavier told her. How he had come across it he didn't explain. It had probably belonged to his aunt.

'Ferdinando was a silk manufacturer. *His* mother was French, so you see I have some French blood too! He married my grandmother as his second wife. Paulina was American,' said Xavier. 'So I have some Yankee blood as well!'

Flora wondered why his father had not taken him with him to America. Paul Leopardi would surely not have got on with a Fascist father? Another time Xavier told her that it was Tante Jo, never his father, who had looked after him in childhood. She thought, well if he wants me to meet his aunt, he must like me. Older French people on the whole did not invite people much to their homes. She told Colette that Xavier wanted her to meet his aunt. Colette mentioned it to Michel who said: 'She's honoured – but perhaps his aunt has been pestering him to be more sociable?'

*

The first visit took place on a Thursday afternoon, and Flora was a little nervous beforehand. When Xavier opened the door a tall, thin, middle-aged woman with a big nose and rather greasy hair in a bun came up behind him. But Flora found her welcome much more friendly than she had expected. Indeed, Joséphine Duvallier seemed grateful for the visit. She led Flora into a dark, sparely-furnished sitting-room. Xavier disappeared for a time and the aunt and Flora made the kind of small talk Flora regarded as a test of her abilities in French conversation. After a little while Madame Duvallier said: 'You will have to excuse me in a moment as I must go to meet my daughter from her religious lesson. Then I shall offer you all some *pain au chocolat*. . . .' She went out of the flat and Xavier came back into the room.

He said: 'My cousin Solange is being introduced to God.'

'Was Solange born in France?'

'Oh yes, here in Paris. About a year after we left Menton.'

'So when exactly did you leave Italy?' she asked, more for something to say. He sat down, obviously disposed to chat.

'In August 1939, a month before war broke out. Uncle Edouard wanted to be in France – thought the Boches would be pushed back. Optimistic wasn't he? They all knew war was coming and that old Musso would join up with Hitler.' She wanted to ask him: But what about *your* father? Tell me about him.

Indirectly he answered her unspoken question when he said 'I wanted to come to Paris. They told me my father would be here, but he wasn't, not at first anyway.'

She waited.

'He'd gone to the States, as I told you, when I was seven, to join my American grandmother in Chicago. He didn't get on with my grandpapa. I suppose that's why he never came back

54

to Italy before the war, but returned instead to France.' As she had guessed, there had been trouble between Xavier's father and grandfather.

Xavier went on: 'I saw him once in the South of France. Afterwards he was in the Resistance and we never saw him again throughout the war, though my aunt had a few letters. In the end the Gestapo shot him. Sometimes I think he was punished for not taking me with him in the first place. Can you understand that?' He said all this in a deadpan way and she didn't know how to respond. That a man should pay with his own life for the dereliction of his child was not an idea she had ever encountered before.

'You do understand that Grandpapa was a Fascist and that his son was on the other side,' he said again with deliberation.

'Yes, of course. But where was your mother?'

'They told me she was dead,' he replied. 'I don't want to talk about her. I like talking to you about my father. I don't speak of him much to my friends.' She sensed a sort of despair under his words.

'That's my story then,' he said, quite jauntily. 'Now I shall boil some water for coffee.' He got up, went through a door into a kitchen which, she could see, looked more like an old-fashioned scullery. She heard a tap run.

'Can I do anything?' she asked.

'No – sit down and tell me about yourself.'

What was there to tell?

She heard a child's voice as the outer door to the flat was opened. 'Is Xavier back?' it asked.

A pasty-faced girl, still wearing a pale blue *tablier*, and with big brown eyes behind pebbly spectacles, sidled into the room followed by her mother. Flora got up and shook hands with the child, as was expected. Solange Duvallier looked long and hard at her, reminding Flora immediately of a child she'd known at home in the war, a refugee from Poland. Wanda had also been rather fat and pale.

'Your *goûter*, then your homework,' said Solange's mother and went to busy herself in the kitchen.

Solange devoured her *pain au chocolat* from a tray that had appeared with bread and milk for her and coffee for the others. Flora too was, as usual, hungry. Xavier was silent as they gulped and chewed. The aunt ate nothing, only sipped at her black coffee. It was such an ordinary scene, Flora thought, but she sensed currents underneath that she did not think arose from her imagination. When Solange went off to her room and Tante Jo to the kitchen once more, Flora said: 'Your aunt, she lowered her voice, 'is your father's half sister?'

'Yes – and Uncle Ludo is her brother. They are the children of my grandfather's first marriage. Ludo's in Italy, holding everything up – probably selling second-hand cars. He was in the Italian army – he fought in Sicily.'

'What else did your grandfather do?' she asked. 'I mean apart from being on the side of Mussolini?'

'I told you – he was a silk merchant,' replied Xavier, looking at her over the rim of his coffee cup. 'We were rich.'

She wanted to ask him too about his American grandmother and to press him further about his mother but dared not just then. But she did begin to wonder how exactly this grandfather of Xavier's had died.

After this visit to his aunt's flat Flora met Xavier quite often. They sat in cafés and on benches in the Luxembourg talking about poetry and politics and religion and music. She did not feel that he was really very interested in her as a person, though she knew she should be honoured that he wanted to tell her all he did. In spite of his saying he would like to speak English with her, they were always to talk French to each other. Flora had realized that she expressed herself slightly differently from the way she would have conducted a conversation with a young Englishman, and there was a tiny additional uncertainty: that as she was not completely bi-lingual perhaps there remained little nuances of his conversation that she did not quite understand, or might have misunderstood, and this added to the mystery Xavier Leopardi had for her. She hoarded all the details he let slip of his romantic Villa, and constructed a life for him in her imagination.

Flora had felt very alone to begin with among the swelling Parisian crowds in the Métro, with not one single person who knew her as she stood swaying with them in the cheapest carriages, drinking in the smell of Gauloises and garlic and cologne and petrol. She had not minded not knowing anyone at first because she had welcomed the challenge of living in a new city as well as in a new country and speaking another language. Soon though she came to feel she belonged to Paris.

She realized that anything she might feel for Xavier Leopardi was already set apart, was not an integral part of her Paris experience. She got to know him there as she got to know Colette and the others, but she needed to make no effort to become interested in Xavier, as she sometimes did with the others. Eventually he consented to discuss her own character with her, perhaps aware he must make some effort to reward her for listening to him for so long. He said to her once: 'You are a Romantic,' and another time: 'You are quite intelligent.' Did he mean 'not very' intelligent or 'rather intelligent'? 'You are more interesting than your ideas,' he added.

Xavier aroused her imagination in a way that the others, good friends though they were, did not, and thereby sowed the seeds of what was ready to blossom into a romantic passion. But Flora was wary at eighteen of the sexual side of young men. Not that Xavier had ever given her a moment's real worry that he might suddenly pounce on her. To him, she stood perhaps for normality, perhaps even an ordinariness, that had not yet existed in his life.

When eventually and with extreme reluctance she had to return to England, all Xavier's compulsive talk of his child-hood and his Villa remained vividly in her mind. But he himself still remained a partial mystery. And mysteries breed romance.

She thought she might never see him again, even though if it depended on her she was determined she would.

At first she had a lot of other things to do and think about. There was another new life of university studies upon which to embark. She missed Xavier, but sometimes she would ask herself if she had invented him.

Except for the days she received his letters. They wrote off and on to each other, but four years were to pass before they met again face to face.

Lago di Como
27 Sept. 1952

Dear Flora

I was very sorry not to be able to see you in Paris last month. Why do the English always come to Paris in August? – It is a dead month. I was obliged to come here to begin to arrange my Uncle Ludo's and Aunt Josephine's business affairs as well as my own. The great news is that the Villa Carolina has at last been signed over to me by the Lombardy administration. They have 'taken their time!' How do you like my English idioms?

But it means that I must save more and more and invest my money in good places to begin to repair and decorate bit by bit for it is in a very bad state. Our old housekeeper Edwige Rouart is living there at present. Tante Jo is not eager to return to Italy for good. I hope that by next summer a few rooms will be cleaned and ready for human habitation so that you may visit me in Italy if you wish. Some of the furniture is still there but much has gone. If you come I shall make you talk Italian although I would like to perfect my spoken English also. Is my

English not improving?! I hoped perhaps to come before Christmas to an English course in London but now I shall be too occupied.

I passed the first part of my Economics exam in Paris and my great-uncle Alexander Moirier – Sasha – has promised to help me find work in Italy where he still directs the silk business that was my grandfather Ferdinando's before the war. He is the brother of my grandfather's first wife, Feodora, half Russian and at least eighty years old.

Please write to me -

Ever your friend -

Xavier Leopardi

London

October 17th 1952

Dear Xavier

I was very disappointed not to see you but very glad you have passed the first part of your <u>licence</u>. Congratulations. Will you not continue with the second part? I was in Paris for a month and did wish I could have seen you there. Never mind. I went in August because I had to start work in September and until July I was at home, then in London, looking for a place to live. I too have passed my exams. I am not very keen about my first job and do not intend to stay there. It's an administrative post and I am very bad at it. I would like to use my French but that seems impossible here unless I become a <u>professeur</u> or a translator.

I would love to come to Italy next summer if it is convenient then, but won't you have too much work to have someone stay? Send me a photograph of your Villa – and a recent one of you if you have one. I enclose one of myself. I still have that one Colette took of you at Les Deux Magots.

Give my best wishes to your Aunt Joséphine and her daughter. Your cousin Solange must be growing up now. My days in Paris seem thirty years ago rather than three. But I have never forgotten them – or you.

Best of luck with your business schemes – will your old

uncle make you a partner – or must you invest a lot of money in it for that to happen?

With all my love

Flora

London

March 1953

Dear Xavier

It was wonderful seeing you on Tuesday – if only you could have stayed longer. But I realize how important it was for you to get back with the orders. Somehow I still can't see you as a businessman and still think of you as a student. I know that making money is only a means to an end for you. I loved seeing the photographs you brought with you of the Villa and can quite see why you are so besotted with the place.

I can't imagine what it must be like to own a place like that. What a responsibility!

You have not really changed to look at – that photo you sent me last year wasn't much like you.

Sorry if I talked too much on Tuesday – sheer nerves – but I always talked a lot, didn't I?

Did you mean it when you asked me to come over in July? Would you give me a definite date?

With love from

Flora

By the time she was twenty-two, the idea of Xavier had become more enticing, more glamorous to Flora. She had 'wasted' him when she was younger! Seeing him in the flesh intensified her new feelings, which were melancholy as well as exciting. She really had no idea what he felt about her. Her growing infatuation for him made the feelings she had nursed for other, less mysterious, men, seem lukewarm, thin-blooded. Perhaps she was just ready to fall in love?

She must see him again soon! But when she did, she must not give him the impression of a besotted young woman.

TWO

Larve d'Amore

i

The Villa

1953

She was standing on deck, looking over the side of the little passenger steamer that went over hourly from the wooded promontory to the opposite side of the lake. It was a hot sunny day and the lake water was coloured turquoise, reflecting and even deepening the brilliant sky.

Now that she was finally to see Xavier on his home ground she felt both nervous and excited. After four years of only occasional letters, and that one meeting the previous March, could she expect anything more from him than they had exchanged during their long conversations? For the last year she had woven a whole tapestry of love around him, and she needed now to get to know him better. She must try to wait and see what he felt; she did not know whether he had ever experienced anything but friendship for her. Women were always supposed to wait, but Flora was an impetuous young woman.

He would not have asked me to stay if he didn't feel something for me, would he? was the questionable hope that was at present going round and round her head.

She was being silly! She must not expect him to fall in love with her as suddenly as she appeared to have done with him.

In her experience, men did not usually fall in love the way women did. Flora was only twenty-two but knew herself well enough to realize that she had believed herself in love even more frequently than most young women. None of these passions of hers had been reciprocated. There had been plenty of young men who lusted after her; alas, never the ones she loved. She had privately called her feelings 'love'; you were not allowed to mention the word to most young men, who would run a mile if you did. Her friend Clare Goodwin said it was just a word women gave to their sexual passions, whereas men were more cagey, and distinguished between 'love' and 'sex'.

Flora felt sure Xavier Leopardi had had many affairs. Maybe not affairs of the heart though – and that was what she wanted with him. Sometimes she said to herself: 'He's in love with his Villa – there isn't room for a woman in his affections.'

She pushed these thoughts away for the time being. She was too introspective. Why could she not prepare to enjoy a holiday in such a beautiful place without tying herself in knots?

The further shore was coming nearer. She could distinguish a church and a large hotel, then nothing but woods bordered the lake where it curved round a little. Behind the curve on her left lay, she knew, the Villa Carolina – or Paulina as it was sometimes still called by the locals with whom she had spoken the previous evening. For some twenty years in the past it had indeed been called 'Paulina'. In answer to her questions the old barman in her small hotel had said: 'Oh, the Leopardi place? They say the family's come back. Villa Paulina it was before the war.'

'Did you know Ferdinando Leopardi?' she had asked him. He had been quick to say 'No', but had added that it had been a bad business. 'Very bad,' and then he had murmured something that sounded like *darsena* but she couldn't be sure and she had not been able to find the word in her small Italian dictionary.

What did the past and the rest of the Leopardi family matter? It was Xavier who had invited her, Xavier who now owned the place. He'd said on the telephone that he'd be waiting at the landing stage. Very soon she'd be able to see him, and everything would fall into place.

There was only a handful of people on the boat, mostly young men who crossed over from one shore to the other for work, and a middle-aged English couple who both wielded cameras that were in constant use.

'Look at that church, Dennis!'

'What are those trees? Are they laurels?'

'Isn't it pretty!'

'I'll take a snap of the boat when we get off.'

'Let's each do one of the promontory.'

'It's too hazy for distance shots.'

And so on.

Flora could hardly believe that this was an ordinary place for ordinary tourists, not a magic one to which she alone had been given the key. She had been told that Verdi had stayed near here, and Stendhal, and heaps of other writers.

She looked back to where they had come from, now a distant village, a huddle and clutter of red roofs, with mountains as backdrop, their summits hazy in the heat. The man called Dennis said: 'They say there's a beautiful old villa further on.' He pointed vaguely away from the church. Flora turned away, irritated. Hurry, hurry, boat!

The boat was doing the opposite of hurry: they were now almost at the shore and it was slowing down to line up by the landing-stage – just a strip of boarding and several bollards. A sailor prepared to cast a rope round one of them. Soon he threw it round the nearest and was ready to jump off the boat to secure it.

There was a little hut, a bicycle leaning awkwardly against it, and a bench with a few people now getting up unhurriedly to get on to the boat for the return trip.

Where was Xavier? If he wasn't there, what would she do?

Flora looked down at her heavy suitcase, heavy because of the books she'd crammed in. She ought to have looked at herself in her handbag mirror; probably she was all greasy and sweaty. Her heart was thumping. The engine stopped. Then a figure that had been hidden behind the others detached itself from a bench near the hut and she saw Xavier Leopardi in an open-necked white shirt and cotton trousers. She waved. He put out a cigarette, ground it down with his heel, raised a hand and then stood quite still as the boat rope was secured to its landing bollard.

She must not appear excited, or in a hurry, so she took care to be one of the last off. Another sailor took her case in one hand and with the other helped her negotiate the gap between boat and dry land.

Xavier was strolling up as she waited and was soon by her side. The sun must have acted upon both his hair and his skin, for his hair was fairer and his skin darker than she remembered from their last meeting. His casual attire had a certain flair that was never, in her opinion, achieved by Englishmen.

He smiled as they shook hands. 'Flora! The car's waiting over there.'

'Is the Villa far away? I couldn't see it from the boat.'

'Only about half a mile – you can't see it from the boat – they cross at the narrowest point.'

He was business-like, took her case, and she followed him to a dark green car.

'Generally, I use my Vespa – but we've just got the old car going again – a miracle!'

Xavier put her case on the back seat and Flora got into the

front seat next to him. Once their drive began she divided her gaze between the trees that came down steeply to the edge of a wood on one side, and the lake on the other, its irregular shining mosaic slatting through the leaves of evergreens planted on a downward slope. She allowed herself then to look at Xavier's wavy hair, now somewhat longer than she remembered, and curling over his collar. Now she would be able to discover what he was really like and would – at last – see the famous Villa.

Eventually, the car was driven up a sandy-covered slope, trees still crowding in on each side, their branches pattering against the windows. They came up to a gateway in a high wall, two white pillars still there to guard the empty space where once the gate had been. As the car went through, she saw a white façade that seemed to be the side of a house, for there were only three long windows, each on top of the other, the top one under a crenellated roof. It must be the Villa? Perhaps this was all it was and Xavier had made the rest up?

A tall woman was standing at a narrow door as the car came into the semi-circular courtyard. She must be in her late sixties but her hair, parted in the middle, was still black.

'Here we are,' said Xavier. 'Back door, I'm afraid. Cars can't get round to the front at present. Only lake transport there.'

He stopped the car, got out, lugged her suitcase from the seat and opened the door for her. She tumbled out into great heat and great silence. There was a scent of pines, and a sudden squawk high up in the trees.

The woman still stood there, saying nothing, making no movement, until she suddenly twitched into life as Xavier walked across with Flora's case. Flora followed and the woman disappeared inside.

Flora followed Xavier down a long corridor on the left, at right angles to the vestibule entrance. Over his shoulder he said to her: 'These rooms are the only ones ready so far.' He stopped before a door, saying: 'Here's yours.'

He opened the door into a narrow room with one window at the far end. Facing the window there was a high wide bed and on the left hand side of the room was an enormous mahogany wardrobe with a long, somewhat tarnished mirror.

'Running water next door,' he continued. 'There'll be something waiting for us in our temporary dining-room when you're ready.'

'Thank you.'

Then he was gone, closing the door quietly behind him.

Flora leaned against the bed for a moment, shutting her eyes, and then she opened them and walked to the mirror. She saw a girl dressed in a long black crumpled skirt with a pattern of green diamonds, and a sleeveless green blouse. The girl had big eyes and a bright lip-sticked mouth and darkish skin turning even browner from that morning's sun.

She would love a wash. Should anyone else be partaking of the lunch she had better appear respectable. When she was introduced to the family she supposed she would have to muster her Italian. It was a pity you couldn't always guess it from your knowledge of French.

She tried to see through the window but it was a little too high to be of any use unless she stood on tiptoe. The room appeared to be at the corner of the house, for she could just glimpse the end of a terrace with a crumbling balustrade on the right. She stood on a chair to pull up the sash and warm, flower-scented air immediately filled the room. She guessed it would be hot at night, but she would leave the shutters open for now.

Next door was a stone-floored room with a sink and an ancient lavatory with a British patent. At least Xavier had got water going there! So far she had received a strong impression of making do. He had warned her about that; it was only during the last year that he had begun to set the place to rights and it might take years to get it back to its former glory, if that could ever be. He'd achieve it in the end though, she was sure.

As she washed her hands and face with the English soap she'd thoughtfully brought with her, and dried them on an old roller towel hanging by the basin, she wondered whether her presence might be a nuisance. She must offer to help him, since it was he who had invited her here.

When she came upon the dining-room she found things were a little less primitive. She guessed these rooms on the ground floor must once have been the servants' quarters. In the *sala da pranzo* there was a long oak table, and two people already sitting on two of the six heavy oak chairs ranged round it. On the right side of the room stood a large moveable dark wooden screen. A matching oak sideboard fashioned like an altar reared up at the far end; next to it an open door led, she assumed, to the kitchen. Through that door now came the tall dark woman, carrying a tray. The two men sitting at the table looked up as Xavier himself entered the room behind the woman.

'Uncle Sasha!' he shouted to the older of the two men who sat by an ear trumpet placed on the table before him. 'This is Flora Russell, an English lady.'

Flora advanced and shook his hand as he turned to gaze at her. He obviously wasn't going to get up. The other man, whom she guessed to be about fifty, did however rise to his feet.

'Ludovic Leopardi. You are welcome,' he said in English in a quiet voice. He was tall, and she noticed, as he came towards her, that he had a slight limp.

The woman carrying the tray put it down and Xavier said: 'Edwige, you must be introduced to Flora.'

Oh, what black eyes she had! And what a searching look

she gave her. She was an intelligent woman, thought Flora, going up and shaking the woman's hand. It was immediately retracted, to busy itself setting out plates of cold *prosciutto di Parma*. She took a large wooden bowl of salad from the tray and then went back into the kitchen.

'Edwige won't eat with us, I asked her again,' said the man called Ludovic. He was quite handsome, but he had a mournful expression in his rather cow-like eyes, eyes that had mauve circles underneath.

'It's up to her,' said his nephew, pouring amber coloured wine from a large pottery jug into everyone's glass. 'Your health, Flora,' he said, lifting his own glass as he smiled at her. Flora responded with a quick swallow of the cool wine, which was delicious, flowery, summer-sweet. Poor Xavier – he had his hands full with all these relations and that old house-keeper. She remembered his talking about her years ago in Paris.

'You ought to have finished your economical studies,' said Uncle Sasha suddenly as they passed round the salad. Turning to Flora he went on: 'He's a clever boy, you know.'

'Yes, I know,' replied Flora, trying hard to understand the old fellow's Italian. It was true that Xavier had never finished the second part of his economics degree at the Sorbonne.

'I learned quite enough,' Xavier said, but his great-uncle seemed not to have heard him. Xavier picked up the ear trumpet and put it to the old man's ear, saying: 'You do not need a degree in economics to make money!'

'No indeed! *è vero!*' said Uncle Ludo mildly.

Flora decided to enjoy the food. She might try a conversation with the younger uncle, Ludo, later. She could not see herself shouting inadequate Italian into an ear trumpet.

'Are you going to show your friend all you intend to do in the house?' Uncle Ludo asked Xavier as he speared a thin wafer of Parma ham on to his fork.

'I shall show her the outside first – she hasn't seen the front yet.'

A woman younger than Edwige, a woman in her late twenties, appeared at the kitchen door, bearing another tray on which was a plate of fat spicy sausages.

'We don't eat much during the day, but we send out for food from the hotel sometimes in the evening,' Xavier said. 'This is Delphine. I don't know what we'd do without her.'

The young woman smiled at Flora, her gaze lingering on her with frank curiosity. Flora thought the woman very elegant, even in an apron over a brown dress. When the woman went out Xavier said: 'She worked for us when she was only fourteen. I can remember her – and a maid called Cécile Agostini. Ludo remembers them, don't you Uncle?'

'Vaguely,' replied Uncle Ludovic, his manner suiting his reply.

A delicious chilled dessert – *semifreddo* – came next, followed by cheese 'to cleanse the tongue,' said Uncle Sasha. After all this, coffee was served in cups scarcely bigger than thimbles.

'Have you a hat?' Xavier asked Flora, getting up. 'The sun is very hot.' He blotted his lips on a large linen napkin, which he then returned to a silver ring on which was engraved a large X. Ludovic and his uncle were about to disappear, the former helping the tottering old man with a languid arm.

'No, I haven't – I didn't want to look like a *turista*,' replied Flora.

'Then I shall fetch you an old linen hat of Aunt Jo's. Wait here and we'll go out at the front.' He disappeared behind the large screen at the side of the room. Delphine came in with an empty tray on which she briskly piled the dirty coffee cups. Flora wondered how you got round to the front of the house. She had her question answered when Xavier appeared, a little breathless, from behind the screen.

'Here – this way.' He handed her a crumpled linen hat and

she followed him behind the screen which concealed a door into the courtyard. Round the side of the house they went, Flora in the hat that was a little big for her, and came out on to a terrace.

'There!' said Xavier, and she drew her breath in sharply in surprise. This terrace was the highest one, set above a sloping, urn-bedecked, tree-shaded lawn. In the distance glittered once more the lake. Although this terrace was on the ground floor level of the house it was still high above the lake, for the villa had been built on a hillside.

'I apologize for the small lunch – and for the back of the house,' he said. 'You'll see – next time you come it will all be different. In the autumn we start on the other rooms at the front.'

Flora stood staring down at the view, holding on to the end of a balustrade. 'It's beautiful – and the lunch was fine.'

'The great gardens are on this side,' he said. 'But it's the wrong season for them, the azaleas, rhododendrons, camellia hedges, they're all overgrown at present. You'd have to come in spring to see them. But the oranges and lemons are ripe further down there.' He pointed to the right. 'I got a gardener to begin on them – there wasn't so much to do there. The Germans – and then when they went, village volunteers from the Committee of National Liberation and their successors – kept them going so they could pick the fruit. Come, I'll take you down the path and then on a grand tour so you can see all the terraces rising up from the bottom.'

They walked down a path on the left bordered by conifers and tree-ferns, down, down, past a garden of tropical plants – palms and cacti – till they came out level with the bottom terrace. Xavier pointed to the garden further down on the left and she saw pergolas, paths, and trees with glimmering yellow and orange and green fruit. It was the first time she had ever seen orange or lemon trees.

'It's like paradise,' she said.

'Paradise after Adam and Eve have left,' Xavier suggested. 'It is a great responsibility, you know.'

'And you own all this?' She gestured from left to right. She had turned round to see the front of the Villa, white in the sun, with pale grey steps edged with stone banisters leading from terrace to terrace, forming a pretty pattern up to the top.

'Yes, all of it. I had to borrow money at first to pay servants and workers – not that we have many at present. Fortunately – until the will is finally proved – there's a demand for silk. How long for we don't know – we may have to diversify into the new synthetic fibres – but Uncle Sasha is hopeful.'

Money was just a means to an end for him she thought – for restoring the Villa.

'May we go right down to the very bottom and then walk up the terraces?'

'Of course – if it is not too hot for you?'

'No, it's fine.' She loved the warmth. 'Nobody lives in the rest of the Villa yet then?'

'Edwige kept a room or two almost until the end of the war but then got chased away for a time by the Americans. She came back in 1946. I've still got my own room at the top as well though it hasn't been redecorated. We've made a start on the ground floor. The bedrooms were all on the top floor – ten rooms to clean out – troops from both sides had used them. They were in a terrible mess.'

Flora looked back again at the square building whose ground floor and beneath were half obscured by overgrown privet hedges at each side, and then once more at the four central terraces with their curving stone balustrades all meeting at the central entrance portico.

'And the middle floor?' she asked, noticing that unlike the ground floor and most of the top floor all its windows had their shutters closed.

'Ah!' he said. 'Those are my special rooms. I'd love to make one of them into a music room. So far I have only an old phonograph downstairs – the grand piano was removed by a German officer. Look, on the left up there – four windows – that's two rooms. In the centre three windows – that's three more rooms, two of them interconnecting and big enough for a concert hall! And on the right again four windows – two more rooms. . . .'

'Yes?'

'One of the rooms on the right next to the interconnecting rooms was my "Violet Room", Flora. You remember? Where I smelled the Parma violets?'

She remembered vaguely something about scents that they had discussed in Paris and how he had talked about the perfume of the violets he remembered from childhood but she could not remember the details.

Abruptly, he changed the subject, saying: 'Uncle Ludo has begun to have his top bedroom painted. Tante Jo will take a suite on the ground floor at the back when she stays here. Edwige has her rooms on the ground floor now, not too far from the kitchens below. You see, at the back, what is the ground floor there is above the ground floor at the front because of the slope. . . .'

'It's so big – all of it—' Flora was lost for words. All the grounds, the gardens, the terraces, his plans for all the rooms he so glibly talked about – why did one small family need all of this? She wanted to ask him: why do you have to have them all living here?, but said instead: 'I suppose all the family will help – I mean financially?'

He looked at her quizzically. 'My uncle Sasha Moirier has a flat in Como but at present – just for the summer – occupies a room here. It's better for his health that he stays in the country. Aunt Jo will want Solange to have a room too, but Edwige may not wish to stay on.' He sighed. 'They all depend on me to get the place to rights. Uncle Edouard died, you know, and left Solange some conscience money. As for Ludo, at present he pays his way doing odd jobs, though he says he'd like to work in Como. I regard the place as my investment. The bank loan sees to things at present, but all my grandfather's money will be released eventually. You'll see!'

She still did not quite see but forbore to ask him any further questions. It was obviously his Shangri-la and he was happily occupied restoring it.

The place was truly beautiful, a value in itself, like some Platonic ideal! Flora sensed it would be spoilt for her if it were dragged into the world of money. Xavier must have divined her thoughts for as they walked up the first flight of stone steps and paused to regard the large waterless fountain at the front, he remarked: 'A pity that wars and arguments got in the way of it all.'

'Will you soon make the fountain play again?'

'Of course, but for the present it is necessary to use the water we do have for washing ourselves, and for the cooking and cleaning. The water engineer is going to unblock the fountain works, then you see it will be eternally recycled. The same water will rise to heaven—' He raised his arm, '—and return to earth—' He lowered his arm '—only to rise again!' He raised both arms this time.

'Eternal rebirth,' she said.

As they arrived at the level below the first terrace where there was a stone bench, she asked: 'Is your Uncle Ludo a good craftsman?'

'Surprisingly good! He's not the most energetic person in the world but he does know what to do – he remembers how it all was in his own childhood before the first war.'

She looked back at the weeds on the surface of the fountain basin. It was cooler sitting under the terrace.

'Three more flights of steps to the grand entrance,' said

Xavier. 'Would you like a cigarette before we climb up?'

She accepted one, though it only made her feel hotter. 'Then, on the other side we used to have the *cascata* – what is that in English?'

'Cascade – waterfall.'

'Over yonder behind the house on the other side.' He pointed with his cigarette.

'"Yonder" is very poetic!' she said.

'What should I say then?'

'"Over there" – but yonder is a more beautiful word.' Talking about words rather than things she felt their old friendship return at last. 'It's a very poetic place,' she went on, still unable to take it all in. But ruins were always poetic, though she could not say that to him. They walked up a flight of stairs, and came on to the first terrace where bougainvillaea spilled down from wall to wall like a stair carpet that had not been properly nailed down.

'My favourite colour!' she exclaimed.

Overgrown greenery hung over the next flight of steps. These brought them to a level from which rose the final curve of the terrace; in its centre was a stone portico with a large black door. At last she was going to see inside the rest of the house.

'We are now on a higher level than the room where you ate your lunch,' said Xavier solemnly, and for a moment she thought he sounded like the guide to a stately home. 'Shall we go inside? You might find it rather creepy – Delphine says there is a ghost. There's no furniture left in these rooms so it doesn't matter if we leave the shutters open. There is nothing the sun can spoil.'

He had lapsed into Italian and she listened, only half understanding. She wanted to ask him so many things. How had his grandfather Ferdinando died? Why had he himself abandoned his degree in mid-stream? Was Edwige any sort of relation? Why did Uncle Ludo have a limp? She did not know the Italian for that. Limp Uncle Ludo had a limp . . . she was rambling. It must be the sun. She had liked Ludo. He had smiled at her in a kindly sort of way.

'Why does your Uncle Ludo limp?' she asked him.

'Because he had a piece of shrapnel or something lodged in his leg in Sicily,' replied Xavier. 'He didn't want to fight – I believe he hated the whole idea – but it got him away from here and from his father. I expect he met lots of nice soldiers too!'

As he was opening the outer door with a large iron key produced from his pocket, she asked: 'When will your Aunt Josephine and your cousin Solange come on a visit?'

'September or October, I believe, but Tante Jo is fussy – she won't come unless she can be comfortable.'

All her possessions would be in Paris, thought Flora, but she might want to look for things she had left here fourteen years ago when she had been obliged to make her home in another country.

'Solange has never seen the place,' Xavier went on. 'Aunt says she must finish at the lycée before she comes to live here for good, if she ever wants to. That's at least another six years. And perhaps she will not want to come. Her father didn't really belong here.'

He pushed open the great door and relapsed into silence as Flora followed him into the vast hall: high, marble-floored, half-lit, with only one or two open blinds. A staircase rose upwards from the centre of the room to the floor above. Despite the great heat outside it was a little chilly here. She shivered. In the half-light she saw a balcony running round three sides of the floor above, with carved figures on a stone frieze.

'There were marble sculptures here once,' Xavier said, 'but the Germans took them all away. Come through.' They went under the staircase to where another room opened out. The smell was of dust, and perhaps attar of roses – not unpleasant. 'I'll show you the top floor, but the lift is not working yet. We can go up these stairs here.'

There was a staircase rising from this back room and she toiled up it after him. He did not pause on the first floor but went on climbing till they came out on a lighter central landing, the end windows unshuttered, late afternoon sun coming in. He pointed above to a scooped-out dome in the roof.

'Up there next to the dome is the clock room. The clock has stopped of course, but I shall see to that. Do you mind heights?'

'Yes – I always feel giddy.'

'Then I shall not take you there. I have been only twice myself.' He went to the window, saying: 'Look. From here you can see the whole of the front!'

She gasped at the view: the great fountain, the high hedges of privet, which from here looked impenetrable, and the first terrace. From this height the other terraces were hidden and the eye was led down to a pair of enormous traceried cast-iron gates, the lake shining behind them. It all dazzled her eyes in the bright sun.

'I think they built it for the view,' he said. 'I will show you some more of the rooms later, but I think you may be tired?'

'Yes, it is a lot to take in.'

'And as it is now five o'clock, though the clock has stopped at midnight, unlike your Grantchester one that always stood at ten to three, it is time for English ladies to take tea. It will be Italian tea though, with our own lemons.'

'Oh Xavier it is all so beautiful! But there is so much to be done!' She thought, too much.

'Yes, but it will be done. I shall do it. You like my house!'

He was both overweeningly proud and a little pathetic, she thought disloyally. He seemed more foreign here. Yet he was so kind and attentive.

They went down by another side staircase, passing his own room. He murmured: 'That is my old room,' but did not open the door. At the bottom of the stairs a door led into the kitchens. Delphine was sitting there in a rocking chair knitting. There was no sign of Edwige.

'Go into the dining room and I shall bring a tray of tea – or is it a tea-tray?'

'A tray of tea – you put the cups on a tea-tray.'

At least he was getting some free English lessons. She might even learn from him how to speak passable Italian. He had assured her it was important for him to learn English, 'Because of the Americans – they have all the money and I need that!' She thought, his grandmother was American. Is she dead too?

Over the tea she asked no more questions and when he said he must meet some workmen at six o clock who were to come over from the nearest town, she found her way back to her narrow room, intending to write down her first impressions. But instead she fell into a heavy doze, waking only in time for supper.

They ate a delicious meal of lake fish washed down by a local white wine, drier than the one they had drunk at lunch time but just as cold. After saying, 'The fish is good today,' Uncle Ludovic was silent throughout the meal. Flora imagined he probably kept his own counsel. Even if he disapproved of his nephew's plans he would probably know better than to outwardly disagree with him. How much of Ferdinando Leopardi's money would go to Ludovic, who was after all his son, not his grandson?

Sasha Moirier was talkative, once he had dealt with his fish-bones, or rather Delphine had come in and delicately removed them for him.

'Edwige cooked this?' he asked the maid, and on her affir-
mative reply he said: 'Thought it wasn't hotel muck.' At least
that was what Flora thought he said. His speech was not easy
to understand. A few moments later he looked at Flora,
saying quite out of the blue: 'Ferdy was a hard worker – took
his pleasures hard too.'

Xavier muttered: 'So hard he had to get himself killed,' but
the old man did not hear him. Flora looked at Xavier in
surprise. Perhaps she was now going to be told how
Ferdinando had died. But Xavier said no more. Ludo woke up
then and said: 'Father was a good businessman.'

'Eh?' said the old man and took up his ear trumpet. Ludo
patiently repeated his words, to which Sasha replied: 'Never
lent me a cent, you know, not even when Feodora begged him
to. Still, I had the last laugh,' and he wheezed as he now
laughed once again.

Edwige came in then, bearing an apple tart, and Sasha
stared at her with a fierce expression. She returned his look in
full measure as she looked up from fussing round Ludovic
with the dish. When she had gone out Uncle Sasha said: 'Why
do you keep her on?'

'You wouldn't have any dinner without her,' said Xavier.
Flora was baffled by all these undercurrents.

After the meal, Xavier said: 'I found the old phonograph,
Uncle Ludo. I thought we might take it next door and listen
to a few old records.'

Next door, turned out to be a sort of anteroom to the dining
room: you could scarcely call it a sitting-room. Three sides of
the room were lined with three old sofas, each flush with the
wall, and there was a small table in the middle that looked as
though it had once belonged to a nursery, for Flora saw child-
ish drawings on its deal surface. On it stood a box from which
Xavier extracted a pile of His Master's Voice records. Sasha
had disappeared.

'Wherever did you find them?' asked Ludo.

'Up at the top of the house,' replied Xavier, giving no further details.

Flora went to look in the box. There was a smell of dust and mildew, and another scent a little like that attar of roses she had sensed in the main part of the house. Suddenly Edwige was in the room with them, holding a duster which she gave to Xavier.

'Don't go, Edwige, stay and listen to the music,' said Ludo. She raised her eyebrows. Flora had never seen anyone enact such an eyebrow-raising.

'There's some Gigli,' said Xavier.

'Oh Gigli – I *love* his singing!' exclaimed Flora. She probably had some of the same records? *Che gelida manina* and *Salve dimora*.

Edwige sat down on one of the horsehair sofas, her hands folded in her lap.

'You can choose one first,' said Xavier to Flora. 'Then we can have a concert.' He fished in his pocket and produced a tin box of needles which he placed on the table; he began to wind up the handle. It certainly looked like one of the original machines. Flora joined Xavier at the table. Uncle Ludo was now looking wistfully out of the window. Flora looked carefully at each record as Xavier handed them to her. They did not all feature Gigli; there were some singers she'd never heard of but Puccini's operas were well represented. 'What's this?' she asked. '*L'alba separa* by d'Annunzio Tosti? Who is d'Annunzio Tosti?'

Somebody replied: 'Two people! D'Annunzio was a poet, Signorina.' It was Edwige who spoke. They were the first words Flora had heard the woman address to her personally.

'Who was Tosti then?'

Xavier exclaimed 'You don't know *Tosti*, Flora! When he was your dear old queen's music master?'

'Which queen was that?'

'Why, Victoria of course! And he wrote lots of songs for the Italians as well as the English. Do you want to hear this one? It's a setting of a poem by d'Annunzio, one of his finest.'

'Signor Leopardi was a great admirer of Signor d'Annunzio,' Edwige said. 'I will stay and listen to this.'

'Then I shall show you some books,' said Xavier to Flora, giving the handle a final twist. Flora had been wondering when books would appear in this house. 'My grandfather had all his poems.'

She waited. The turntable squeaked slightly and then a voice began to sing – a long liquid line, melancholy yet powerful, almost ecstatic. She watched Xavier as the song finished. He had his head thrown back, his eyes closed. When the last note died away, Ludo said: 'Oh what memories, eh, Edwige?'

Edwige got up. 'You chose well,' she said in Italian to Flora. Then she turned and went out of the room.

'It was her favourite – you could not have chosen better,' said Xavier waking up. 'I shall choose Tosti also – his great "Farewell".'

Flora was enchanted by these songs. Why had she never heard them before?

They went through all the records in the box, then Flora said: 'May I hear that first one just once again before I go to bed?'

Xavier looked at her curiously. 'Yet he was a Fascist too, you know,' he said softly.

'Who, Tosti?'

'No! No! d'Annunzio. Like my sainted grandfather.'

'I'd like to read his verse even so,' she said.

'Then I shall find the books for you.'

He put the record on again and she liked it even more the second time.

In her diary that night she wrote about the music, and about Edwige Rouart, whom she could not make out.

'I shall never forget this evening, for it was the occasion for my hearing for the first time the beautiful sentimental songs of Tosti. I had the feeling that Xavier was glad I chose Gigli and those songs. I feel that somehow Xavier wants me to buttress his own feelings, wants me to tell him he is not wrong to feel as he does about the house, wants me to feel it too. Although he did not say, I believe that music has memories also for him.'

Flora Russell stayed two weeks in Italy that summer. At the back of her mind had been a notion that Xavier might possibly ask her to stay on longer – or she might find a new job in Italy or France. But after a few days at the Villa she knew she must not stay for more than two weeks. If she had been a plumber or a painter and decorator she might have offered to work for the family for her keep, but any talents she possessed were not in that line.

He was still the old Xavier she had known in Paris, but now she felt that he was partially hidden under a new shell of business and plans, all arising from his passion for the Villa. During her first week, which she spent helping him with accounts, or reminding him of English words in exchange for Italian ones, he did no more than touch her hand or take her arm or look at her in a friendly fashion. In the cool of the evening they sometimes went for a walk round the place and she saw the dried up *cascata* and the other parts of the garden. She sensed that Ludo, and even Edwige Rouart, thought she might be his 'little friend' as the Italians said, or even that he was in love with her. Perhaps it was obvious that she was in love with him. She had never been one for hiding her feelings, and why else would she come to stay with him and his odd family?

Now and then Xavier would disappear on business and Flora would be left to her own devices. She did not in the least mind this, for she was of an independent spirit, never at a loss to find something to do or to think about. She had also brought plenty with her to read. But how, if at all, she fitted into his scheme of things, was still uncertain. It did not seem that he intended any physical intimacy, yet she had the strong impression that she was there to be observed, and that he had plans for her future.

After the first week she evolved a little routine for herself. She saw no great need to get up early if Xavier was in any case busy. At about nine o'clock she would go to the dining-room, deserted at that time, drink her coffee and eat a roll or two, all brought to her by Edwige who never said more than 'buon giorno'. Then she would look for Xavier who had made himself a little office in an old cloakroom and was usually to be found there, more often than not talking on the ancient upright telephone. She would ask if there was anything she could do for him before luncheon. Once or twice she helped him by writing in a little black exercise book which he always carried with him his plans for the rooms: colours, paint, furniture; or the garden: lists of plants in Latin. But usually there was not a great deal she *could* do except keep out of the way. He had warned her before she came that he would be busy but would still be delighted to see her, and she had taken him – and still took him – at his word. She did not need to be entertained. 'But couldn't I help Edwige with the cooking?'

'No, no! she has Delphine – we run a simple household.'

The two uncles stayed out of the way in the mornings, Ludo in his room, which he said was quite clean enough and needed no further embellishments, and Sasha resting in a small bedroom not far from her own in the old servants' quarters.

It seemed, then, that Flora was at liberty to explore alone

before lunch, before the heat of the day became too extreme. They were having a hot summer. She would wander in the overgrown gardens, learning the names of the plants from Xavier's lists; some of the original metal labels still remained from the time when gardeners had tended the place.

There was a tiny strip of road between the great gates of the Villa and the shore. One morning she decided to cross it and explore further down by the lake. In a southerly direction, across the water in the direction of Como, the view was open, with thickly wooded slopes stretching behind occasional scatterings of red roofs belonging to distant villages. Northwards, however, beyond the promontory opposite, the lake gave a sharp turn, and the rest of the shore was a mystery.

She sat down on some steps by the side of the lake near a stone arch. There were more steps leading down to the water, and a balustraded wall of the same design as the terraces, also bearing statues and urns, led up the other side to the top of a small stone building smothered in greenery. This must belong to the Villa too? Lake water came through the arch and a small rowing boat was anchored by the steps. It all looked extremely ancient. Craning her neck she looked through the arch. It must be the boathouse? She must ask Xavier about it. She walked back up the slope and descended the stairs on the other side, running her hands on the stone balustrade as she came down to the arch she had seen at first. It was so pleasantly cool and shady that she decided to sit there hidden. She sat on there for an hour, wishing she had brought her camera, but too lazy to go back for it. The steps and the urns were elegantly photogenic. She would bring a camera tomorrow.

At about half past twelve she crossed the road again and went back into the house. Xavier was in the courtyard at the back.

'A pleasant walk, Flora?' He had a few smudges on his forehead and she thought he looked tired.

'I was down by the lake. I found a beautiful little place –
there was a rowing boat tied up there. Is it yours?'

'Oh, that would be Luciano's – *we* don't use the boathouse
any more.' He used the word *darsena* which Flora presumed
must mean boathouse.

When they sat down at the table in the dining room Uncle
Sasha was already there reading his newspaper.

Ludo came in soon after. 'I found some more records!' he
said to Flora, handing her the large wooden bowl of different
kinds of lettuce which Edwige had brought in. 'Gigli again –
you'd like them.' He turned to Xavier: 'They were up in the
top lumber room. They may have been Jo's. *La Paloma* was
among them – do you remember when you were a little boy
she used to listen to that?'

'It was a tango,' said Sasha.

'Tangos are hard to dance well,' Flora said. 'But I'd love to
listen to more Gigli, Ludo!' He had asked her to call him by
his first name.

'I'll bring it down then – there was some cabaret music too.'

They all mixed their own salads. Flora took some crisp and
curly lettuce and some dark red slices of tomato from the
bowl, sprinkled a little salt on them, took some chopped basil
from a little dish, then dripped olive oil over the lot, mixed it
well and twirled it around. *Insalata* was eaten as a main
course at lunch time and was delicious. She loved the Villa
food – the *panini* (little bread rolls), the grilled peppers, the
slices of mozzarella, the *polenta* cooked in all sorts of different
ways, which Xavier said was peasants' food, and the lake fish,
especially the *avarello*, a sort of bream. She devoured fresh
fruit – grapes and peaches and melons – all washed down
with Soave, or Lugana from Lake Garda. Everything tasted
delicious.

'You like our food then?' asked Ludo, seeing Flora enjoying
her *insalata*.

'Flora likes everything here,' said Xavier complacently.

Sasha said: 'I expect Edwige would prefer to cook à la française.'

'We have neither the staff nor the facilities for long and complicated dishes,' said Xavier, frowning.

'What does he say?' said Sasha. Xavier seized the ear-trumpet which had so far lain unregarded by the old man's side and poked it towards Sasha's ear.

'Edwige has too much to do,' he shouted.

'Yes, yes,' said the old man testily. 'It would be more sensible for him to sell up, wouldn't it, Signorina Flora?'

She was not sure what he meant but replied: 'I don't think that it is always best to be sensible, Signor.'

Xavier smiled. Sasha gave no sign that he had heard her reply.

Later that afternoon in her room she thought, well of course it would make more sense for Xavier to sell the Villa. With its grounds he could get a good price, but she supposed it was his obsession to recover all he had lost, to recover his lost childhood.

The next morning she decided to go to the little shops on the other side of the hotel about half a mile away to look for souvenirs to take back home. She must buy some postcards of the place.

They were very cut off at the Villa. She might be in Italy but she had seen more of Italy on the day of her arrival than since. Here it was just 'The Villa', with, to be sure, Italians to get to know, the Italian language to listen to and Italian food to enjoy – but all belonging to a distinctive family, probably not a typical one. It seemed however that the shopkeepers knew quite a lot about the Villa. Flora bought her postcards and a silk scarf for her mother, and then decided to buy a newspaper to improve her Italian. The woman behind the counter said: 'Staying at the hotel are you?'

'No, I am staying at the Villa.'

'At the Villa! Well well! Giuseppe, do you hear that?' She shouted to a man who was busy at the ice-cream counter. 'This young lady is staying at the Paulina.'

The man looked up, shrugged his shoulders. The woman turned to Flora. 'They're making lots of changes there, then?'

'Yes, it is all being restored,' said Flora in her best Italian.

'Restored? We heard there was a lot of damage done – we were away in the war. My husband's parents are from near here – his brother once worked for the old man.' She smiled, did not seem hostile, though certainly curious. Her husband looked up then.

'A lot of damage!' he echoed. 'Apart from the *human* damage.' He tittered unpleasantly.

The woman said in a low voice as she handed Flora her scarf wrapped up in green tissue paper: 'I always say some things are better forgotten, signorina. It wasn't as if he was killed in the Villa itself, was it?'

Flora did not know what she was talking about and could not help asking: 'Do you mean Ferdinando Leopardi?'

'*Si, si* – the old man. Oh! We heard lots of stories about him – but let bygones be bygones – I expect it was mostly gossip – apart from the politics. . . .'

'How did he die?' Flora was impelled to ask.

'You know – the ones who killed—' she dropped her voice '*Il Duce* – they should have taken *him* to Milano too – but it seems they couldn't wait. . . .'

'Hanged in his own boathouse,' said the man. Flora felt suddenly cold. Had she heard aright? *Darsena*, that was the word.

'So you're helping them out at the Villa, I expect?' the woman continued.

'Yes,' said Flora faintly. 'Er – I think I will have a *gelato*.' She could think of no other way of stopping this conversation.

The man served her quite cheerfully now and both he and his wife said *'arriverderci'* when, clutching her ice-cream in one hand and her purchases in the other, she turned to go out of the shop.

She walked slowly back to the Villa, thinking that only yesterday morning she had sat by the old boathouse. Had it been there that the old man had died? The more she considered, the more she felt reluctant to say anything to Xavier about it. Perhaps he might tell her in any case – though it wasn't the sort of thing you could just come out with casually. She had given him an opportunity the other day when she had mentioned the boathouse, and all he'd said was that they didn't use it any longer and someone called Luciano did.

How many other family secrets were hidden? The two uncles must know all about their brother-in-law's and father's death. Most likely neither had been anywhere near when it happened. She remembered, when she was about fourteen, reading the accounts of Mussolini, executed by the partisans, his corpse then taken to Milan, to be hung by its ankles on public display by the side of his mistress Clara Petacci, and she knew already that old Ferdinando Leopardi had been a follower of *Il Duce*. So had many other people; indeed, she even remembered when she was a child an old aunt of hers saying that the man was at least getting the Italian trains to run on time. Her father had been scornful, had talked about the war in Abyssinia.

Flora resolved to try to forget what she had heard.

One evening during that last week, Ludo put *La Paloma* on the old gramophone and she and Xavier danced together to the catchy sad rhythm. It was physically the closest they had come together since her arrival and it gave her a sort of heady excitement. Edwige and Ludo and Delphine watched them dancing together, then Uncle Ludo danced with Delphine and they ended up listening to some German cabaret songs. When Xavier was out of the room Ludo remarked to Delphine that Xavier's father had brought them back from Berlin about twenty years ago. It was the first time that Paul Leopardi had been mentioned among the family. Flora thought that Edwige looked uncomfortable.

The next evening Xavier, perhaps aware that, as her host, he had been neglecting Flora, perhaps realizing that she should not yet be expected to share his passion for the Villa Violetta, took her to an evening open-air concert in the old town of Bergamo. She was to look back on that concert and the time they spent wandering along the cool alleys, under the arches and across the cobbled squares as a high-spot of her holiday. That night, unable to sleep, she wrote in her diary:

At the concert in Bergamo tonight I heard Wagner's 'Star of Eve' from Tannhäuser. It was mellifluously perfect, glowingly sad. Xavier was very quiet throughout the concert and I wondered what he was thinking. Afterwards, he said he had not really appreciated the Wagner and that made me unhappy, because straight away that song spoke to me of a twilight far away in time and space. I was perhaps three or four years old, sitting in a push chair that was being wheeled by my mother at dusk into a little cemetery. The voice ceased and the strings took up the melody, but I was still back in a distant childhood, a time long before Xavier, long before Paris.

The music that spoke to me of another time, another place, stirred and shifted the self that lies underneath my newer self that is here in Italy with Xavier. Here in Italy I have less subtle yearnings. Italian music seems to speak to those parts of myself that lie nearer the surface of my life, not the same 'layer' that saw the evening star for the first time.

*

Two evenings before Flora was due to leave for England there was a sudden thunderstorm. From the top floor of the Villa they watched the lightning flash over the lake.

Xavier invited her to look through those books he'd told her he'd found there. In a tea chest there were several volumes of poems by the writer Ludo had mentioned, Gabriele d'Annunzio, along with children's books in Russian and French that Xavier said had belonged to his grandfather's first wife Feodora; there were some American children's books too.

'Those were *my* grandmother's, I expect. Oh, look! There's a book I remember reading when I was about six!' he exclaimed when a garishly-coloured copy of *Pinocchio* turned up. After that they emptied all the books out on to the floor. Apart from the poems they all seemed to be children's stories. Suddenly Flora's attention was caught by an inscription in a copy of *Uncle Remus*: To dear little Paul from his Mamma. Christmas 1917.

'Is that your father?' asked Flora.

'Show me. Yes, that's him.'

More than ever before she wanted to ask him: 'Where is your mother in all this?' but something held her back.

It was with a conviction that the mystery of Xavier's mother was about to be explained that she readily accepted his invitation, the following morning, to go up with him to the middle floor of the Villa. As they climbed the stairs he said: 'I think you'll find these are the most beautiful rooms in the whole Villa.'

They reached the corridor and he flung open one of the doors to the many rooms facing the lake. It was furnished with Empire sofas and small tables, all dimly visible behind closed shutters. An inner door led to a second room.

Beckoning Flora to follow, he opened it, and then marched to a window and flung wide the shutters. She gasped in surprise when she saw a fine carpet, velvet armchairs and an Empire bed with a silk cover.

'Good heavens. Where did you get the furniture? Was it there already?' she asked.

'I haven't bought the curtains yet,' said Xavier. 'What do you suggest?'

'Long cream drapes?'

'Mm?'

She was looking at the ceiling frieze.

'That needs to be painted,' he said.

She looked down at the floor.

'The carpet is not right,' Xavier said. 'I'm thinking of bringing back the marble – the Germans stripped the marble from some of the rooms, you see. I've only opened up two of these rooms. There are others – the best ones – that I shall do up this winter or later.'

'Are these your Violet rooms?' Flora asked hesitantly.

'Two of the others are really those, but these two also belong to my Violet Villa.'

'May I see the others?'

'Oh, there is nothing to see there yet. Can you smell violets, Flora? I'm sure I can!'

She was obliged to admit that she could not. The smell was the same as everywhere else, the smell of the past, she thought.

'It doesn't matter. You know, Flora, I shan't open up the other rooms until I have more money to do them justice.'

'May I not just have a look at them?'

'Oh, there is nothing to see.'

They went out into the corridor again and she looked along it towards an oriel window, projecting outwards. She felt a curious sensation in her chest, a sort of constriction. Yet, out of impatience, or curiosity she could not seem to help wanting to push him further.

'Just tell me which ones they are.'

'If you must know.'

He went up to the next door and leaned against it. 'Come here. You see – it is locked.'

He pulled her roughly to him and she thought, oh, now, at last, he is going to kiss me. But instead of the hot kiss on the mouth which she knew she wanted, he smoothed her hair and kissed her gently on the forehead.

'There, Flora – you are so fresh and good it would be a pity to spoil you.'

What did he mean? Surely he did not imagine she was still a virgin pure and unsullied? Her experience might not have been vast but she had made love with one or two young men.

'I am not a child,' she said. 'And I love you, Xavier.'

Before she spoke the words she had not known she was going to say them. What had spoken from inside her? Was it just frustrated desire?

She had a sudden brain-wave. These must have been his *mother's* rooms – that was why he had such a 'thing' about them. His dead mother. With her in mind, he would not want to kiss a young woman other than purely. Latins were odd about their mothers – something to do with Catholicism perhaps?

'Were these once your mother's rooms?' she asked him as he held her hand in his and looked earnestly into her face.

He sprang back as if she had shot him.

'My mother's? Oh no! No, certainly not.' He leaned against the wall. 'Why do you say that?'

'Because you never speak of her – nobody does – and you once told me you had been told she was dead. . . .'

He made a visible effort to control whatever emotions were raging in him. 'I believe now that she is dead,' was all he said as he turned away and marched down the corridor towards the stairs. She had perforce to follow him.

'Xavier – tell me – what was her name?'

He did not slow down and she hurried down the stairs after him.

'Victoire,' he flung over his shoulder.

She caught up with him at the bottom of the stairs. 'I'm sorry, Xavier, that I upset you – I was just puzzled, you see. . . .'

'Don't let's talk about it.'

His mother must have abandoned him, then. That must be why he was so odd about her and why nobody else would talk about her.

He turned before they reached the door into the servants' quarters. '*They* don't want to talk about her either,' he said. Or about your grandfather, she thought.

He took her hand again. 'Flora, I trust you,' he said.

'Then let me love you – one day,' she replied. The intensity of his tone was a little frightening but perhaps she frightened him too. Women were not supposed to declare themselves.

He did not reply except to take her hand again and kiss it gently.

The next day she left the Villa.

He took her in the car to the boat and was again friendly and attentive. She felt, paradoxically, frustrated. Whatever was the cause of his mystery was not going to be revealed to her now. She had made it clear she loved him, had cast herself metaphorically at his feet, yet was not sure whether he had rejected her or not. There was something in the way he treated her that she still could not understand. If she roused his sexual appetite he gave no evidence of it. If he found her a bore he did not say so. He had seemed to want her to be there, had treated her on the whole like a friend or

– she searched for the word – an old-fashioned sort of *fiancée!* Perhaps he categorized women as some Englishmen did, into those whom you respected and those with whom you slept?

She did not want to say goodbye to him in this miserable state of indecision. As they stood waiting for the boat to arrive she ventured:

'Are you angry with me?'

He looked astonished.

'Why no, Flora – of course not.' They were speaking French. 'I don't want you to go,' he said. 'But you must. Things are still fluid here – I shall be better organized next year. Next year you will see; it will all be different!'

'You want me to come again then?'

'Of course – *mais naturellement!*'

So he saw her as semi-permanent fixture in his life? She was puzzled.

'I should like to see you in France,' she said. 'Or at home, away from all your – preoccupations. . . .'

'We shall have to see. Write to me, Flora, and I will write to you.'

So they parted, and it was over a year before she saw him again.

ii

Menton

1954

In the spring of 1954 Ferdinando Leopardi's will was finally proved. The Villa Carolina was to descend to Ferdinand's grandson, Xavier Bruno Leopardi, provided he went on living there. Money for its upkeep had apparently been stowed away in Swiss bank accounts; Ludovic Leopardi was to receive an annuity; Josephine a much smaller one. Edwige Rouart, however, was left a diamond necklace which had also been deposited in a Swiss bank, thus fortunately escaping the ravages of war. In April Sasha Moirier died.

It was also in 1954 that Xavier publicly renamed the Villa the *Villa Violetta*.

Xavier explained all this to Flora in his letters, for the two continued to write to each other.

Sometimes Flora wondered if there was any future for herself with Xavier; at other times she felt sure she had been destined to meet him.

He was even busier this summer, he said, and did not want her to come for another visit until everything was perfect. Flora half agreed with this. But there must surely be somewhere else that they could meet? Away from the Villa, she and

Xavier might have a different sort of relationship?

She had always wanted to visit the south of France, so she decided to ask him if they could be together for a few days in Menton, the town where he had lived when he first left Italy. If he did not want to meet her there, well, she might go by herself. She needed a holiday. Her latest job as secretary to the manager of the export branch of a large publishing house was more congenial than the last, but she still tired of London and its rush hours.

She was sure Xavier would be different if he could be detached from the Villa! She felt that if he could not enter upon a relationship with her that she could regard as adult, then she would feel free to look elsewhere.

I don't want to play games with Xavier, she wrote in her journal, *but it would be morally right to become his lover!*

All her instincts now said to her: Get to know him better. It isn't a sin to love someone and want to make him happy.

The only matter that worried her was the possibility of the pregnancy that might follow such rashness.

Another more rational – or judgemental – part of her told her that Xavier himself might not see her love as innocent. Girls who expressed themselves physically were not good girls. She dismissed this possible reaction as not being worthy of the sophisticated Xavier she knew.

She quite often dreamed of him. Sometimes he was making passionate love to her; at other times he was cold, and she felt spurned. These dreams haunted her. She was prepared for Xavier not to be in love with her in the way she now knew she could be, perhaps already was, in love with him. Even in her previous affairs she had found that disappointment often followed ardour, but this had not made her any the less keen to pick herself up and try again. And Xavier *was* different from the other young men she had known. Without idealizing him she knew that was true. Maybe when she knew him better – certainly if or when she knew him physically, she would understand him.

She received further letters from him in a mixture of French and English and Italian but still knew nothing more about his mother. She even contemplated writing to Tante Jo to ask her about Victoire – but feared Xavier would be angry. She had no right to pry. About the death of Ferdinando Leopardi she had dared ask no one in the family, though she had gone to the Newspaper Library to see if it had been reported in 1945. She had drawn a blank. Probably he had not been famous enough.

May 13 1954

Dear Flora

I sometimes wonder how free we all are. I mean, we are made up of our childhood experiences and our language and our social class and our religion and the country where we were brought up, none of which is within our own control at first. Can you imagine a little Xavier brought up in your English town speaking English and with no horrible war to separate him from the house he loves . . .?

Reading this, Flora thought: he does not mention his parents. Yet a person's mother and father must be the most important influences on their life?

Are we born with a certain temperament? Do our genes account for all of us? If so, how can we possess free will? Remember our philo classes – the endless discussions about environment and heredity? I think of such things as I labour away here. Things are looking good! I have already given up my office work at the silk factory and Ludo has decided to take over Uncle Moirier's post for the time being. Should I have offered him some of the money left me for the Villa? He does not seem to care that the place is not his – and of course he will

live here for as long as he wants. I am determined to be generous. . . .

We inherit our environment, thought Flora. Within the
constraints of money and time and place, a certain sort of
person makes a certain kind of life for him or her self – and
then their children will have parts of both the heredity and
the environment. And so it must go on. . . .

Villa Violetta
July 27 1954

Dear Flora
I received your letter about Menton yesterday. If I visit France
in September and meet you there it will probably be my last
real holiday away. I am finding it more and more difficult to
tear myself away from here even to go to Como. But I am
taking your advice about making an effort of will – just to see
if I can . . . and so, yes, I shall be able to spend one week with
you. I will leave you to make the arrangements. . . .

Flora went ahead and booked two communicating rooms in a
small hotel near the sea, with a garden, away from the busy
centre of Menton. Xavier had not said whether he wanted a
room of his own, so she played safe. It would be up to Xavier
to tell her if he wanted to spend his nights with her.

On the first day of her holiday she wandered alone all over
the town, sat on the promenade looking at the sea, and fended
off the advances of several youths who could not understand
why a young woman should be by herself. It was hot, so she
doused herself liberally with the lemon-scented perfume
which was sold all over the town.

During the morning of her second day there, she sat reading in the shade at a table in the garden of the hotel. I am
perfectly content just now, she thought, 'and yet I know I shall
either be miserable or elated this time tomorrow.'

Xavier was to arrive from Ventimiglia at six o'clock that evening at the railway station in Menton.

She went to meet him, a jumble of sensations warring in her: fear that he would not be there; worry that she would suddenly fall out of love with him the moment they met again; hope that he would be the old Xavier; delight that at last they would be alone together.

Yes, he did look a little different – a little less thin perhaps. He put his arm round her and sniffed her hair.

'Lemon shampoo,' she said.

He asked, 'Is it far? We'll take a taxi if it is.'

'About half a mile – too far to walk in this heat.'

They were speaking French. Suddenly she was filled with happiness.

On arriving back at the hotel she waited as he signed in and then said, as they went up in a tiny lift to the second floor: 'Your room is next to mine.'

'I hope you have chosen me a good view?'

'The view is of the gardens – there was nothing left overlooking the sea. It's a lovely place. Where did you live when you came here at the outbreak of war?'

'I think it was the other side of town – nearer the harbour – but I have really forgotten.'

She thought: yet he remembers so much from before he was even here.

'I shall go down to the garden whilst you unpack,' she said, when he had opened the door of his own room and she had pointed to her own.

'Oh, there is little to unpack – I am not used to holidays, Flora.'

Then he pulled her to him and kissed her eyes as she stood there, murmuring: 'It is strange finding you here, Flora – but I am glad.' He had apparently decided to make it plain they were to be more intimate than they had been the previous summer. She kissed him back and then withdrew from him a little.

'I shall order you a drink and we can eat here in the garden.'

'Flora – I –'

'You can see my room later,' she said.

She went down to the garden to the chair where her magazine still lay and found she was in an emotional turmoil. She knew that nothing put most men off so much as a too eager anticipation of their own desires. He would have to make it easier for her if he wanted to make love to her. As she sipped her glass of iced Cinzano and soda she found herself almost wishing that they were embarking on a purely sensual affair. That way there would be no embarrassments, no high mutual expectations. Don't expect anything, she kept saying to herself, he may not want you as a lover. Then the feel of his skin against hers as he had kissed her just now overrode her resolution to be reasonable.

'What are you thinking about?' he asked as he came to sit by her side. He had changed into a white open-necked shirt and she thought he looked very handsome.

'Oh I was thinking about you, Xavier!'

'I am flattered.' He smiled.

'I thought you would never be able to leave your Villa. Tell me all the news. It's so lovely to see you here.' He took the glass of vermouth she had ordered for him, and sucked the lemon peel.

'Did I tell you I thought up a wonderful way of making some money to invest in my Villa Violetta?'

'Something new?'

'Yes. I thought we could offer one or two of the rooms to intelligent foreigners – the high class sort, you know. They say the Americans are going to buy one or two of the other villas on the lake and convert them into holiday centres.'

'You wouldn't want to run a hotel, surely?' she said quickly.

'No, no, not a hotel. Just one or two rooms we could – how do you say – "do up"? – and make a little income from them.'

'Are you so short of money? I thought your grandfather's will had made everything OK?' She was already wishing they had not embarked upon this conversation.

'It is enough to live on, you know, so I need not bother any more with the business; Ludo is enjoying himself in Como sorting things out there. But I was getting impatient with the rest of the restoration and it means I shall need ready money to hurry it up. I have nearly finished the painting of the best rooms—'

'Not your Violet Rooms! You wouldn't put visitors in there?'

'No, of course not. Those rooms will be for me – and perhaps for you too, Flora, when you come next time!'

She wanted to change the subject, but he went on: 'Some Americans came to look at the gardens thinking they were public. As children in Chicago it seems these people knew my grandmother! And once met my father when he visited her in 1938. It was pure chance they turned up and got talking to Edwige!'

This might be a good time to ask him all the questions she had never before dared to ask, the kind you could not really broach in letters. She took her courage in both hands and said: 'Who exactly is Edwige Rouart? Does she work for you all for nothing?'

He was silent for a moment and then replied: 'She was nursemaid to Tante Jo and to Uncle Ludo after their mother died when they were quite small – before my grandfather married my grandmother, Paulina. Later he made her house-keeper and when I was a child I believe she also entertained his friends after his wife had gone away.'

'She's French, isn't she? Not Italian?'

'Oh, she's quite acclimatized now, I think. She helped bring me up too, you know, till my uncle and aunt took over. I told you old Ferdy left her a necklace?'

'Yes. I thought it a little odd. Was it a very valuable one?'

'Oh, it was valuable all right! She's always saved her money, too. My grandfather paid her well.'

'Doesn't she ever want to leave you all? She must be getting on?'

'She's seventy next year.'

'I think she's a little frightening – she says so little.'

'She likes you – she said I was to treat you well.'

'You *do* treat me well, Xavier,' she said, laughing. 'And I love your Villa – it's so beautiful. But. . . .' She wanted to add: I like to meet you away from it, but there was a tiny constraint between them which she thought might disappear only when he had made his intentions clear – when they had become lovers. If he loved her even a little in the way she already loved him, in spite of all her questions and self-questionings, he would make love to her tonight.

'Flora,' Xavier said now, 'it is like a tapestry here, you sitting under the tree! You look very cool and collected. Edwige thinks I do not live in the real world – and that you do.'

'I thought she'd be your ally in making your villa so beautiful it could be *apart* from the real world,' Flora found herself saying.

'Edwige doesn't like wasting money, and she has no high opinion of young men. But that's enough about me and my affairs. What about you?'

Flora tried to gather her wits, to tell him about her work, her new job, the books she'd been reading, the films she had seen since they were last together, and the general tenor of her life. But whenever she tried to describe her ordinary life in words, it all seemed to have taken place years ago and thousands of miles away.

He suggested they should walk over the road to the sea before dinner and she agreed.

It was a little cooler now but the sea was still that deep Mediterranean turquoise. Xavier pointed over to the old town on the left where a maze of old alleyways led down to the harbour. 'I think we used to live at the back of the town, on the hill,' he said.

'Do you want to see if you can find it tomorrow?'

'I don't mind – *ça m'est égal*. But it was not a very happy time of my life. Perhaps I don't want to remember it.'

Back in her room Flora changed for dinner into a thin sleeveless dress, and glanced at the magazine she had brought up from her chair in the garden before going out to meet Xavier at the station. It was a literary review and that morning she had been absorbed in it. It seemed to belong to a Flora who was only herself when she was alone.

They ate a leisurely dinner in the garden-room with the doors open to the summer night and shared a bottle of chilled white wine. Flora was thinking, after coffee they would not be able to put bed-time off any longer. Should she assume he would want to share the night with her? She was glad that at least she had her own room and decided she would leave the communicating door open.

'I'll order a bottle of Vittel water,' Xavier said. 'I'm thirsty – shall we have a night-cap together?'

'OK – I'll go up now,' she replied.

There was soon a knock at the communicating door. She opened it to find Xavier there, balancing a tray with two glasses, a bottle and slices of lemon.

She gestured him to come in and pulled out one of the two

chairs. The room was still warm and she opened the outer shutters to the night to cool the air. Xavier poured them each a drink of the mineral water, sat down and said in a matter of fact voice: 'Tell me, Flora, I assume you are an advanced woman and do not object to sharing your bed for at least part of the night with me?'

'Is this a definite proposal?' she asked with a smile, though she could not help her hand trembling a little as she took the glass from him.

'Well, I would not like to act in an ungentlemanly fashion,' replied Xavier.

For answer she put down the glass, went up to him and kissed him. He looked a little surprised. 'I think we may both be a little tired tonight,' she said, 'but it would be nice to stay together.'

He took her hand, turned it over and kissed her palm. She shivered. With his other hand he took his glass and drained it, put it down and then enfolded her in his arms. His shirt smelled like her own hair – of lemons – she thought confusedly, and his breath a little of the wine they had drunk. They sat on the bed and he kissed her forehead and then put a tendril of her hair back behind her ear. She felt her insides melting like snow to liquid in the sun, but then he straightened up and said:

'I should not do this to a good young woman – we Latins are not like *les* Anglo-Saxons who are "pals" together.'

'But we are friends, Xavier,' she murmured.

'I want us always to be *friends* until I am *ready* or *rich* enough to ask you to marry me, Flora!'

This was not what she had hoped for from Xavier. 'Oh, I don't know about marrying!' she said lightly. 'Xavier, I want to be close to you *now* – you don't have to promise your future away!'

She took her water and drank thirstily. It made her feel a

little cooler. She wished she could act as coolly as she had intended. But she realized that Xavier might not know what he wanted either. 'Let's cuddle up together. We can fall asleep like children tonight,' she said. 'I'm tired and I'm sure you are.' Let's see what tomorrow will bring, she thought.

He stretched out on her bed and they embraced. He must have been very tired for when she woke from a doze she found her arm still around him although he had turned away and was fast asleep.

Flora's thoughts were milling round her head. Xavier had made her a sort of proposal of marriage, yet he had refused to make love to her. Further sleep eluded her until after dawn had broken. When she woke again it was to find Xavier kissing her neck hungrily. Then he suddenly jumped out of bed whispering: 'Forgive me, Flora!'

'Come back,' she whispered, and held out her arms.

'No – you need to sleep a bit longer—'

'I love you,' she said softly. 'But perhaps you were right to wait—'

He turned, bent down and kissed her again, this time on the forehead. Then he went quickly back to his room through the communicating door. She decided to stop worrying about whatever his problem was and to go back to sleep. Things always looked less gloomy in the morning.

They took breakfast together in the garden.

'At least I got some sleep!' she'd said cheerfully, on finding Xavier already there at a table under the trees when she went down rather late to the coffee and croissants that were brought to them by a neatly dressed young woman. She was determined to enjoy all the hotel offered. Having saved up for a year to afford this one week abroad, it would be criminal to waste a delicious breakfast that had been paid for in advance even if the other meals were not.

Xavier put his hand over hers. 'Do you think everyone believes we are married?' he asked softly.

'I shouldn't think so! The French are supposed to be the ones who encourage illicit honeymoons, aren't they?'

'For a well-brought up English Protestant girl you are extraordinarily advanced, Flora,' he said.

She wanted to reply: those are the very people who *are* 'advanced', but thought better of it. 'True,' she said. 'Do you disapprove?'

'It is not so simple,' he replied after a pause, staring into his empty coffee cup. He had poured and drunk a cup before she arrived.

'You need not worry about me, Xavier – I'm not a baby, you know!'

He looked up at her. His eyes looked cloudy. 'There are women – and women,' he muttered.

Oh God, she thought, the ones you love and those you want to possess. He went on: 'You are the sort of girl who should – will – marry—'

'For love,' she said. 'But men – do *they* marry for love? I thought arranged marriages were still quite common in Italy and in France – more common than in England – except for royalty, of course.'

What a silly conversation to be having on a sunny morning on the first day of your mutual holiday. Now they might discuss some abstract point, and then she could change the subject.

'Michel has married,' he stated. 'He is "in love", I am told. He is only my age.'

'My parents would say he was too young,' said Flora stiffly. She had endured an argument with her father about early marriages when she was eighteen, being then of an age to think she should know her own mind.

'And what do *you* think, Flora?'

'People are all different – but perhaps women are more grown up than men of the same age?'

'Grown up in some ways, yes. But is being "grown up" always a good thing?'

'It is if you want to marry, I suppose?' She poured them each out another cup of coffee. Xavier must have done a lot of thinking after leaving her bed early that morning.

'Did you have a happy childhood, Flora?' he asked.

Had they not talked about this before? *Had* she had a happy childhood? Mixed, she supposed, like most people's – but mainly happy. '*I* was very unhappy sometimes – at other times wildly happy,' he went on without waiting for an answer. 'Never in-between.'

'I loved both my parents – and they were fond of – loved – me,' said Flora, and waited.

'There, you see, you were luckier than I was. I can't say I loved my father because I hardly remember him. Even when he was living with us at the Villa he wasn't close to me. I think Tante Jo loved me – in her own way.'

'And your mother?' pursued Flora.

There was a longer pause. Then he said: 'Oh, I do remember my mother, you know – before she went away. They separated when I was about four years old.'

'Did you ever know why?'

'Tante Jo just said they did not get on.'

'But you once said to me that they told you she had died—'

'That's what was said – I think it was only to spare me. I came to the conclusion she left my father for another man—'

'But why not take you with her – if your father wasn't terribly interested in children?'

'I don't know – it's all long ago.'

'If she'd taken you with her you'd never have gone on living in your lovely Villa!'

'I know. I'm still not sure that she's dead – I don't think about her much now. If she'd wanted to see me she could have tried – she'd have heard I was back in Italy, wouldn't she?'

'Perhaps she's left the district – or even the country? Doesn't your aunt know? Or Ludo? Have you never asked them since you grew up?'

'I'm sure Tante Jo has no idea. You know, she's very inno-cent . . . she doesn't believe in couples separating – even when her own husband – oh, well, never mind—'

'Your Uncle Ludo might have some idea. If you really wanted to know – you could press him—'

'No, I'm sure the only person who might know is Edwige – and I daren't ask her.'

'Daren't?'

'I know it's ridiculous – but perhaps I think she might tell me things I don't want to hear.'

'Does she ever talk to you about your grandfather – how he died?'

'No. Never.'

'I think we have to live in the present,' said Flora. 'Whatever happened in the past, it's over, isn't it? Maybe your mother – Victoire – wasn't "grown up"? I'm not sure that I am myself. But I'd marry for love – is that wrong?' He made no reply, so she went on: 'You can't know a person of the other sex really well – understand them – unless you become lovers.'

'Oh, is that your experience?' he asked a little coldly.

'No, it's just my instinct. You might just want happiness – sex,' she said carefully, 'but when you already know someone quite well – in other ways – it would seem a pity to deny yourself a deeper knowledge.'

His face muscles slackened as he looked her full in the face. 'I can't love people,' he said. His eyes were suddenly dull.

'Have you tried?' she asked lightly.

'I may have done. Or I may have tried with the wrong people. Men do that – they take what's on offer.'

Now he was being brutal but she refused to consider the implications. She felt it was said to punish himself.

'Perhaps you can't get a deeper knowledge of some people in any other way?'

'Or perhaps you might spoil what you already have?' He sounded like her best friend Clare whose fiancé talked in this way about having children one day. Should she say: Nothing is for ever? Except children, she thought. She hated his blowing hot and cold. She said, 'Life is full of risks.'

He said no more on the subject, but for the rest of their week together that particular conversation stood like a ghost between them.

They spent a pleasant first day – she enjoyed it anyway – walking on the beach, poking around in the market, drinking pastis, eating cheese and crusty bread and peaches for lunch, and in the evening a deliciously cooked meal.

It did not seem that she had burned her boats as far as marriage with Xavier was concerned, for he was still talking about her next visit to the Villa. In some indefinable way he seemed to hold on to the idea of her as 'his'.

And on that night of their first full day together Xavier came to her and made silent love to her. Flora was happy, because she loved him, even more so because she knew even as he entered her body that she would never have the whole of him. There would always be something more to know, to desire. In other ways it was as he had once said – but about a different matter – not so simple.

His caresses were tender and good but Flora knew enough about men to know that he did not find it easy to give himself. He was aroused – but in a lukewarm way. He did not need her; or his mind desired her but his body was a little reluctant to oblige. Yet for her it *was* good, his very difficulty lengthening the process of love-making. She thought it could not have been very satisfactory for him, whatever he said when he finally sighed and groaned. Never had she felt so tender towards him, yet she could not allow herself to say why. He would be hurt if she were tactless. Really she did not mind for herself, only for him. He might think she did not know how hard it was for him to achieve that physical consummation – perhaps would not wish her to know. She sensed that physically he might need some other kind of woman, though she could not imagine what kind exactly.

A few moments after he had ceased his effortful straining towards pleasure, he said: 'You are so good – to me – I do not deserve it.'

It will be better later when we have more practice, she wanted to say, but the words stuck in her throat. She would say nothing, unless he hinted, however delicately, that he was not satisfied. That she had not satisfied him? Yet she felt she had been right to welcome him with open arms, felt quite contented herself, because it was Xavier and because he had come to her.

He had fallen asleep on his back, one arm shielding his eyes. Light was coming into the room; it must already have dawned outside in the garden. She lay quietly, wishing she could go and smell the morning air.

Suddenly from the adjoining room on the other side from their connecting door she heard a moaning begin, a woman's voice. It rose in a mixture of panting and shouting.

Xavier had not made her feel like that.

But I don't want to see myself as an animal, she thought, unless the man who loved me could also become an animal I could trust.

Had Xavier made love to other women? He must have

done. Other women who squealed and screamed and moaned? His desire for her had been dreamy, slow. Hers for him too. She shut her eyes and said to herself: now I am his. Even if it is more of an agony for him than a joy, I am still his. He is not mine though, was her last thought as she too fell into a short sleep, to dream of a butterfly, a Painted Lady that was caught between the two of them as if between two layers of tissue paper that protected it.

For the rest of the holiday the nights that they spent together were no different. Had he noticed that she realized it could have been better for him? His caresses were tender and she found she thought of him sometimes as a child who needed comforting. Xavier was eager to make sure she felt good herself, but she took care not to appear too passionate, not to overwhelm him with any appetites of her own. That feeling she had, that he might have had many other women, remained unresolved; she was not going to ask him. If she were not the right person for him he was free to tell her.

She wanted him to feel she was strong.

She was convinced that the spectre of his mother still haunted him.

But Xavier did not refer to her again.

One morning they had walked to an old square behind the main street near the church and looked down on the sea from a gap in a wall. They sat down on a bench in the shade.

Xavier said: 'I think we used to live behind this square – I can't even remember the name of the street, but we rented a flat somewhere near here. Uncle Edouard bought a wireless and batteries so we could hear the news of the war.'

'So the war came almost as soon as you'd arrived?'

'Yes, war was declared a week or two after we came here.' He began then with no forewarning to speak of his father and once more of his American grandmother, Paulina. 'I think if the war had not come he *would* have taken me to America.'

'Is your grandmother still alive? How old would she be?'

'Edwige once said she was born the same year as herself.'

'When was that? Do you know?'

'1885.'

Flora did a rapid calculation. 'So she'd be only sixty-nine. American women live for ever!'

'We always assumed she'd died.'

'But surely, Xavier, for whatever reason she left the Villa she'd still want to see her grandson, wouldn't she?'

'Tante Jo did write to her last address after the war to tell her that my father had died, but she never got a reply. Maybe she knew by then in any case about his death. A friend of his could have written to her.'

Flora was wondering why the grandmother had left her husband, old Ferdinando. The Leopardis – the branch that Xavier was connected to, anyway, appeared to be a disunited family, forever leaving each other.

'Did your Aunt Josephine ever say *why* your grandmother left your grandfather?'

'No – I don't think she knew. As I keep telling you, Flora, Tante Jo is an innocent. She always spoke of her stepmother as a very clever woman. Not a good housekeeper, she said. But my grandfather had adored her—'

'So what year was your father born? Was he a lot younger than Josephine and Ludo?'

'Not a lot – I know he was very young when I was born. But Paulina must have had him almost as soon as they married. She didn't take over Ludo and Josephine though. Edwige was the one who looked after them – and then she looked after my father too! Perhaps my grandma didn't really like children . . . she was there, I think, for Grandpapa to display to others – for showing his family and neighbours and people in Como and

Milan that Ferdinando Leopardi had a beautiful young American wife who painted and played the piano and read modern novels—'

Flora interrupted him. 'Did Edwige like her American mistress?' The more she tried to disentangle Xavier's family the more she felt that the key to it all lay in that formidable old woman Edwige Rouart, to whom the old man had left a valuable necklace.

'From what Tante Jo told me, they didn't get on. My aunt would never say anything unkind about anyone, but I think after the first war, when Jo would be in her early teens, there was some sort of row, because she and Ludo saw little of their stepmother – afterwards.'

'When did Paulina leave you all then?'

'I don't remember. I must only have been about four. I've a vague memory of her in the garden with a large parasol but I can't remember her ever talking to me—'

'It was before your mother went away then – and certainly your father?'

He flinched. 'I remember Papa much better than my grandmother! I know more from Uncle Ludo about his and Jo's own mother. *She* was born in St Petersburg with a Russian mother and a French father, who was a diplomat – she was delicate, she died after Aunt Jo was born. You remember Sasha? He was Feodora's brother. The family went to live in Paris – and then Italy – it must have been in the 1880s. Lots of foreigners came to the lake at that time, you know. It was Feodora's father who first bought the Villa. My grandfather leased it from them when he married their daughter. He bought them out later, in the twenties. I suppose money was in short supply for Russian émigrés by then. Do I bore you with all the past history of my family?'

'On the contrary, Xavier, I find it most interesting.'

Her interest in his family surprised even herself. Every small scrap he let slip was picked up and remembered by her, all of it belonging to the exotic creature Xavier had become for her.

The day before their holiday was to end they went on a little shopping expedition, and each bought the other a present. Xavier's for Flora was a soft silky scarf in pink and mauve and purple. She would wear it in London, and it would remind her of him. Flora bought Xavier a book, a collection of philosophical extracts, a very French volume. Later they sat inside a café, for the sun beating down on the pavement tables outside made it too hot to read or even to think. Flora was feeling sad that her time with Xavier was so soon to end. She half feared that when they said good-bye this time, it would be for ever, that Xavier had made love to her only to please her, that he did not regard her as a serious love.

She looked at him sitting next to her drinking a cool *bière blonde* and knew she would be bereft when they parted. When she was with him she could not concentrate on her usual reading; her normal life was suspended. So long as she did not think of Xavier she would be content, even happy, to return home alone, to begin again to live in her old way, with friends, busy with work. But though she sensed a future full of the wish to be with him, she also realized that she needed a life of her own that was not consumed with this longing.

'You look very serious,' he said. This was unusual, for he did not often notice her own moods so long as she was happy to fit in with his.

She decided to tell him part of the truth. 'I shall miss you, Xavier – just being with you. But I know you'll be busy, and perfectly all right without me.'

'I shall be busy – but I shall think of you often,' he said. 'I'm glad I came here and that we have got to know each other – a little – better.' He paused. 'I once told you that you were the marrying kind – don't forget I may ask you myself!'

Was he teasing her?

'I believe you did ask me!' she said, herself half teasing him.

'Did I? Well, that will depend on your coming back to Italy one day – what about a whole summer?'

She could not make him out. 'I cannot stay a whole summer – because of my work,' she replied.

'So sensible, Flora!'

'No, I am not very sensible – I will come if you want me to.'

He took up the book of extracts she had bought him and began to turn its pages. When he wanted to concentrate on something else, he did. Flora wished she could be like that.

'Let me have a look at it,' she said, and held out her hand.

'An inspired choice,' said Xavier. 'Old Kant, and Hume – one of your lot. Your Hobbes is here too—'

'We only studied bits of Kant at the lycée,' said Flora. 'I wish I knew more about the British philosophers.' She looked at the table of contents. In the shop she hadn't had time to look, but it had seemed interesting, or at least the sort of thing that might interest Xavier.

The Animal and the Spiritual – Kant and the Christian ethic . . . Hobbes and the humanistic approach . . . she read.

'Why must spiritual always mean religious?' she asked. 'I mean, Christian – I hope I'm not governed solely by animal instincts – and yet I'm not a believer.'

'Don't you wish you were?'

'I used to, but not any longer – I suppose we're all heirs of Christianity though.'

'Kant was a Protestant,' said Xavier. 'Remember?'

'He sounds like the Book of Common Prayer,' said Flora. She read aloud:

Taken by itself, sexual love is a degradation of human nature, for as soon as a person becomes an object of appetite for another, all motives of moral relationship cease to function, because as an object of appetite for another, a person becomes a thing and can be treated and used by everyone. . . .

'Ugh!' She riffled the pages and found a passage more to her taste. 'Guess who wrote this:

The appetite which men call lust . . . is a sensual pleasure, but not only that; there is in it also a delight of the mind for it consisteth of two appetites together, to please and to be pleased; and the delight men take in delighting is not sensual but a pleasure or joy of the mind. . . .

Well, so long as by men he means women too!'

Xavier was looking at her with a strange expression on his face. Finally he said: 'Your Hobbes sounds like an idealist there.'

'But that's just what I feel!' She wanted to say: Love *is* a joy of the mind – I know it is for me. She thought: the Christians say marriage is for children and to put an end to lust, and for mutual help and companionship – but they don't mention being in love!

Xavier said softly 'I'm not using you, Flora—'

No, she knew he was not. The trouble was, sometimes she wished he were. In spite of her own feminist inclinations, she wanted him to be able to lose himself.

Had he never before met a woman who thought there was nothing fundamentally bad about sex? Most men, Italian or English, didn't worry about the morality of their sex lives. Perhaps they returned later to the Christian beliefs that had been instilled in them. When they were old, or dying.

Echoing her thoughts, Xavier said: 'Your average man takes all that with a pinch of salt.' He produced the English phrase triumphantly.

'Women are expected to behave themselves,' she said.

He did not follow up this remark but went on: 'Others, like my grandfather – whom even you might have called decadent – made a virtue of not believing what the Church had to say. Some good it did old Ferdinando!'

'Even I?' she said. 'But I'm not decadent.'

'Precisely – that was my point – it depends on your definition of virtue. And of course you were not brought up a Catholic.'

'Protestants are supposed to be even more puritanical at home,' she said. 'The Irish especially – both Catholic and Protestant. Must be something in the air. Was your grandfather an intellectual?' She remembered he had called Paulina that.

'I believe he would have considered himself one – he wasn't, of course. He followed his hero d'Annunzio who wasn't so much romantic as a man who made a religion out of what you call sex. He was very promiscuous, had lots of mistresses – and worse—'

'It's only when things are forbidden that they become exciting for some people,' she said.

'You think sex is all just good clean fun, then? *I* don't.'

For answer she said: 'Your English *is* coming along!' She thought: where are women in all this? Just the lust-objects of dirty old men, or of husbands, or of randy young men? But she did not always feel 'randy' with Xavier, only at certain moments. Was not a romantic passion beautiful and exciting in itself, something set apart?

'Perhaps I'm just lucky,' she said aloud, thinking once again that a clever woman would pretend to be cold in order to arouse, then to be wooed. It was apparently the other way round for the two of them. 'I hate conflict,' she said. 'Why can't feelings be simple?'

'Sin is both horrible and exciting,' he said. 'There is a dark side to life, Flora.'

Yes, she thought, unrequitedness, or feeling a different sort of love from that of the man you love. But love and desire unite in physical closeness. She hoped it wasn't true that only in marriage would a woman be able to give and receive both.

'Happiness – marriage—' said Xavier, 'impossible! Unless you prefer to live at a lower pitch. My grandfather married twice – and he had lots of other women too. I wonder if he had the gift of making them love him?'

Flora handed him back the book she had bought for him, wondering if her choice had been sensible after all. 'Your Aunt Jo is a fairly happy person, isn't she?' she said. 'And Uncle Ludo?' Even if you are not, she thought.

'Aunt Jo has found that only God is worthy of being worshipped, and Uncle Ludo prefers men – in case you didn't know.'

'No, I didn't, but I can't see that it matters.'

'When I think about my grandpapa, I realize he was a bully,' mused Xavier. 'But we are told that some women prefer bullies.'

'Is that why your grandmother left him, do you think? After all, she was rich – had enough money to free herself. Rich American women are freer than most.'

'She couldn't have left him unless she had a fortune of her own. Money is what makes the world go round, Flora.'

'I don't believe that, Xavier—'

'You don't want to believe it. I do. People can be controlled with money.'

'Not everyone.'

'Not good well-brought up little Anglo-Saxon girls.'

'Don't be horrible—'

'Sorry – perhaps you will rescue me.' She wondered from what.

All the way back to the hotel and back in her room when, for once, he wanted to make love to her in a more abandoned

119

fashion – all the time she had the impression that he had retreated far away inside himself and that it might not matter to whom he was making love; she felt that he might be revenging himself on something that had little to do with her.

She might never understand him; he did not think she could. To make Xavier Leopardi happy would entail a sacrifice of some of her own independent desires. She had yearned for experience, and here she was being given what she thought she had wanted, although her real self might be temporarily suppressed.

The next day they parted, Xavier on the train for Como and Flora on her journey to Nice, Paris, and the Channel. The day after that she found herself back in the familiar routine of her life in London.

Mixed up with Flora's sadness at being once more parted from her enigmatic lover were to be her constant and uneasy thoughts about his family, especially his grandfather. She was glad he was dead.

Xavier wrote and said he hoped she would come to stay at the Villa again whenever she could get away from England. She wouldn't recognize the place when she came! It was still being transformed. He was going to buy a large painting to hang at the end of the middle corridor. More about it in his next letter; he was just off to Milano.

Dear Flora

I must write and tell you of this wonderful painting. I bought it yesterday. For a long time I've wanted to own one of the pictures painted by a compatriot of yours, a member of your Royal Academy with a rather French sounding name. I believe he died about 25 years ago so it's not a modern picture – none of your Picassos for me! It's one of a series of pictures he painted in Italy over forty years ago, before the first war. I saw copies of them for the first time in some book and the book said one of the originals was in London. When I came to London last time I went to look at it. I never told you because it seemed something too personal, too private.

But now I feel we know each other better I can tell you that I have found in Milano one of the other studies, very like the London one. It is of a woman, probably a peasant, though she is young and beautiful. Barefooted, wearing a strange turban. She is employed pouring a basket of violets on to a sheet where the petals are to be collected to make perfume. There is a sack already packed and the petals are floating down like purple butterflies. All this inside a sort of barn with rafters and beams and the sunlight dappling the walls. An old donkey waits to be unloaded and in the distance is another woman bending down to load him up again. I can't tell you what pleasure this painting gives me – I can almost smell the violets . . .

Flora's twenty-fourth birthday came and went. In the new year of 1955 she attended the weddings of two of her friends, for people were pairing off, and in these conformist 1950s they married. It was on one of these occasions that Flora met a kind young man, one John Thornton, who was studying economics. He loved France as much as she did though he said he did not know Italy very well. John was the only man to whom she mentioned the Villa. She felt there might be no hidden depths in him, nothing she could not get to know, nothing she really needed to know about him that she did not already sense. He had read the same books as she had, toyed with similar ideas and doubts. He was sceptical about the kind of philosophy taught in France, said the present fashion for existentialism was just a modern version of Rabelais' *'fay ce que vouldras'* – do as you will. If there *were* depths in John Thornton she did not wish to explore them in the way she felt compelled to explore Xavier Leopardi's.

'Leopardi is a poet's name,' John had said to her. 'Is he related?'

'The only poet they spoke of in Italy was d'Annunzio,' she replied.

'*He* was an interesting man, but a bit of a fraud,' said John. 'I gather he led a decadent life?'

'As far as I remember, very much so. Took the sadism from our own dear Swinburne and added cocaine, erotomania, and incest elevated to a mystical practice!'

'Good Lord, I'd no idea!'

'But at least he wrote some highly regarded lyrical poetry – and did mad things after the first war – flew a plane and founded a new Republic – himself as President of course—' John was as usual depressingly well-informed.

Somehow she did not want to introduce him to Xavier, should he ever visit England again. This did not appear likely.

In the letters that arrived quite regularly from Italy there were many descriptions of the Villa as it was now shaping up to his notions. Even Josephine approved, he said, and they planned to have several Americans to stay. Flora had never really believed in these Americans but apparently some were to come next spring to see the gardens and explore the area. She suspected Xavier was disappointed that a larger Villa a mile or two away on the other side of the lake was about to be turned into a conference centre. Violetta might be chosen in future only by tourists, not by the writers and intellectuals Flora believed he secretly hoped to meet.

At the end of June a letter arrived from Xavier still talking about the painting he'd acquired.

Dear Flora:
Yesterday evening I listened to your Gigli and thought of you here with me. All is freshly painted and awaits your holiday self. I have worked hard almost like a little Protestant. My

picture is up and looks even more beautiful in the evening light. I took a short motoring holiday with my uncle to Cremona and Parma and Mantua and returned convinced that nowhere matched up to this place. It's not as old, but who knows that the foundations were not laid here for a building in the time of the Romans. You knew the Roman poets visited our lake?

Aunt Jo is to come too, with Solange, at the end of the month so I hope you will be there then also. . . .

He was beginning to see her as one of the family! But he never alluded to their physical life together in Menton, which she thought strange. Was it some *pudeur*? Whenever she felt exhausted by his elusiveness, she would read English Romantic poets. Xavier seemed to exist in the same place as those poets to whom she returned so often: *'O aching Time! O moments big as years!* She had once quoted Keats's words to him; they seemed to have some connection with Xavier's feelings for his childhood, the childhood that continued to exert a powerful pull upon her, as if her own childhood were of no account.

John said it was only when you were older that you became nostalgic about your childhood. Flora wasn't sure whether he was right. She might not yet be nostalgic about her own childhood, but for Xavier's she felt that mixture of nostalgia and mystery, something hidden at the heart of things, that had been there whilst the nations fought, whilst men and women were killed and chance exerted its malign influence upon the innocent. Then she would tell herself not to be over-imaginative.

There was something about Xavier that aroused both her pity and her tenderness. In Menton she had found him physically attractive more on account of some future promise than for what had been for them both the exigencies of the moment. In some indefinable way she was the prisoner of his past.

She had a dream in which she had to rescue him, but from what, when she awoke, she could not remember. Her dream self had known, if not in words. There had been a narrow door and a thin black shape that came through it.

Another night she dreamed of Ferdinando Leopardi in the clothes he had worn in that old photograph of him she'd once seen. She knew he was dying, and that Xavier had killed him.

After these dreams she woke with a feeling of jealousy, of rivalry, for which she could not account. She had always thought she might one day have a female rival, but this imaginary rival was formless, shapeless. . . .

She wrote to Xavier, having arranged to take all her annual leave in one go, possible only because she had finished one publisher's commission and was waiting for another. If she didn't mind taking half of her holiday as unpaid leave she could stay away for a whole month. One of her grandmothers had just died, leaving her a few hundred pounds. She might not be a rich American, like his planned Villa guests, but the money made her feel a little more independent.

The Villa was now officially re-christened *Violetta*. Was it in honour of his childhood memories? Or of the painting he had hung there?

Or – which was more likely, she thought, somehow in honour of his mysterious mother, Victoire?

iii

Summer

1955

This time the boat was a new one. The Fiat that awaited her was also new, with Xavier in a smart linen suit at the wheel. They left the car at the bottom of the lane by the lake and entered the Villa this time by the main gates, which opened on to freshly laid gravel. The fountain, now restored, was sparkling in a silver plume in the hot sun. The stucco of the Villa walls had been repainted and shone as dazzlingly white as the lilies she noticed in the flower beds. A man was tending the garden, a basket of weeds on the gravel next to him.

'Çiao, Enrico.'

'Çiao, Signor Leopardi.'

The bougainvillaea bloomed deep purple over the rising terraces, geraniums of every shade of vermilion and scarlet were spilling over urns. Up the path they went and arrived at the front door which this time was open, leading into the marble-floored hall she remembered.

'We've got the lift working again,' he said as they turned left and walked past the staircase that rose to meet the next floor.

The lift was a cage – a gilded cage, she thought.

'All the family bedrooms are on the top floor now,' he said

as they went up in the lift. 'Not all finished but liveable in. Visitors are on part of the middle floor.'

'And your painting?'

'Yes, you'll see it in a minute.'

When they got out of the lift, he led her to the first room on the right. The door was open.

Delphine was just coming out of it. On seeing Flora she smiled: 'All ready for you.'

Flora entered a large room with the facing window open, and another, set at a right angle, shuttered. Xavier put her bag down.

'You'll want to wash and unpack? Then come along to the middle of the corridor where the staircase comes up – and I'll show you my picture!' He went out.

It was not the room she had been shown before. That decorated room was further along the corridor and was now probably reserved for American paying guests. Xavier had told her there weren't any staying there at present.

On the little table by a brass-knobbed bed, which was covered in a white cotton bedspread, there stood a glass vase of violets. Perhaps he put them everywhere as the emblem of the new Villa?

She washed her hands in a large porcelain basin – another innovation – the water pipes must have been extended – and then stood looking at herself for a moment in the long mirror that faced the shuttered window.

Then she walked out into the corridor along to the centre staircase. As she approached she saw the enormous gilt-framed painting on the staircase walls. It depicted a dark-haired woman with a scarlet turban, just as he had described it, with the petals from thousands of violets shucking down from her sack on to a cloth.

'You can see it better from below,' Xavier's voice came from the foot of the stairs.

'I like it – I suppose it is the motif of the place now?'

'That was my idea.'

He looked a bit sad, she thought, as she walked down to meet him. He had made his Villa into something else, but by restoring it had he lost whatever the old scent of the *Violettes de Parme* had meant to him?

'We are to lunch in the new *sala da pranzo*. Tante Jo and Solange are already there.'

'And Madame Rouart?'

'Oh, Edwige doesn't approve of my improvements. She's got a little apartment downstairs – often eats there alone. But she's just bought a little house up near the village, and she says she'll move there permanently in the autumn.' He looked cross. Then: 'How do *you* like what I've done, Flora?' He looked as if her reply really mattered to him.

'It's magnificent, Xavier!' But it must have cost a fortune she thought.

'Once the will was proved there was more in the coffers than we had guessed,' he said diffidently. 'Even with the taxes and all the bureaucratic fuss – of course here in Italy you have to grease several palms whatever you do or plan – but the Como business is making a profit too now!'

'Is your Uncle here?'

'No – he's in Como at present.'

Talking, they walked to the ground floor where Xavier led her into a long bright room that looked out on the courtyard. Through the windows, behind the trees, she could see the silver glint of water falling. It was all transformed from her memories of it.

'I suppose you've brought it back to life – just as it was?' she said.

'As far as I could remember it, but Edwige says it was better before!'

'Old people don't like change.'

Seated already at the table were two people, a woman and a rather overweight girl of about fourteen. Flora advanced to shake hands. Tante Jo rose.

'Solange – you won't remember Xavier's English friend, I don't suppose?'

'Yes I do, *Maman*.'

The child did not get up but stared at Flora after shaking hands.

'How long ago is it? Six years? Seven?'

'Six years,' said Flora.

'And how do you like what my nephew has done with the Villa? Isn't it splendid?'

'Wonderful,' Flora murmured, and sat down at the table with its pristine white linen cloth.

Delphine came in with plates of tomatoes and basil, and the oil and salt were handed round. Xavier poured the same wine she remembered from last time.

Menton seemed not to have happened. He gave no indication that she was his girl friend, only his old friend. She supposed he did not wish to shock his religious aunt. Looking at Tante Jo, Flora suddenly realized how ugly she was when her face was slack in repose: too long a nose, a thin mouth, small eyes, wispy hair. Flora knew she was a kind woman, well-intentioned, and it had not struck her when she met her in Paris that she lacked any redeeming facial feature. When she smiled the ugliness left her face.

Flora M. Russell
JOURNAL
Private

20 July 1955 . . . Solange tucked into her lunch with a vigour not usually found in fourteen year old girls, whom I have often found picky. She is a pale, heavy child, stolid, but I imagine also timid. Her mother did not fuss over her but neither did she address many words to her. She may be bored, tucked away in this place away from her friends. I said to her: 'I expect you are glad school is over until October?'

She looked at me warily. She was not wearing her glasses – her eyes are a pale brown, and large – rather nice.

'I have to repeat a year,' she said. 'I had bad marks in English and French.'

I said, 'Perhaps I can help you with your English?'

I feel that I may need occupation here for I do not want to impose myself upon Xavier and it might be a good idea to show him I have something to do – until I know exactly what he wants of me. I thought I might help Solange with her English, and when I suggested this Tante Jo said: 'Oh that would be very kind, mademoiselle.' Solange looked frightened, so I added: 'I could talk to you a bit in English – it might help you.' Xavier said, with a slight smile: 'I'm sure Flora is a good teacher.'

In the afternoon he was busy with the man who is making the new address plates for the Villa and comes all the way from Como with them: VILLA VIOLETTA in curly bright blue capitals on a white background, special ones for the front gate and the big porch and the lakeside and smaller ones for round the back.

Tante Jo said: 'It's a pretty name,' but reserved her opinion as to the change. She must have known the house as both 'Carolina' and 'Paulina'. Odd! She herself hardly ever speaks of the past. Xavier took me at about five o'clock into another ground floor room he calls the library. He opened the shutters and I saw a table, a few bookcases – not all filled, and on the wall and over the mantelpiece several portraits. Over the mantelpiece in a heavy frame similar to the one surrounding the lady on the stairs was one of a man I immediately recognized as Ferdinando Leopardi. It must have been painted in the

1920s for he looked as though he was in his forties, but not much different from the man in the photograph.

'Here is his first wife too,' Xavier said. 'Feodora, that is. Not my grandmother. We found it in the cellars where he must have put it for safety at the end of the war.' I saw a sweet-faced brown-haired woman with a look of Ludo about her in the mouth and forehead. It was a much older painting than the one of her husband. I asked Xavier whether there was a painting of his own grandmother, the American. 'Oh, no,' he said. 'I expect Grandpapa burned it after she decamped!'

There was a small painting too of Ludo and his sister Josephine as children, he in a sailor suit, she in a frilly pink dress with a dog at her feet. Ludo didn't look at all like his father. Josephine had a look of Solange, but did not resemble her father or even her mother. Perhaps Solange does have a look, though, of her grandfather.

'Is there a portrait of your father?' I asked Xavier.

'No – only photographs – and Tante Jo says most of those must have been lost – there were albums of them, she says, but we can't find them. I believe the only one I have of him is the one I was given as a child after he had gone to America. They always said he had a look of his mother Paulina – he was quite fair and tall,' he said.

'You are not all that dark – for an Italian,' I said.

'Oh, lots of Italians from this part of Italy have fair hair and blue eyes – we're all bastards – a mixture of the Swiss and French as well as northern Italians.'

Xavier looked sunburnt, and, I thought, handsome, as I stood by him in the library. I said: 'Your little cousin Solange does have a look of her grandfather – what was her own father like?'

'Edouard? – rather nondescript, I always thought. He wore natty suits and spats and made a great thing about being French rather than Italian. He was very boring and he had no

patience with his daughter – I do remember that. I think Tante
Jo was relieved when he departed, though she'd never admit it.
He died in Nice, I believe – in insalubrious circumstances.'

I did not ask him to elucidate as I knew already that 'Oncle
Edouard' like Ludo Leopardi had been 'queer', but he went on:
'I think it was Ludo he really liked! but Ludo was always
discreet.'

To change the subject and because I was not really interested
in Uncle Ludo I said: 'Solange looks the sort of child who might
be bullied, I think.'

'She's better than she was – Tante Jo says she's just shy. It
was kind of you to offer English lessons.'

We looked at some landscapes of the lake painted in the early
years of the last century and then Xavier went off to see about
some repairs to the wrought iron of some of the balconies.

He says there were some Americans here last week.
Apparently, he lodged them next door to my room on the
middle floor and they spent a lot of time sailing on the lake and
meeting friends from Como. He told me that British royalty
sometimes come to the lake for a hide-away and a rest . . . He's
off to Como himself tomorrow to talk more business . . . .

I came across Madame Edwige in the garden yesterday
afternoon, had hardly seen her so far this time, since she keeps
to herself in her own quarters or goes back to her mysterious
little house in the village. I wonder what she has done with the
necklace she was left? She was wearing a large sun hat and I
didn't think she'd want to stop and talk to me, but she did and
greeted me with a Bonjour and a stiff smile. Apparently, she
was off to gather herbs. She has a little kitchen garden she
tends up by the waterfall. I wonder if she knew what Xavier
and I were up to last summer in France? I feel there's not
much she misses, yet I can't help feeling she doesn't like me
and wishes I were out of the way. Still, she did smile at me. I
still have the feeling that she knows more about the family

history than anyone . . . .

Uncle Ludo came back today and seemed very pleased to see me. 'Have you seen our portrait gallery?' he asked. I told him I had. 'I wish we had a later picture of Father,' he said. He never alludes to his father's politics or to how he died. That old man must not have had a great opinion of his elder son – to leave the Villa to his grandson instead? I get the impression he was tyrannical from all they say. 'He always went around with a cane with a silver knob,' Ludo told me.

'I still think his ghost might be here somewhere! He was such an impressive person, you know,' Tante Jo said unexpectedly, and then with an earnest expression she added: 'His political friends had far too great an influence on Papa – he might be still alive if he had listened to Edouard.'

So Edouard had had some uses – trying to deflect the old boy from the pathways of Fascism! Edwige happened to be there bringing some flowers into the drawing room as Josephine was speaking, and she looked at her most peculiarly; it was almost a look of dislike, but who could dislike Tante Jo?

We had a delicious risotto today for lunch. Why do things taste so different here?

Uncle Ludo talks to me in Italian and I do my best to follow. He treated me last night to a long disquisition on business and silk manufacture in general. It would seem, according to Xavier, that he has a new lease of life. I think he must have been bullied by his father, but he never says anything too derogatory about him.

Xavier has found two more maids to help with the guests and the meals and the cleaning. Delphine bosses them around. I'd like to talk to her, since she was here as a teenage maid when Xavier was a child. I'd like to chat to Tante Jo too about Xavier's mother – but it would be presumptuous to do so, I know, until I know her better. The occasions are still rare when she wants to talk about her past here. Yet she's always amiable. She says little *to Edwige, almost as though she were afraid of her.*

I am reading Gide's Counterfeiters *and a novel by another Frenchman, Montherlant, who writes about women but seems to hate them. I prefer the novels of Colette. Xavier has many French novels in his room (he says) but I have never been invited to see them . . . .*

At dinner tonight Ludo spoke again of his grandfather's idol, the poet d'Annunzio. I asked when did the poet die, and he told me, in 1938, at the age of 75. Then he quoted some lines which I must say sounded beautiful: L'alba separa dalla luce l'ombra, E la mia voluttà dal mio desire . . . . I think it means: 'The dawn divides the darkness from the light, and my sensual desire from my will.' Ludo said it was about a man who killed himself.

'You can see his own villa over by Garda,' he said. 'The Vittoriale.' Xavier said: 'I don't think Grandpapa liked his poetry much – it was more his way of life!' Ludo went: 'Tsch tsch . . . .'

It struck me again how the others now defer to Xavier who is after all of a younger generation. Is it because he need not have them to stay here, since the Villa is his? Ludo has never in my hearing complained that he ought to have been the one to inherit, since he was the eldest of Old Ferdy's (as I call him now to myself) children. Like Tante Jo, I sometimes feel that at any moment he will come round the corner of a corridor with his silver-topped cane. I haven't told Xavier this. It isn't that I'm afraid of ghosts, more that I know Old Ferdy would have thought I could not really belong here.

I believe Xavier loves me in his own way and I am still free to concentrate on my own emotions. Unrequited love – if that is what it is – makes one more not less infatuated . . . but yesterday I found myself thinking of London as home. Out there is a world I want to understand, but here it seems remote and unconnected with me. All last year I was thinking about setting my mind in order when I had time. Here, servants accomplish all the mechanics of living for us, so I have the time now if I want to do some thinking. But the more attention Xavier has paid to me in the last few days the less I have felt I belong! though I long for him to make love to me again and make all right.

I've borrowed a little volume of Italian Romantic poets and I took it to a shady seat on the lower terrace today and found poetry once more a solace. I have the poems of that other, more famous, Leopardi too – one entitled Primo Amore *is very lovely. I practise my accent reciting it! Ah! come mal mi governasti, amore . . . .*

This morning I felt the need to work so I found Solange and we walked in the garden. To begin with, we chatted in French. Then I said simple things to her in English – she is quite intelligent. I asked her what I was doing when I was for example watching a butterfly or fastening my sandal or walking up to the waterfall. She soon cottoned on. It's only by speaking that you learn to speak, and she got quite pink with pleasure when I told her she had a good accent.

I had a dream last night about the boathouse – but it wasn't quite the boathouse. I can't remember exactly what it was there that frightened me – it wasn't old Ferdinand. There was some sort of a mirror and I saw myself in this mirror being carried to a bed and I said: 'I am too heavy to be carried.' I knew it was all wrong because there was someone else's face there already on the pillow, and a red hat on a chair, but I couldn't see who it was and I thought, there are going to be three of us. When I woke up I asked myself if Xavier had made love to a woman in the boathouse. Was my subconscious trying to tell me something? But at lunch today he was very attentive and smiled at me and took my hand when we went for a little walk under the trees. Of course, I didn't tell him about the dream . . . .

*

Flora looked up from her journal. She had spent a pleasant afternoon with Xavier exploring the woods above the Villa, with no talk of the past, neither their mutual one nor Xavier's childhood.

The next day, her second Friday, she went into the new kitchens for a glass of water. Delphine was standing there drying her hands. She poured a glass of mineral water for Flora and then said: 'I think I need one too – why don't we sit in the courtyard?'

They sat down companionably. Delphine had never acted in a servant-like way and now she asked: 'Are you American or English?' She must have forgotten, thought Flora.

'English,' said Flora swallowing the fresh water with relief.

'We've had a few Americans here – not as many as *he* expected though,' said Delphine. '*Turistas.*'

'I suppose I'm a sort of tourist too,' replied Flora.

'Oh no! you are a friend of Signora Josephine and Signor Xavier! It's not the same. I knew an American lady once – Signora Paulina – but I was only a little girl when she went back home. I remember her though – she used to give me *candi* – like the GI's in the war.'

'Why did she go back home?' Flora asked curiously.

'Perhaps she was homesick?'

Flora guessed Delphine was the sort of woman who loved a gossip. She must have been at the Villa when Xavier was born – but she would not remember. Delphine went on: 'It was my mother's opinion, Signorina, that Madame Paulina knew too much about Signor Ferdinando – her husband.'

'You mean his politics.'

'Oh, I don't know about politics, Signorina, but he had lots of secrets. Mr Paul – Mr Xavier's father – *her* son – he was a nice young man and always spoke to me too. Mr Paul never stared at me like some men did. I knew old Signor Leopardi was keen on *Il Duce* – later we had lots of queer men in black come to meetings and things at the Villa.'

Flora made an encouraging murmur, fascinated by the conversation.

'Signora Paulina was a beautiful woman but I don't think she ever fitted in here. Mr Paul was like her – always reading a book – like you! She talked to everyone who came here, but Mamma said she didn't like some of her husband's guests. Mamma thought that she persuaded Mr Paul to stay on in Italy with his Dad so he'd forgive *her* for pushing off! But he never did forgive her, my mother told me. She packed up, Mamma said, one day when the old man was away in Gardone with a friend, and when he came back she'd gone. I wasn't here then – I was with my uncle learning to work in his little hotel. I was only a kid but they started me early on work! Oh, there was such a to do, Mamma said, and he was shouting all the time to Madame Edwige and Signor Paul. Signor Ludovic and his sister kept well out of his sight. Mamma said the mistress had left him a letter, though she never saw it . . . .'

'What happened after that?'

'Well, Mamma told me it wasn't the last of the troubles . . . the mistress left before another trouble . . . poor Mr Paul, he had his hands full working for his father in Como! They say he was interested in politics. Everybody else said Musso was brilliant and he'd sort us all out – especially those lazy sods from down South. But Signor Paul didn't like him. "Mark my words, Delphine," Signor Paul said to me once. "That Benito" – he meant Mussolini – "isn't going to do any of us any good." Well, he was right, wasn't he? *I* didn't realize till the war that the men that old Signor Leopardi was in with were Fascisti. The Black Boots, we called them. Signor Paul and his father couldn't have had much to agree about, could they? He took after his mother. Mamma heard her once begging her husband

to cancel an invitation to some of his friends. "It's my house to
do what I want in and invite who I like," he said, and it can't
have been long after that she packed her bags and left. Of
course they didn't think she'd gone for good, but she had!'

'Did he destroy her portrait then?'

'I don't know about any of that – they changed the name
back to Carolina, I do remember that, but everyone'd got used
to Paulina . . . . Well, I mustn't sit here gossiping.'

Flora wanted to ask her whether she'd known Xavier and
what he was like as a child but saved it for another time.
Delphine got up to take both their glasses back to the kitchen.
She'd only talked as she had, Flora thought, because she
regarded Flora in the same light as Signora Paulina, all those
years ago: an outsider. Paulina had apparently been kind to
the little Delphine. Funny that Xavier had said she didn't like
children.

Flora had now been over two weeks at the Villa, still waiting
for Xavier to give a sign, even if it were a negative one, that
he had not forgotten all that had taken place in Menton. So
far he had said nothing, although he had smiled, been pleasant, and just as attentive as on her first visit. Everything
hung in the balance, but she had no idea what she must do
or not do, say or not say, for him to evince whatever feelings
he possessed for her. She was certainly now on good terms
with the Villa inhabitants, accepted by Tante Jo and Uncle
Ludo – when he was there – and by Solange, who had
become less shy, less sullen, and more chatty, and by the
servants, as 'Xavier's friend' – even perhaps his unofficial
fiancée.

At dinner a few days after her conversation with Delphine
she asked about the Americans. Were there to be any more of
them? Was her room intended for American visitors?

Xavier answered a little wryly: 'So far none but Americans

have been able to afford my exorbitant prices! But I'm disappointed that so few have answered my adverts.'

'I'm sure they'd think the Villa worth their dollars,' said Jo. 'Look at all you've done – you've brought the old place back to life. I'm sure Ludo agrees.' Ludo said nothing, only looked vague and took another helping of pasta. 'Though it's no longer home to me as you know – still, I'd hate to think of its being sold and not appreciated,' Josephine went on.

Ludo looked up and said: 'Americans are to take over the villa at Varenna completely.'

'That's different – it's no longer a family home. I like to think of Xavier here one day with his family – just like the old days,' Tante Jo went on sentimentally.

'Have you persuaded Edwige to take a holiday yet?' asked Xavier, offering the bottle of wine to Flora, who declined it. She found too much wine late at night, far from making her sleepy, kept her awake.

'She has promised to visit us in Paris,' replied Jo. 'Do you know, it's fifty years since she was there!'

'She's forgotten France,' said Xavier. 'Perhaps in the same way as you've forgotten Italy, Tante Jo.'

Jo did not appear annoyed. 'But we still take holidays in our old places. Edwige never has, I don't think. She could have taken holidays away when we were grown up, but she never did. She was too fond of us all, I suppose!'

Xavier looked sceptical.

'Was she here all through the war?' Solange asked. There was a moment's silence and then both Ludo and his sister spoke at once: 'She moved into the village when the Germans came,' and 'she took Italian nationality so as not to be deported.'

'Poor Papa,' said Josephine, after a pause. 'What would he have done without her!'

Flora wondered if it had been Edwige Rouart who had

found her employer dead in his boathouse. But nobody spoke
of that, and she was sure Solange had not yet been enlight-
ened. Solange knew about Xavier's father though, for she had
told Flora that *Maman* lit candles in the church for him as well
as for her father and stepmother Paulina. She must assume
Paulina was also dead. Tante Jo obviously did not judge
people according to their political beliefs. Flora could imagine
what Xavier would say about the candle-burning.

The next day Flora was once more sitting in the courtyard
with letters to write. Xavier had gone over to the other side of
the lake and Josephine was shopping in Como with her
brother. Solange had said she had a headache, which Flora
thought was code for 'the time of the month'.

She felt a little bored, which was unusual for her. Xavier
had promised to show her other rooms on the middle floor,
saying he'd like her advice about colour schemes. But he held
the keys himself for what Flora now thought of as the tourist
apartments.

She sat there in the shade with a writing pad and envelopes
intending to write to John Thornton and to her best friend
Clare Goodwin to whom she had told a little about Xavier
and his Villa. But she found it hard to strike the right tone of
voice to them, apart from describing the place and the people.
What was she waiting for? She knew she was waiting for
something. Was it a formal proposal of marriage?

She heard the kitchen door open, and shortly afterwards
Edwige emerged with a basket of flowers. Did she decorate
the church or were they for some sick person? Flora said good
day to her and the old woman paused and came up to her,
putting down her basket carefully on the flagstones.

Flora had the feeling once again that for some reason the
woman did not like her. Perhaps it was just because she was
English. Some of the French did not like the English. But
Edwige sat down beside her and said: 'It is hot isn't it?' It took

Flora a moment or two to realize she was speaking French.

Had Delphine mentioned to her the interest Flora took in the past? There were so many things she'd like to ask the woman but one couldn't start to ask abrupt questions; it would be rude. Questions such as: What did Feodora die of? What was Ferdinando really like? Had Edwige approved of the Fascisti? What had she thought of Signora Paulina? What had Xavier been like as a little boy? Edwige, however, appeared to want to ask a few questions herself of Flora, for she began:

'You saw the portraits, Mademoiselle? Xavier is very like his grandmother to look at, don't you think?'

Flora had not really thought that Xavier and Paulina were much alike, so she made a non-committal murmur, and then waited politely.

'She had a strong character, that one,' said Edwige, smoothing her apron.

'She put herself first.'

'Women cannot usually do so,' Edwige agreed. 'But they should.' She looked at Flora searchingly as if she wanted to know whether Flora also was a strong character.

'It's easier for men,' Flora said, and waited.

Edwige said nothing so Flora went on: 'I suppose Xavier's grandfather always put himself first?'

Edwige looked at her in surprise. 'Of course – his was a powerful personality.'

'You must have known him well, Madame?'

'Forty two years, Mademoiselle.'

'Xavier has told me about him,' said Flora and hoped that Edwige would consider that meant he had told her about the man's end.

'His first wife idolized him,' said Edwige.

'I suppose he idolized his wives too?'

'You might say so – it was one of the things they had to put up with,' she said dryly.

Why were they having this conversation? Edwige was clearly leading up to something. Could she ask the woman about Xavier's own mother? She seemed to know everything!

'It's worse for women to idolize men,' said Edwige. 'Take my advice – most men are animals, though some are beautiful beasts. Few have souls!'

Flora looked at her in surprise but the other woman smiled, took up her basket and went off briskly.

What sort of experience must she have to say that? Why say it to her unless she meant it as a warning about Xavier? Paulina, the outsider like herself, had left her Leopardi husband. Was it because he had no soul? According to Delphine, Edwige had not liked Paulina – yet today Edwige had sounded as though she were generally on the side of women.

Tante Jo seemed to agree with Flora that it was Ferdinand who would haunt the Villa, if anyone did. She always mentioned his name with reverence. He seemed to have been the sun around whom all the family planets revolved. The idea of a dead Fascist haunting the place was disturbing, especially when the details were so mysterious. Xavier did not appear to be interested in that part of the past. Should she mention to him her conversations with both Delphine and Edwige? Tell Xavier what Edwige had said about men? She resolved instead to talk to Tante Jo, who might shed a more benign light on people.

After dinner that evening Flora and Jo were taking coffee together in the *salotto*. Xavier and Ludo were in the office with accounts to prepare, bills to pay, and all the problems of real estate to attend to and Solange had eaten her supper in bed and gone to sleep.

Tante Jo gave Flora the chance she had been hoping for when she said, Delphine having left the room: 'It's so nice she came back here – she used to worship my half-brother Paul, you know – when she was a child.' At last Tante Jo was volunteering some interesting information.

'Why did your step-brother leave Italy? Was it to live with his mother again?'

'Has Delphine been gossiping?'

'Oh, no! – I just wondered . . .'

Was Tante Jo so prejudiced towards her own family that even a faithful servant could not be trusted to speak the truth!

'He just decided to rejoin his mother in America for a time – and after that he preferred living in France.' Josephine looked at her blandly: 'Does my nephew talk to you much about his father?'

'No – but I think he's proud of him.' Now was the moment to ask about Xavier's mother.

'Would you like another cup of coffee?' she asked instead.

'No, thank you – it stops me from getting to sleep – Italian coffee is so strong, I find.'

'He has spoken to me a bit about his mother,' Flora said, and Tante Jo looked up in surprise.

'Oh, but he never knew his mother – he was only tiny when she . . . went away . . . .'

'He said she was called Victoire,' said Flora, trying to sound vague and uninterested. 'I wondered if she were French?'

'It was an unfortunate marriage,' said the other woman firmly. 'She behaved badly – though it was not her fault – her own mother was not a very nice woman.'

'Xavier has the impression that she died.'

'My father told me that she was dead,' Aunt Jo said stiffly. 'Have you been talking to Madame Rouart?'

'No – not about his mother – a little about when he was small.'

'Oh, he was *such* an intelligent little boy,' said Josephine, her face lighting up. 'I was the one who brought him up after his papa left for the States.'

She was clearly relieved to have changed the subject slightly, and Flora decided not to press her further. It was Edwige Rouart to whom she must direct any questions she might have about Victoire. Had Ferdinando had his own reasons for telling his daughter she was dead?

Tante Jo said: 'Don't believe all my housekeeper says – the war disturbed her – all the unfortunate circumstances – people blamed her for . . . things, but she did her best.' Was she alluding to the death of her father? 'The family will always owe a debt of gratitude to Edwige, but she will be better off now in her own little house. Xavier will have to take on more staff if more visitors want to stay here.'

Flora supposed that if his letting off rooms in the Villa to Americans was to be successful he'd certainly need more servants. The tourists might or might not eat here, but they would use the Villa as a base for their sight-seeing.

When Flora went up to her room that night she opened the shutters and looked out over the lake. It was dark; the moon, which rose on the other side of the Villa, was yet to travel over to the south, whence it often woke her through a corner window with its brilliance. As she undressed, she thought of Tante Jo's words: She behaved badly.

Tante Jo was so rarely judgmental that she was sure these were the original words used by Ferdinand Leopardi to her. Had he said the same to his grandson? Surely not? As far as she had noticed, Edwige Rouart avoided Josephine. They never said much to each other – yet they must once many years ago have been close.

She was sure, as she closed the shutters and got into bed, that old histories were the reason for Xavier's problems, whatever they were. It might be better to forget them if she could, and try once again to bring him back into the present.

I might be here on false pretences, she thought. Yet Tante Jo seemed to accept her as Xavier's friend, and even appeared to like her. She felt sure that Jo had not liked her stepmother Paulina – people did not usually warm to step-parents.

But that was a relationship lost in the mists of days before the war – and none of her business.

The next morning was slightly overcast. It was hot and humid and there was the tiny hint of a storm in the air. The lake was a pale greenish-grey. Today would be a good day to offer Solange a lesson and Flora mooted this to the girl who arrived at breakfast still a little heavy-eyed but less pale.

'If a storm does not break we can sit by the cascade,' she said.

'I wish I could go shopping with you,' said Solange. 'I need a pair of sandals. *Maman* can't be bothered to go to Como again for them. We could go over the lake one morning to Bellagio perhaps? Then you could tell me all the English words for shops and things!'

'OK – but shall we take a book to the waterfall today?'

'I've got an Agatha Christie,' replied Solange, 'but it's in French!' She giggled.

'*Méchante fille* – naughty girl!' said Flora. She thought: at her age I didn't expect a grown-up to talk to me much, or even go shopping with me. Perhaps Solange thought of her as not grown up.

In the event they spent a peaceful morning sitting in the shade of conifers, the scent of pines all around them. After lunch the sky darkened and the birds began their pre-storm twittering. Flora decided to finish her letters in her room. Xavier had not been at lunch, had once more disappeared on business.

The drum roll of distant thunder began at about three o'clock. By English standards this was going to be a huge storm. Flora enjoyed thunder and lightning so long as she was inside a house with no fear of being struck. She went out on to the corridor outside her room at about half past three and was surprised to see Xavier on the landing looking at his picture.

He did not hear her at first as she went up to him and she too became absorbed in the painting. Then he sensed her presence and turned his head.

'I hope storms don't worry you? Delphine has her head under a cushion – she's frightened of the noise and the lightning.'

Just then there was an enormous clap of thunder that seemed to come from the roof of the Villa itself. Scarcely had it stopped resounding than there was a flash and crackle of lightning followed by another even nearer thunder-clap.

'I rather like the elements,' she said. 'I thought you were going out – you were not at lunch.'

'No – but I didn't fancy driving through a storm. What have you been saying to Tante Jo, Flora? She came to talk to me in the courtyard this morning saying something about your being interested in my parents.'

'Did she? I asked a bit about your mother.' Flora suppressed what Tante Jo had actually said about Victoire.

'Oh?'

'She mentioned your father, and your maternal grandmother, but she didn't seem to know very much – she didn't seem to mind talking to me about the family. Did she say anything else to you?'

He said nothing for a moment and returned to his contemplation of the painting. Then: 'If there's anything you want to know why don't you ask me?'

'You don't appear to know very much either! Anyway you're always busy.' She wanted to say: if you want me to marry you – though I'm not even sure about that – I ought surely to know a little more about your family? Aloud, she said: 'You haven't talked very much to me about anything this summer!'

He looked at her then and said: 'They all think she's dead, my mother.'

'And you don't?'

'Oh, I think I agree with them now. If she was as bad as they say, she'd be back now I'm a rich man, wouldn't she?'

'I didn't know they *all* said she was bad.'

'It's the impression I got when I asked Edwige last year.'

'You did? You never told me you'd asked her again.'

'Well, I did. All she said was I'd better stop thinking about her because she wasn't going to come back.'

'She didn't actually say she knew she was dead?'

'No, she was careful not to say that. Does it bother you?'

'Xavier,' she put her hand on his arm, 'I've come here because you asked me to, yet sometimes you treat me as a stranger. I can't help wondering about your family – since it seemed once to have such importance to you.'

'Well, it doesn't now, Flora. As you say, I asked you here and I'm sorry if I've been busy. As far as I know we're all sane. Especially Tante Jo.'

'Who doesn't like Edwige – I've noticed that!' There was another loud thunder clap. He took her arm.

'Since we're up here, let me show you some other rooms – I mustn't look at my picture too often or I shall spoil it for myself!'

He began to walk along the corridor towards the rooms on the other side of the staircase, furthest from Flora's own. She followed. He stopped at a door that had not been repainted. 'The best window for a view of the lake's in here,' he said, opening the door.

The room was completely empty except for a truckle bed, two rickety-looking chairs and a long pier-glass. The walls and woodwork had not been repainted either, and there was a faint outline of old paper that had faded so much it was now just a shadow on grey. The windows were still shuttered. He opened one of them and they looked down towards the lake where there was a gap in the trees so that you could see the opposite shore.

He put his arm around her as a deafening roll of thunder resounded and simultaneously there came a tremendous flash of lightning.

'You could choose the decoration for this room if you liked,' he murmured.

'There are two or three other rooms on this side of the staircase that you haven't done anything about, aren't there? They aren't for your Americans then?'

'Oh, I wouldn't have tourists in *them!*'

He wouldn't desecrate them, she thought.

'The room you did up – further along – was sort of Regency?' she suggested. 'I mean, that's what we call it in England.'

'French Empire,' said Xavier. 'About the same period.' She was looking out of the window as he went on: 'My grandfather's second wife, Paulina, was keen on interior decoration. They tell me so, anyway. Tante Jo said all the rooms up here were done up by her in the Twenties. At least, I don't suppose she did them herself, merely offered suggestions. After she went away he just let them go to pot – until he had one or two refurbished in a different style.'

'So when you saw them – when you were little – they'd been done up again?'

'I suppose so – I don't ever remember seeing them in daylight.'

It was dark now, dark enough to imagine night had fallen. Suddenly there was a spattering of rain on the window, then a lashing and a streaming as the storm broke. They both looked out again. Great sheets of rain began to fall and the lake was suddenly invisible, the sky a pewtery purple over the far hills.

'It'll pass quickly,' said Xavier. 'When the rains come without a storm they can go on for days, but the storms are soon over – until the next time.'

'It does make things a bit cooler,' said Flora, moving to the long mirror on its stand and peering at herself in it. He came to stand behind her and she had the curious feeling that she was two people. One Flora stood there looking much as usual in the half dark; the other was a second Flora, eyes like giglamps, slender, strained, with a taller figure behind her whose chin she reached with the top of her head. The first Flora was independent, strong; the second one an object, an object brimming over with love and unrequited tenderness, frailer, not in charge of herself. She remembered her dream of the boathouse.

She put her hand up behind her head and searched for Xavier's hand behind her. He grasped it, pulled her round and kissed her roughly on the lips before drawing away quickly.

I ought not to keep asking him about the past, she thought. We ought to think of the present and the future. Xavier studied himself in the mirror for a moment and then turned and went out of the room. She followed him downstairs, and he made an inconsequential remark about the way the older generation in Italy still had power in the Church and in the family.

Has he forgotten that he is now the one who has the power here, she wondered. One day he will perhaps be like his grandfather and rule the roost!

Xavier's kiss went on burning her lips for the rest of the day even when the sun came out again and the rain stopped and the lake became turquoise once more.

In the evening she felt troubled, and in order to dismiss certain questions from her mind – and banish them from her conversation – she wrote them down in her journal. She knew no one at the Villa would read it for it was always kept in her suitcase, brought out only late at night from time to time.

Leopardi Family Mysteries

1. Why did Paulina Leopardi leave the Villa? Was it something her husband had done? Something she'd just discovered? (She must soon have realized what sort of man she'd married?)
2. Was this before or after her son Paul married the Victoire woman? (I think it was some time afterwards.)
3. When did Victoire disappear? Xavier thinks he was about four years old at the time, so it must have been in 1934?
4. Xavier remembers his father better than his mother so Paul Leopardi must have left the Villa after Victoire left? How long after Paulina left? Did Paul join his own mother in America?
5. Who was really in charge of Xavier? Xavier seems to regard Tante Jo as his main childhood guardian. Edwige Rouart didn't go with them to Paris, but he told me she helped to look after him when he was a baby.
6. When did the Germans begin to occupy the Villa in the war? When did Edwige move away? Did she later betray Ferdinando Leopardi to the authorities?

Flora then managed to put all this out of her head for a few days, but her curiosity always returned in the end.

It was another stiflingly hot day. The new girl who helped Delphine had gone home to Menaggio for a week's holiday. Flora offered to help prepare the vegetables, so Delphine brought them into the courtyard where Flora was seated on her favourite stone bench. The young woman joined her there behind a table she had loaded with peas and beans.

'Were there many maids before the war?' Flora asked her idly.

'No – not really – some came for the times when all the family were together – I think the village women used to help out a bit then. Chiefly it was Madame Edwige and my mother and me.'

'Was there a maid called Cécile? I think I've heard Xavier mention her.'

'I don't know. I believe Madame Rouart did have some other girls to help with the sewing and the spring cleaning, so there might have been one called that. Ask her – *she'd* remember.'

'Can *you* remember any of them?'

'I met one of the girls who used to help here. It was in the munitions factory in the war – but she was called Lilia. She died of TB.'

Flora waited a moment before asking: 'Did all the servants go to the wedding between Signor Paul and Xavier's mother?' She had not been able to resist her curiosity overcoming her scruples.

'I believe they were married in Como. My mother told me it was a sort of elopement. I suppose they might both have been under twenty-one, him and his bride.'

'Victoire?'

'Yes – that was her name – I'd forgotten. I never really knew her because I wasn't old enough to work here then.'

'She didn't stay long?'

'I don't know – Mamma might remember. I'm sure Madame Edwige would know.'

'She appears to know everything,' said Flora, eating one of the peas she'd just shelled.

'Perhaps she does but' – Delphine lowered her voice – 'I wouldn't trust her. Even when I was only a teenager and worked for her, I thought she told fibs.' She looked nervously behind her shoulder, adding: 'I shouldn't say so but I think she had a shock in the war – she was *that* devoted to the old master.'

'Well, she never talks about him. I suppose you know about his death?'

'Only what I was told – I was away till '46. My mother worked in Como in the war too, so she knows only what *she* was told.'

Flora decided in spite of Delphine's relish for gossip she really knew little more than she did herself about some matters. She felt a bit ashamed of giving way once more to curiosity. If she really wanted to know anything more she'd have to ask Edwige Rouart. She changed the subject.

When she thought it over she realized that they *had* been married, Paul and Victoire. It was not as she had imagined: Xavier was not a romantic bastard!

For the rest of the week Flora wandered in the Villa grounds, sometimes alone, sometimes with Solange. Her sense of the past was not so much in the gardens or on the terraces as in the Villa itself. Even there it was only in some rooms that she had that feeling she had experienced on her very first visit, a feeling of constriction in the chest, almost a dislike of herself, like nausea in the mind. In the rooms where she had stayed at first, in the old servants' quarters, the feeling vanished, but it was there a little in the entrance hall of the Villa, and strongly there on the first floor middle corridor. Her own bedroom seemed to have no effect upon her; the room from where they had watched the storm had it a little, but she was convinced that if she ventured behind other doors belonging to the rooms on the other side of the staircase, it would return.

Was it fear? she asked herself. No, not exactly. It was almost as if there was something that exuded dislike – perhaps a dislike of women. She dismissed it as a fancy, a fantasy woven around the strange ups and downs of her relationship with Xavier. Xavier himself seemed not to sense anything unto-ward, for he loved every inch of the place. What if she took

Solange to the rooms where the feeling came over her, saying nothing, to see if they had the same effect upon her? Adolescent girls were said to be very sensitive to atmosphere. Flora disliked any impression that she had no control over her own reactions. This never happened to her in England.

After lunch one day Solange asked her if she would teach her to play chess and Flora seized immediately upon the idea. 'Why not come up to my room? It's cooler there if I close the shutters.' They went upstairs.

'I haven't seen this part of the Villa before,' Solange said. 'Are they bedrooms?'

'Some of them are for the planned American tourists,' replied Flora. 'Others are not yet decorated.'

Solange was looking at the picture on the stairs. 'It's pretty,' she conceded. Then: 'Have you been on the very top floor?'

'Once or twice.'

'Uncle Ludo has a room up there – I like him—'

'Yes, I agree – he is nice.'

They went into her own room. The chess set was on her little table and she pulled a chair up to it for Solange and sat on the bed herself. She had intended to ask Xavier up for a game, perhaps with an ulterior motive, but had put it off.

Solange proved a quick pupil. 'It's easier than learning English!' she said.

'Are you good at maths?'

'Mm – they say so at school. Mother isn't interested in my maths report though.' She looked up. 'Are you and Xavier going to get married?'

'I don't know,' said Flora. 'Men have to do the asking, you know!'

'I don't think I shall ever marry,' Solange said. 'Boys are so boring!'

'They improve as they grow up,' said Flora, wondering if this were true.

When they had finished a game they got up and went out of the room. Solange sped along the corridor in a sudden burst of energy. She noticed the unvarnished doors. 'Let's go and explore these rooms. Perhaps they're like those in Bluebeard's Castle!'

Flora shivered. 'No! – no – they're private, I think.' But Solange was already trying the doorknob of one of the middle doors on the other side of the stairs.

'It's locked,' she said in a disappointed voice.

'Leave it then, Solange.'

'It's funny up here,' said the girl, now following Flora decorously down the stairs. '*C'est curieux.*'

'In what way?'

'I don't know – too many rooms, I suppose. Were they all bedrooms do you think?'

As they came down the stairs they passed Edwige who stood aside to let them pass. Solange said in French, '*Non, Madame* – please go first,' and Edwige stared at her, before a sudden smile creased her usually stony features and she replied: 'Thank you – it's nice to have young people with manners around again.'

'I expect those rooms were used, you know, by the Germans,' whispered Solange when she had gone. '*Maman* told me they came in the war. We had enough of them in Paris, though I was only a baby then.'

'Your papa knew the Villa,' said Flora.

'I know, and he didn't like it. Too many women, he said. *Maman* told me!'

Flora felt that the Villa, with wives and daughters – and mistresses? – living in it in the old days, had paradoxically been a place built for men.

That evening Xavier asked her to have a game of chess with him and she agreed. He seemed friendlier, less remote. Was the neat head that bent down over his chess pieces the one that she had once caressed? Were those clearly chiselled lips the ones that had given her a violent kiss? Did Xavier see life – and love – as a game of chess that had to be brought to a conclusion through the imprisonment of the king? But the king never died, could not even be killed in battle, would always be resurrected in the next game.

Flora had learned from Xavier to play a bold game with her queen. Tonight, since she was playing white, she decided to begin with her queen pawn. In truth she preferred to be black and to play a defensive game, but there was sometimes no choice: you had to attack.

For once, and by a sheer fluke, which she pretended she had been planning all along, she began to demolish his other pieces. But her endgame was always her worst. Through lack of practice she could never capitalize on her advances. Little victories there might be, but the grand final victory usually eluded her. This time however she managed, if not to win the game, to bring about a stalemate when only the two kings and a pawn each were left.

'*You* should have won that!' exclaimed Xavier, laughing. 'All your moves were better than mine – didn't you see what you should have done with your rook before I took it?'

'It's always the way,' sighed Flora. 'I played a few times last year, you know, and I may have improved a little – but I can't swoop in to the kill!'

That night there happened to be a full moon but Flora fell asleep immediately. She woke suddenly out of a deep slumber. Moonlight was streaming through the unshuttered windows; she got out of bed and went to look out at the scene below.

The silver was unearthly, more like a bright firework that would not burn itself out, everything in its light etched clear: the trees, the fountain which she could just see if she leaned out a little further, and the traceried high gate at the bottom of the garden. She felt restless, as if she had stumbled on a natural secret that yet looked unnatural. She had never seen moonlight so bright. Then she heard a floorboard creak outside her room and was instantly alert. She went to the door and opened it. Xavier was standing fully dressed there in the corridor. She stared at him.

'May I come in?'

He came in and she shut the door. He sat down heavily on her bed.

'I could not sleep,' he said.

'It's hot – I woke up too. I was looking at the moon—'

'Oh Flora – you must be angry with me?'

'For coming up to me? Why?'

'Because I know I've neglected you. Come here!'

She went to sit beside him on the narrow bed. The moonlight made her face look mysterious, remote.

'Poor little Flora,' he said. 'Why can't I love you properly?'

Her heart began to jump.

'I love you,' she said, and silly tears started to her eyes.

'Perhaps marriage *is* what I need?' he went on, looking away out of the window. His profile stood out against the silver of the sky outside.

'Nobody has to *marry* me!' she said.

'They all want me to settle down with you, you know – Tante Jo and Ludo – they like you.'

She thought, I'm not marrying his family!

'If you really knew me you might not like me,' he said, still looking away. For answer she put her arms round him.

Suddenly he kissed her as he had done a few days before, probing her lips and inside her mouth, and then her neck where her light summer nightdress was open. She remembered Menton, and lay back passively whilst he slid his hands up her back and then round to her breasts. She felt a swoon of desire, and a need to caress him back slowly. But he did not want to wait, and entered her violently.

They might be in some dark alley in a low part of a city: a sudden animal-coupling, exciting because it was impersonal. He was not hurting her – but she knew without doubt that in a curious way he was hurting himself a good deal. He groaned, even swore, seemed to be fighting some unknown invisible opponent that was hidden in her body.

It was soon over, with no cry nor groan nor yell, but instead a sound like a hiss, an emptying of air, that fought through his throat as he was overcome with a pleasure that sounded and looked more like pain. For a few minutes he was silent, his eyes fixed and staring, his breath coming in great rasps.

Then, as he lay now heavily upon her, he began quietly to weep.

Please don't let him ask me to forgive him, she prayed. She said in a choked voice, drawn out of her before she knew what she was saying: 'Why can't I be enough for you, my Xavier?'

He stopped crying, rolled over on to his back. 'Did I hurt you?'

'No – did you want to?'

'For a moment – to stop me hurting myself.'

Flora thought, if she had wanted a violent man, a man whose sensual victim she might want to be, she would not have chosen Xavier. She whispered: 'You could try differently – with other women?'

'Yes.'

In a primitive way she had even enjoyed this sudden coupling, and she knew she loved Xavier. But her feelings for him and the pleasure she might take in his desire for her were completely separate. Was it like that for him too?

Quietly, she asked: 'Why can't we be enough for *each other*, then?'

'There is something in me that is stronger than love,' he replied.

Your mother, she thought.

'Nobody can put it right,' he went on. 'Except —' and then he was silent.

'I don't want to control you,' said Flora. 'I want you to want me – just like you did – but more happily.' He had retired into himself again and she must drag him back. 'I think it might need a long time for both of us to feel right,' she said finally.

He sat up. 'Oh there is nothing wrong with you, Flora – I shall lose you to a better man!'

For answer she put her arms round him again and felt maternal. 'Lots of men don't fall in love,' she said. 'I don't go round expecting men to fall in love with me!'

'But I want to love you – all those good feelings I have with you – I shan't love anyone else in that way – and then I go and spoil it all—'

'Nothing is spoiled,' replied Flora firmly. 'I was glad you wanted me.'

'You will want more than I can ever give you – women like you do—'

'I can be all sorts of women Xavier! Just now I feel a bit – motherly.'

'I realize that. But you can't be the one who releases me. No, *you* can't!' He stood up, once more in charge of himself. 'You are not my mother *Flora cara*. If my mother had been like you I think I would be happier now.'

'Don't go, darling Xavier – don't go! don't be distant to me – treat me badly if you want – but don't ignore me!'

But he kissed her hand and glided away so that she was left alone in a pool of moonlight.

For the rest of her holiday Xavier treated her like bone china, ignoring once again all that had happened between them.

'You don't have to be so polite,' she said to him in the garden one morning, a day or two before she was to leave.

'You'd rather I was a brute?'

'No – neither—'

'Then I shall be your friend – like an Englishman,' he said.

They stood in the salon on the last evening of her stay, and suddenly she wanted to hear the music from the old gramophone again.

'You never made your music room,' she said to Xavier.

'I'd too many other things to do – I shall get round to it, I suppose,' he replied, but she thought he sounded indifferent.

'May I listen to Gigli again?'

'Of course you may, *Flora cara.*'

She put on Gigli singing *La Paloma*, which she had not heard for two years, and then the same tenor singing *Parigi O Cara* from *La Traviata* and thought her heart would break. Since Solange was there listening, she tried to control the emotion that welled up. Violetta was dying and there would be no Paris together ever again . . . . *I am not dying though and I have a remote possibility of happiness*, she thought, but for the first time she feared for her future with Xavier.

That night, she dreamed of a woman standing by Xavier's painting and pointing to it mournfully. The woman turned and Flora saw she had no face, before she disappeared through one of the unvarnished doors on the middle corridor. Could she have been Edwige Rouart? But Edwige was not Xavier's mother, though this wisp of a speculation must once have been in her conscious mind, before it was rejected and returned to her subconscious. The dream woman had not been Edwige; she was sure of that.

It was the day of her departure. The vision of next week back in England stretched ahead: beginning with the dull desolation she would be sure to feel on the first Monday at work. She might bear it if things were settled between herself and Xavier, but nothing was settled. And there was the possibility that this would be her last visit, that he would not invite her again, that their affair had ended; that her status of unofficial betrothed was no longer to be considered.

Xavier said nothing at breakfast, not unusual for him. He always hurried out after drinking his coffee even if she were there, and now did so even on her last day.

I shall never get to know him better, she thought, and a sense of despair invaded her, which she firmly pushed away. She did not want to leave, but she must. She had already packed ready for her journey to Milan. Xavier was to drive her to the airport this time. There would be no journey by boat, either over the lake or over the Channel.

She went into the courtyard, since she was not to start her journey until the afternoon, the flight being in the evening. Delphine joined her there in the sun.

'He wants me to get one of the upstairs rooms cleaned,' she complained with a sigh. 'Some Americans are to arrive next week.'

Flora noticed that she talked familiarly to her now. 'Have you ever been in the rooms that have not yet been altered?' she asked her.

'Which ones?'

'On the middle corridor – the other end from me.'

'Madame Rouart was hoping *she'd* have them, I think! She used to sew in one of the rooms up there. But she's now in her little house beyond the wood.'

Flora had never been invited there, though she knew that Solange had once visited the old lady in her new house. As a treat, Tante Jo had said.

'Mind you, I think Signora Giuseppina would prefer a suite of rooms up there if she came back for good – but I don't think she will.'

'Solange might, one day.'

'She likes it here, does she?'

'I think so, but she might change her mind when she grows up. You don't really know what you want at fourteen,' said Flora.

'Those rooms are meant for *you*, Signorina Flora, I'm sure!'

'For me?'

'Yes – when you marry Signor Xavier!'

'How do you know I shall marry him?'

Delphine looked at her in bafflement. 'That's what he's always said – those rooms are for my future wife!'

That may not be me, thought Flora.

'He has never said anything about that to me,' she said stiffly. Then she remembered he had said she might decorate that dismal room they'd been in.

'Madame Edwige told him a young woman would want a house of her own. But I told you not to take all *she* says at face value!'

'I don't believe everything that is said by anyone – only some of it,' Flora said carefully.

Delphine looked round as she got up and murmured: 'I wouldn't trust her if I were you. She'd prefer him to marry a rich Italian, I'm sure! Never trust the French, my mother always said!'

'What about the English?' Flora was amused.

'Mamma never knew any English people – only Americans. She once told me Signora Paulina – the American lady I told you about – used to have those rooms but they were shut up after she left the Villa.'

That was possibly true, reflected Flora. But Xavier would not keep them as a shrine to a grandmother. Perhaps his father, Paul, had been born in one of those rooms. Delphine would be unlikely to know that.

After a moment or two Delphine said: 'I must be off – I'll say good-bye now. Have a good journey home. I may not see you again!'

Flora, puzzled, shook hands with the young woman, who then smiled cheekily, saying:

'I have a secret – I'm saving up to go to America! To marry a nice GI I met in the war.' With that she was off.

Flora stayed in the sun, thinking over all Delphine had said. Then she walked in the direction of the garden behind the Villa. She sat listening to the waterfall, a book on her lap which she could not read. Xavier would guess where she was. He could come to talk to her if he wanted.

It was as if she loved one Xavier, whom she admired, and pitied another Xavier. As though he were a double personality, like the two Floras she had imagined in the pier-glass. However unsatisfactory for him his love-making had been, she still wanted it, and wanted his slim body by her side. She still admired the sharpness of his intellect, but wanted to succour the child that was still alive in him . . . .

It was not however Xavier who came to stand by her before lunch, but Edwige on her way back from her little house, Flora presumed, to help with serving the next meal, and to keep an eye on the new maids. Flora saw her shadow before she turned to see the woman standing there as if lost in reverie, the sound of the waterfall splashing near by.

It was to be a day of confidences.

Edwige remained standing. What had Delphine said? Don't trust Edwige.

Without conscious thought Flora said in her best Italian: 'Thank you for looking after us here – I have had a beautiful holiday.'

Edwige continued to stare at the far distance and did not look at Flora as she said in French in an urgent whisper: 'His mother is not dead, Mademoiselle, no his mother is not dead!'

Flora got to her feet and looked directly into her eyes. The old woman was still taller than she. Before the shrinking of age had begun to occur she must have been a good five feet eight inches tall.

'What did you say?' she asked, also in a whisper.

'You heard me – she is not dead.'

Flora raised her voice. 'Why do you not tell him so then?'

They were speaking French. The woman said: *'Ce n'est pas mon affaire s'il veut retrouver une félicité perdue. C'est une bête injuriée, notre petit Xavier – toujours enfant.'*

'Why are you saying this to me Signora?'

'To save you – it is too late for him.'

'I don't understand.'

'Elle n'est pas morte, sa pauvre mère – mais elle ne peut pas l'aider,' she said again.

Flora asked: 'Because he cannot tear himself away from this Villa? Because it represents his childhood?'

They were standing side by side now, both staring at the waterfall, neither looking in the other's face.

'You want to rescue him,' said Edwige Rouart. 'Believe me – I know. *He must forget the past*, not bring it back to life – or try to do so.'

Flora had the acute impression that the woman, whilst pretending to see to her interests, at the same time still disliked her, was perhaps jealous of her.

'He is *not* a child,' said Flora severely.

'I have done my duty,' said Edwige. 'Make what you will of me. It was all the old man's fault. Even if he calls the place Violetta' – she sniffed – 'it will not bring back the past.'

'The new nameplates have that name, Madame.'

'You must take him away – if you can,' said the old woman.

'I can't do that!'

'You saw him last summer away from here!'

'How do you know that?'

'I do know. Take him to your country, or to his grand-mother's country—'

'He loves me,' said Flora in a strangled voice.

'*You* love *him*. There have been – there will be – other women. You do not have to believe me, Mademoiselle. I hope you have a pleasant journey home.'

'Please tell him what you have told me,' said Flora beseechingly. But Edwige turned and walked away.

Flora was angry, bewildered – and yet intrigued. The woman had not forbidden her to inform Xavier of his mother's continuing existence, had she? But Flora decided that she could not tell him. That was up to Edwige Rouart. If it were true – which she did not for one moment believe.

The rest of the day – the lunch, the good-byes to Solange and Tante Jo and Ludo, the drive to the airport – passed in a hazy dream. Xavier was kind and attentive but uttered only commonplaces. Before she passed into the airport lounge he kissed her lightly, held her hand with every appearance of tender love and regard.

Her summer holiday – most likely her last visit to the Villa Violetta, she thought, was over.

When Flora said good-bye to Xavier at Milan airport on her way back to London she decided she would write him a long letter as soon as she got back home. Her month at the Villa had made her want to disentangle and sort out anew her feelings for him.

When she had been with him she had always been waiting for him to say or do something, or responding to what he had just said or done. She sometimes felt no longer sure that the feelings she had for him were those of love, no longer even sure what love was. What she felt was a vast emotion: a mingling of anxiety, tenderness, longing, even infatuation still, and also some irritation and a little resentment. And yet she felt sure that he did love her in his own peculiar way.

On long, boring, melancholy, autumn office afternoons she

sometimes felt so depressed that all she wanted to do was fall asleep, to wake up only when there were no practical decisions to be made. Even if she succeeded in making them, there would be no way of putting them into effect without seeing Xavier again. Her life in England was in danger of being lived in a sort of hiatus between the past and the future, and she did not want her London life to be so unimportant to her. Love should add to your happiness, not detract from it.

She decided not to write that long letter immediately but to attempt to distance herself a little from him, to write only in reply to a letter from him. This was a sacrifice, for Flora liked nothing better than to write, and enjoyed trying to communicate her thoughts, however painful. The difficulty was not that her love was unrequited, but that it appeared to be different in nature from Xavier's feelings for her. At first her love for him had been quite simply an infatuation with the mystery of another personality. It had slowly changed into an ache. At the Villa he had possessed her; she wanted him to possess her again, but not in the same way.

She had begun to think he would never write to her again, that it – whatever it had been – was over, when a letter arrived from him at the beginning of October.

He wrote in French, asking her not to abandon him. *Come back soon, and things will be different. I have many plans. Forgive me my inadequacies. Wait for me.*

She replied: *I want you to feel free, for I wish to act freely myself. I need time away from you, time to think – even though I long to be with you always – but not how we were this last summer. If you had never existed I would not now sometimes feel so unhappy and so tortured. I mustn't exaggerate though – must not make a melodrama out of a simple –* she searched for the word and wrote – *incompatibility.* Later she opened the letter again to add: *You must sort your feelings out – if this means I lose you I accept that, for I do so want you to be happy, dear Xavier.*

He replied: *Neither of us is a simple person, Flora. I am sorting my feelings out – as you put it.*

By this time it was late November and she wrote in return: *Perhaps what you need is a simpler person, a woman whom you can love who will not ask you for more than you can give.* Except, she thought, I never *asked* for much.

At Christmas he wrote: *I think I know now what to do – you must wait for me.*

She considered writing to Josephine, to Edwige even, but wrote only to Solange. Solange replied from Paris. In her letter the girl was obviously attempting to sound cheerful whilst feeling far from it, for the contents were rather dismal: the lycée (boring), Paris (boring). She would like to visit England. *Please, please write to me Flora.*

In the New Year of 1956 Edwige Rouart, to whom Flora had sent a Christmas card, wanting to keep open the lines of communication between them, sent her a strange letter.

There are many new faces at the Villa, Edwige wrote.

I am sure that Monsieur Xavier will want you to come again to Violetta next summer but if the opinion of an old woman is of any value I advise you not to do so.

Flora wondered how disinterested Edwige was. She had pondered many times what the old woman had told her about Victoire not being dead, but that might just have been mischief-making; she did not trust Edwige.

Xavier did not write at Christmas but in the following February she had another missive from him.

You may feel free Flora – as you say you wish me to feel – but I promise you that within eighteen months all will be well. Give me a year and come back here next year to find a new Xavier Leopardi.

John Thornton returned to London for a time from the States where he had been following a course at Harvard, and got in touch with Flora.

She went to a few concerts with him and arranged to spend a week of her summer leave from the office in June in the north of England, walking with John. He was a few years older than herself but was still young enough to introduce her to the chaste delights of walking in the hills. He was a friend, not a lover, and in any case the young people who stayed in the simple hostel accommodation were segregated. She could be sure of a good night's sleep when, fortified by fresh air and purged of bad habits among Spartan surroundings, she could allow herself to stop thinking.

John was sensible, calm, rational, quiet, knowledgeable, and appeared to enjoy her company, but he wasn't the kind of man to enjoy a light-hearted love-affair. She wished he were, but alas, light-hearted affairs did not seem to be her forte. Would she feel guilty if she were unfaithful to her strange Xavier? She was well aware that his talk of being free had referred to Rabelais' words: *Do what you will – and let me do the same – and we shall see how we both feel*. That would be risky for her, but better than stagnation.

By the following autumn, however, John Thornton had gone to work temporarily in a university in the north of England, from where he wrote to her from time to time. He still kept on a small flat in Hampstead but appeared to have little leisure to enjoy it.

Her holiday in the north was a fading memory and she had begun to long again for Italy. But she had resolved to go only when Xavier said the time was ripe and there had been no word from him.

She started to dream of white church towers and pink roofs, of wooded emerald slopes falling to lake shores, of balconies smothered in roses, of cypresses, myrtle bushes, gardens with lilies that she could smell even in the dream, of ferns and palm trees and waxy magnolia blooms, dark green glossy foliage – oleanders and citrus fruits – and of bougainvillaea falling like the heavy flounces of a girl's purple petticoats.

She thought when she awoke that the dreams were more poignant even than the reality of which they were the reflections. In the dreams she blinked in strong sunlight, was lulled by the sound of water, lapped in warmth, so that when she woke up she felt little inclined to get up in cooler, underlit London.

To her friend Clare Goodwin she confided that perhaps she was as in love with Italy as she was with the lover who lived there. Last summer, spent in the enchanted land, was as much a memory of a place as of Xavier – yet without Xavier the place might not have exerted its romantic spell. It had charmed her as she knew it had charmed Byron – and Liszt, who had composed some of his best music there. Romantic love had fuelled them all . . . .

She listened to records of the young Gigli singing *La Traviata*, remembering that Xavier had told her Verdi had written much of that opera on the shores of the lake. The music immediately brought back Xavier.

She read Stendhal's *La Chartreuse de Parme* and imagined Xavier as its hero, Fabrizio del Dongo. She read too of the Russian grand dukes who had come to the shores of Como a hundred years ago. Even they recalled Xavier's family, since Ferdinand's first wife Feodora, had been half Russian. Everything that caught her interest now seemed to be connected with Xavier's home. Yet she realized that other parts of herself had been just as capable of being interested in the Venerable Bede when she walked in Northumberland. She remembered her feelings that magic night in Bergamo, when she had listened to Wagner's *Star of Eve*. In one place it seemed she was destined to long for the other; in the North for the South.

'There must be something wrong with me!' she said to her friend Clare, with whom she now shared a tiny flat in Pimlico. Clare said only:

'The grass is always greener!'

Some of her Italian daydreams were less elevated. In the matter of food, for example. She wandered round Soho trying to find fish, and herbs, and ingredients for the sauces she'd enjoyed in Italy, but the results were never quite right. The cheeses did not taste the same as when she'd eaten them at the Villa; the fruits she'd liked best were not available; there were no persimmons or myrtle berries here; the pastries and the coffee and the wine and the lake fish, the chocolate and candied peel did not travel either.

It was no good trying to recreate Italy in London.

To understand the background of Ferdinando Leopardi's life and any influence it might have exerted upon Xavier, she read a biography of Mussolini. It was only ten years since the events of the dictator's last days – and of the last days of Ferdinando Leopardi. Xavier might be amused if he learned how she was trying to understand everything that surrounded him the better eventually to understand *him*.

She felt it had done her good to deprive herself for a time of Italy and Xavier, had put them in better perspective.

But she was sure she would return to him and his Villa.

If he invited her.

THREE

The Secrets of the Villa Violetta

1957

Flora had changed her job yet again in the February of 1957, feeling that she would like to control at least one part of her life. Work was easier to do something about; altering the direction of her love life was harder. Translation from French had been fun at first, but the work was becoming increasingly technical and suddenly she had felt her talents would be better suited to teaching.

Perhaps the memory of the mornings spent with Solange had unlocked the pedagogic side of her nature? She was untrained, so she applied to a coaching establishment and was amazed to find she really enjoyed the work. It would also be much easier to get time off, since she was employed on a monthly basis.

She might spend the whole summer in Lombardy if she wished. But there was little left of the legacy from her grandmother, and to be financially dependent upon Xavier would be awkward. She realized this was to be a summer of decision and she could not help being optimistic. Her own decision was to wait upon Xavier's, but she trusted in an eventual mutual happiness, when all her doubts and his difficulties would be magicked away.

In May she received the letter from him for which she had been waiting. In it he begged her to come and stay. Solange and her mother were not to be at the Villa that summer. She already knew this, for she had received a letter from Solange telling her that her mother had decided they should have a holiday in Brittany in June. No explanation was given, and maybe none had been given to Solange herself, though she did also write: *Uncle Ludo is also to visit Paris, where we shall entertain him.*

Another letter arrived from Xavier a few days later, this time more enigmatic.

> The apartments are now ready for visitors – an American journalist has stayed in the room next to yours. It's a shame she wasn't here at the same time as you – you might have enjoyed talking to her! But when you marry me, *cara* Flora, the best room will be yours!

Her heart beat fast when she read this.

On the heels of this letter another arrived from Edwige Rouart. Flora opened it with trepidation.

> *Monsieur Xavier tells me that he has invited you to stay at the Villa again. Forgive me, but I still think it would be wiser if you did not come! I expect my advice will not be taken. If you do come, I should like to talk to you. Would you visit an old woman in her own house? I no longer live at the Villa.*
>
> She added her address.

Flora was disturbed, all her earlier optimism swept away. But why should the machinations of an old – and jealous – woman put her off?

Her only fear was that when she saw Xavier again she might not be in love with him.

*

She flew to Milan and then took the train to Como. At last she was back! And there was Xavier waiting for her on the station. When she saw him at the barrier she remembered the last time they had met on a railway station. Three years ago. In Menton.

Xavier looked excited. He also looked older, and more purposeful.

'Flora! Soon you will be home!'

He took her arm, placed her luggage in a trolley, and off they went. A taxi, then a boat. After about twenty minutes the Villa could be seen on the left-hand shore, white in the distance, then growing nearer, brilliant in the sun, the windows of the middle storey still shuttered, the bougainvillaea darker than she remembered, the cypresses down by the boathouse surely grown a little?

I dreamed of you all, she thought, and now here you are again.

'We have a new servant girl,' Xavier was saying as they stood before the great door. 'Delphine went to the States last year. Did I tell you?'

'I shall miss her!'

'The new girl is very young – only seventeen – the daughter of a maid who once worked here – I believe I can remember her mother, Cécile . . . .'

A young dark woman was already taking her bags.

'This is Mirella,' he said, and the girl inclined her head. They followed her to the lift. 'I thought – at first you might like your old room – where you were last time?' he said.

Flora thought she would take the bull by the horns. 'I had a letter from Edwige,' she said, her hand on the door-knob, the corridor shadowy behind them.

'Oh?'

'Yes – she said she no longer lived here but invited me to visit her in her own home. Is it still the same little house she lived in – through the wood behind the Villa?'

'Yes. I wish we saw more of her but she's getting on. You must go and see her.' But she thought he did not look too pleased.

'There is a little present waiting for you when you come down to lunch,' he said, and smiled. Flora went into the room she knew so well.

She unpacked a few things and then went to look out of the window. The lake was shining below as it always had; she felt she had never been away.

She was hungry. She went down the familiar stairs to the dining room. The picture of the girl and the violets was still in its place and as she passed it she was sure that the flowers themselves were exuding a faint perfume. Before she reached the room she heard a murmur of conversation through the open door. There must be other guests. That might be interesting.

There were two women standing there, glasses in hand. One was about forty-five, rather plump with glossy black hair, obviously Italian, thought Flora. The other, a younger woman, was thin and elegant and went immediately to fetch her a glass from the table.

'Xavier will be here in a moment,' she said. 'I am Francesca Vitelli, Signor Leopardi's secretary. How do you do?' Flora shook her hand and took a glass of champagne. 'This is Elisa Dawson,' said Signorina Vitelli, and the plump woman murmured a greeting. Edwige had said there were new faces at the villa, but had not mentioned a secretary.

Xavier entered the dining room then and behind him followed the young maid with a tray. Flora saw the table at the far end of the room was already laid and could not help looking forward to one of those meals of which she had so often dreamed in food-starved London. The champagne was already making her feel light-hearted if not light-headed.

Xavier said: 'I'm glad you've all met. Francesca has a present for you!' The elegant Signorina Vitelli picked up a small square parcel wrapped in green tissue paper with a mauve ribbon. 'Join the club,' said Elisa Dawson in English.

Flora saw that on the lapel of her brown silk jacket Elisa was sporting a diamond brooch with flowers of amethyst. She looked at Francesca as the parcel was passed to her and saw round her neck a silver pendant with a cluster of purple drops nestling on her bosom, each drop exquisitely wrought into a violet with the heart of each flower a tiny diamond. Perhaps both the brooch and the pendant were costume jewellery, but she suddenly guessed what she would find in her parcel. For this was the Villa *Violetta*!

'Where are the Americans?' she asked Xavier as she opened her present.

'Oh, we had a lot to see the blossoms in Spring,' he replied airily. 'But no more for the present.'

Flora found a box inside the parcel, and in the box, reposing on cotton wool, a silver ring with a large cluster of violet amethysts. She held it up to the light. It was exquisite.

'The emblem of the Villa,' said Xavier. 'Do put it on your finger. I guessed the size.'

If he intended an engagement, this was not the way to give her the ring, she thought confusedly. It was all very odd.

She put the ring on her middle finger where it fitted perfectly. 'There – just right for this finger,' she said. Elisa Dawson looked at her a little enquiringly, she thought, but the secretary said: 'Everyone who comes to stay here gets a piece of jewellery – aren't they lucky!'

'Thank you, Xavier,' said Flora, but she felt constrained, a little embarrassed. He did not appear to notice any awkwardness.

'This evening I shall show you the new Violet Rooms,' he said.

Lunch was good: smoked lake trout and then veal, and then a cheese called Mascarpone. A great silver bowl heaped with fruit – peaches, apricots, cherries and a melon – stood in the centre of the table. Xavier's 'hotel' must be flourishing!

'This afternoon we could perhaps walk in the woods,' he suggested as they drank their coffee. The two women had gone out of the room. 'Only a short stroll. I want to show you the cascade. My secretary will be busy shopping, or organizing my various enterprises, and Mrs Dawson always takes a siesta.'

What enterprises, and who is this Mrs Dawson? she wanted to ask, but he continued swiftly: 'I have business interests now and investments to supervise in Como and even in Switzerland.' He sounded proud and pleased. 'Mrs Dawson is a sort of *pensionnaire* here,' he went on. 'Her husband died, leaving her a good deal of money.'

'Why did Delphine leave?' Flora asked as they set out for their walk.

'Oh, she went to one of her GIs,' he said. 'You knew she kept up with one of them who was billeted here in the war? A man of Italian extraction. Well, he really did ask her to marry him. Personally I think she was foolish but she'd always wanted to go over there. Let's hope he doesn't beat her!'

Flora said nothing to this. Instead, as they stood looking at the waterfall which plashed over small rocks and looked as if it had been there for ever, she asked: 'Xavier, why did you want me to accept this ring?'

'So you can belong here,' he answered.

'But you know that nothing is decided? It is not an – engagement ring?'

'No – I shall give you a more splendid ring when I ask you to marry me, Flora!'

'I feel I hardly know you any longer,' she said. And yet as she said that, she felt strangely excited.

'I am the same man,' he replied, taking her hand and kissing it. 'But I have perhaps changed a little. I will show you when you come to me in the Violet Rooms this evening!'

'Is it to do with those two women who live here now?'

'You are jealous *cara mia!*'

'No. I told you to feel free – as I wanted to be myself. If you are having an affair with either of them, I can understand.'

'It's not like that –I don't *love* my secretary – or the rich Mrs Dawson.' With that she had to be content, but Edwige Rouart's warning kept coming back into her mind.

Later, in her room she finished her evening toilette. She guessed that life at the Villa would now be conducted more formally, and had dressed for dinner. The place was after all a sort of hotel, and she would show Xavier that she knew how to behave, and might even have secrets of her own. There was a tap at the door.

'Come in.'

It was Xavier, dressed in a paisley-patterned robe.

'I have come to show you the Violet Rooms,' he said.

Flora felt nervous.

'I like your dress,' he said. She was wearing a two-piece – a dark blue satin skirt bought in London and an old halter-neck blouse of the same colour that set off the colour of her eyes. He took her right hand, and she followed him meekly through the door.

He turned towards her, saying: 'Are you still wearing the ring? Let me see.' She held out her left hand. The mauve of the stone did not really go with the blue of her dress; a sapphire would have been better.

She said: 'I have nothing purple or violet to wear, Xavier – I suppose you would like me to match the surroundings!' It was a joke, but she realized, as they now entered a lofty, high-

ceilinged room down the corridor, one of the rooms she had
never entered, that he *would* have liked her to wear the Villa's
colour, for he replied with the utmost seriousness: 'Oh, I
know that violet is not fashionable this year.'

'Fashion has never attracted me,' she replied.

When she took in the surroundings of the room she realised
that they were not fashionable either. By the side of a long
pier-glass at one corner, on the same side as the window, there
stood a Lalique lamp on an octagonal table. On another similar table, next to a divan that lay at right angles to the
window, was placed a large crystal bowl of pot-pourri. There
was an elegant sofa on the other side of the room, and very
little else, except for a bookcase on the wall. She suddenly felt
that constriction of the chest she had noticed before.

'The room is not exactly decorated for *comfort*,' he said
before she could express the same opinion. 'Come and look
out of the window.' But Flora went up instead to the crystal
bowl and sniffed the dried flowers. Violets of course.

'Xavier,' she said, 'did something once happen here? I
mean in this room – when you were a little boy?'

'I can't remember exactly,' he said. He came up to her and
caught hold of her again and buried his face in her shoulder
for a short moment. She swayed a little. 'Then you don't want
to look at the view?'

He raised his head and kissed her lips, her neck, her throat,
his eyes open, returning always to hers, searching them with
a steady intensity.

Then he carried her to the divan. She lay there passively,
forgetful of herself and of time, waiting only for him. Please
God that love-making would be easier for him now. May he not
ask for forgiveness either – or weary her with his guilt. Why
could he not say something, even if it were not: I love you?

Then his passion shocked her.

He was strong, greedy, demanding, took her once more as

a man might take a woman of the streets, but even more brutally; not with complicity, more with an impersonal force. And then he did speak, but they were not Italian words she had ever heard before. She understood he was swearing, talking dirty.

Was this what he needed, what he wanted, from *her*? Pure sex? Desire assuaged? Rutting, swearing, the thrusting male, sure of himself? Herself the object, the vessel, into which he gushed his frenzy. She was shaken. Was *this* what she wanted?

When he loosed his hold of her he fell across her like a fallen tree. There was enough light coming in through the window next to the unlit lamp, and she caught sight of her own body in the mirror behind as though she was in a pornographic film.

Disturbed, she moved slightly, wondering why a demonstration of his desire, unexpected though it had been, and so sudden in its violence, should upset her so. She loved him; he was not a stranger, even if they had been two years away from each other. Was this the only way for them to make contact again? Why could there be no words from him?

He stirred after a few moments and she kissed his cheek, wanting to use words herself, to make the past scene a part of their history, but she would wait for him to speak. After a long silence:

'Do you still feel maternal?' he asked.

'No.'

'Good – it is not just *you* I am possessing – but my pleasure!'

For years she had wished he might be able to abandon himself, but this love making – if you could call it that – was like a sharp rock floating in a sea of nothingness. She felt dislocated. Her body had not been prepared. Why could he not have made love to her in the afternoon – it need not have been gently – in the woods or by the waterfall? He had not even kissed her then, or even held her hand! Or said much at all. He must have intended what had just taken place exactly as it had, and for it to happen without warning. She might not even have been in the mood: he hadn't asked.

I expect he thinks I'm always ready for love, she thought. He may think of me as a loose woman? It's true, I can very quickly want to be made love to, and I've never needed much encouragement from him before. But I don't want him to make excuses . . . no, not this time . . . .

All she wanted was for him to make the connection between this sudden desire of his and the emotion of love, and to acknowledge a mutual need that had nothing to do with looseness or conventional morality – or prurience.

As she was thinking this, he got up silently, went to the long glass, looked at himself in it and said: 'I'm going to change. I'll see you downstairs at dinner. Be sure to wear your ring. And remember – whenever I want you it will be in this room – and you will come here whenever I do. When we marry we shall have other apartments!' Then he went out.

She was too shocked to say anything.

Flora went slowly down the staircase past the picture of the Woman with the Violets, and into the spacious hall where the marble floor, patterned in black and white diamonds, looked more beautiful than ever. The dining room was behind, at the back of the house, and she waited for a moment, gathering courage to go in.

How could she look at Xavier, how speak normally to him after the way he had just spoken to her? As if she were a pros-titute he was paying – but it was not a game . . . . She plucked up her courage, crossed to the door, and went into the dining-room. He was there with the two women: the secretary, Francesca Vitelli, and Mrs Dawson who was already at the table.

He looked up from pouring out a drink and smiled at her

in a politely friendly way just as if they had not spoken since lunch time, when only half an hour ago she had been in his bed.

'Oh, Flora – an apéritif?'

She decided to bring up any still remaining reserves of sang-froid and smiled back saying: 'Oh yes, please – a glass of white wine with a little soda, if I may?' Was the upstairs bedroom scene a different kind of game he was playing, one he had to play if he were to make love at all? Was the rest of his life a pretence?

She felt suddenly, it has always been like this! We civilized people act towards each other as if we were not animals with animal passions. Yet we guzzle in front of each other, and drink, and flirt, whereas nobody but our intimates know what we are like when we are once more as naked as the day we were born; or as we shall be one day before we are wrapped in our shrouds. Was Xavier a little mad?

She waited until midnight in case he wanted her to go once more into that Violet Room with him, but he did not come to her.

She could not sleep, could not get comfortable. Wasn't love-making supposed to make you sleepy and then give you deep slumber? When she did fall asleep at last she kept waking up, each time out of a dream. The gardener, Enrico, was in one of the dreams, with the new little maid, Mirella Agostini; in another she came across a settlement of jolly homosexuals once again in the Villa boathouse.

A woman called Lily was in the last dream which took place in a Violet Room, not the one she had been in that evening, but one near it, two doors away from it, where last time the wallpaper had been grey and everything had been neglected.

Over all these dreams hovered an atmosphere of menace for which she could not at first account when she awoke: the overt content of her dreaming was unpleasant, perhaps, but not sinister. The boathouse might once have housed something extremely unsavoury, but she had never been frightened of the place when she had looked through its door. Neither were the neglected rooms of her dream sinister in themselves; indeed she thought she preferred them to the stylish redecoration Xavier had gone in for.

She awoke in the morning quite late, not at first able to account for the depression that seemed to hang like a lead weight behind her eyes and to lurk in all her thoughts. She got up, washed her face and applied lipstick, and forced herself to go downstairs. A cup of coffee would be very welcome, though she did not feel very hungry.

When she arrived in the *sala da pranzo*, she could not help remembering those mornings only four years ago when – in another room of course, the old dining-room in the previous servants' quarters – she'd used to find Great-Uncle Sasha and Uncle Ludo already installed at table enjoying their cappuccinos and fresh bread and pale curly butter. Then Xavier had greeted her with a smile before going out to see to his 'improvements'. There was no Xavier in the dining-room this morning, only Francesca Vitelli. Had she just arisen from Xavier's bed?

Flora felt acutely miserable. Not principally from jealousy over Xavier's putative lover, but out of a terrible nostalgia, a longing for the innocent past, however unsatisfactory that past had been. Yesterday evening Xavier had made love to her more successfully from his point of view than ever before, if the strength of his own desire was to be the criterion, but it seemed to have left her with a dread of losing control in his presence. Before yesterday, to lose that control with Xavier had been what she had always half-hoped she might be able to do. Now she felt that he would be the last man in the world before whom she would want to drop her guard.

As she dipped a piece of bread slowly into her coffee bowl she saw quite clearly that marriage would mean giving up her individuality and independence. There seemed to be two warring factions in her head so that when Signorina Vitelli asked her if she had slept well she came to with a start and fumbled into a reply in bad Italian.

What had brought about this state of affairs? She could not deny that part of her needed him to come to her again. Not for the sake of an exciting sensation. Yet she might have welcomed pure lust – from anyone but Xavier. She wanted *him* to be tender, and to acknowledge and declare in words that it was she, Flora, whom he wanted and to whom he was making love, not some anonymous female. There must be something wrong with her? Sex need not be so desperate, even if it were exciting. Yet she thought she still loved him. Did she fear lest her romantic passion should suddenly change into a simple pursuit of pleasure? He had changed. Not she.

She had known him too long, knew his weaknesses, still knew him primarily as a person, not a body. She remembered her efforts in Menton to put their relationship on a healthier physical footing. She had failed. Now it was his turn. Xavier's attitude might have changed; had he also been forced to metamorphose himself into another person? It had seemed like that yesterday, even before he had taken her to the Violet Room. What else had he in store for her now?

'Signor Leopardi will be busy in the mornings,' said Francesca, 'but he asked me to tell you to have a look round the Villa and gardens. Go wherever you like. Lunch is at one o'clock.'

Xavier was nowhere to be seen, so Flora decided to take the advice and walk round alone for an hour or two. In particular she wanted to go to the kitchens to see if she recognized any of the servants. Perhaps there might be someone who could give her directions to Edwige Rouart's house.

She went through a side door into the yard where she had so often sat with Delphine Domani. There was a door to the kitchens from there. Yes, there it was, half open. She walked across to the window next to it and peered through it. There were the old sink and scrubbed table. But now there was an enormous Frigidaire, which had not been there before.

A young girl, the one she had seen yesterday, was washing up.

Mirella Agostini. Flora wondered for a moment why she felt she knew her. Then she remembered her dream. She went into the kitchen and coughed slightly so as not to startle the girl.

'Excuse me. I wonder if you could tell me how to find Signora Rouart's house – Signor Leopardi said you might know . . .' It was a long shot. He'd said only: 'The servants will tell you the way.' The girl turned round and Flora saw she was a beauty, with dark fringed eyes and thick black hair. She hadn't noticed that yesterday.

'Yes, Signorina, if you follow the path that goes near the lake by the waterfall and through the coppice you will see a few houses on the top of the slope. Madame Rouart's is the one on the left.'

'Thank you. I did not know there was a lake!'

'Oh it's only a pond, but they call it a lake!'

'I know the cascade so I shall not lose my way.'

The girl bent back to her work. She had not seemed surprised. Maybe Xavier had warned her that Flora might need directions? She was becoming paranoid. Xavier was not a wicked prince and she was free to go where she wanted. If there was any constraint, it was of her own choosing, and came from love.

She decided to go to visit Edwige that afternoon.

Xavier had not been at lunch; there had been only herself and Mrs Dawson who had gone up to her room for a siesta afterwards, so Flora's morning decision held good. Xavier couldn't blame her for visiting Edwige; if he'd wanted to be with her he could perfectly well have come back for lunch.

As she walked along the path through the small wood, the lapping of water still sounding pleasantly on her left, she tried to sort out the questions that she needed to ask the old woman. Then, as she emerged from the wood, she caught sight of the house. Another little path that led to it was bordered on each side with pretty blue flowers. A blue butterfly was sipping from them. The house was two-storeyed with three blue shuttered windows on the ground floor and three above. It did not look like the witch's house that Flora realized she'd been half dreading. It looked more like a fairy godmother's house. But she mustn't let her imagination run away with her again.

A little black cat suddenly manifested itself on the path. 'Puss, puss!' she said invitingly and held out her hand. He looked at her for a moment with his back arched, then turned tail and whisked away.

She knocked on the narrow old-fashioned front door, turning over in her mind what she might say. When the door was opened and she saw Madame Rouart standing there in a smart black dress Flora felt at a disadvantage. 'I'm sorry,' she said hurriedly in French. '*Excusez moi* – but I only arrived yesterday. I did want to see you – I should have written – or telephoned . . .'

'I thought you would come,' said Edwige. '*Entrez*, Mademoiselle. Who told you where to find me? He didn't, I don't suppose?'

'Well, no, Xavier said they didn't see much of you nowadays . . . .'

'True. Well, Mademoiselle Flora, may I offer you a cup of lemon tea?'

Away from the Villa Edwige was still an impressive old

woman who did not look like a former servant. She was wearing a Chypre-smelling perfume, and shoes that were long and
elegant. Flora remembered the first time she had seen her. Her
hair had been just as severely pulled back then and there was
no more grey in it now than there had been four years ago.

She followed her hostess into a small salon at the front of
the house, a pleasant room with a round table before the
window, a table set with a runner, a vase of blue flowers in its
centre. On one side of the room, taking up most of the wall
space stood a large *buffet* or sideboard.

A large ginger cat came sidling in and rubbed against
Flora's legs. She stooped to stroke it. Edwige clearly liked cats
as much as Flora did. It would be something to talk about if
the conversation was sticky.

The room looked comfortable, unpretentious, and the
furniture well-polished. There were several books on shelves
next to the *buffet*, and copies of a Swiss magazine on a little
table. The smell of cinnamon, or something similar, lingered
from the kitchen. Flora remembered that Madame Rouart had
been a good cook in the days when she had helped with the
cooking on Flora's first visit. Had she been taken on originally
as a cook? She knew the woman was an expert herbalist and
often gathered wild mushrooms from the woods.

How could she begin to ask those questions that still
plagued her? If Xavier had made her what she might consider
a serious proposal of marriage, if he had been a happier lover,
she would not be here now. As it was, she felt herself to be an
interloper.

She shivered, wondering how she would find him on
return, and realised that she was thinking of Edwige's home
as a sanctuary. That was nonsense, all due to her own over
heated imagination . . .

She said brightly: 'I thought I would like to see your house
– I never saw it before . . . .'

Edwige gave her some lemony-scented tea in a white cup and sat down at the table with a cup for herself, having pulled up a chair for her guest. 'How are you then? You didn't come last year.' The woman was looking at her over the rim of her cup, regarding her steadily. Seeing that penetrating look Flora knew she could not lie.

'Xavier has changed,' she said. 'You told me not to come to the Villa again. He has a secretary – I expect you have seen her? A Signorina Vitelli—'

'And I hear he has little Mirella too – I believe I knew her mother,' interposed Edwige. She continued to look at Flora steadily. 'Do you love him still? Has he asked you to marry him?' she asked in a no-nonsense voice.

'Well, he did once, but I'm not sure whether he meant it. I do love him, Madame. I want him to be happy . . . .'

'Yes – I would not have written to you if I had not thought you did. But is he not happy now? He's making money. He has these women around him. He has you – waiting to return to him. Forgive me – it is not my business . . . .' She looked down in her lap then suddenly raised her face and looked searchingly at Flora but said nothing.

Flora took her courage in both hands. 'How long were you with the family, Madame?'

'I was at the Villa fifty-four years, if you count the last war, when I had to leave for a time. This spring I decided I would retire.'

Flora thought she spoke a little sardonically. But – fifty-four years! Flora was amazed. Yet when she thought about it she realized that if the woman had known old Leopardi for forty-two years, as she had already been told, that must be about right. Tante Jo must now be well over fifty, and Edwige had been her nanny after Feodora died.

'It must have been interesting – working for one family for so long,' she offered politely, resigned now to talking about

Edwige rather than revealing her own problems.

'Interesting? I don't know about that! It was better than the life I'd been leading up till then, I suppose.' She appeared to want to talk about herself. Perhaps she was lonely.

'Don't you want to go back home? To France? Madame Duvallier would like you to, I believe?'

'Josephine is not expecting me to live with *her*, I don't think! – anyway, I have no other home. I had no home over there when I came here. That was why I came.'

'You were an orphan?'

'Mademoiselle Flora, you have a sympathetic face, but I think you would be extremely shocked if you knew about my early life and experience! It's Xavier Leopardi you want me to talk about, though, *n'est-ce pas*?'

'Well, Madame, it appears that you were warning me off – telling me last year not to come here – and then again this summer. You told me his mother was still alive . . . .'

'Did you tell him?'

'No, I did not, but I think he ought to know. Will you tell me more about the family, Madame? If he does ask me to marry him, I ought to know more – yet you always seem to be withholding something . . . .'

Edwige glanced at her sharply. 'You would not understand anything I had to tell you unless you understood what manner of man his *grandfather* was, and how I came here, and what went on here when Xavier was a child . . . not that he wasn't brought up quite properly.'

A little shiver went down Flora's back. She had always believed dead Ferdinando was the most important person at the Villa. Quickly, she said: 'Why are there so many mysteries here? I understand why Xavier wanted to come back and make the Villa beautiful again, but I don't think he's really happy, and nobody told me about his grandfather's death – I discovered that from talking to people at the shop.'

'But I expect he has told you about his childhood here?'

'Oh, the Violet Rooms and everything?'

'The what?'

'The rooms he loved and remembered – where there was the scent of *violettes de Parme* – you know – the reason he gave the Villa a new name. Now he's even giving guests presents of amethyst jewellery!' As she said that Flora realized how annoyed and hurt she had been that Xavier had seen fit to give her something similar to what the secretary and Mrs Dawson had received.

'You don't sound pleased, Mademoiselle! Soon I imagine he'll be putting little pieces of purple soap in the bedrooms! As for his guests, I'm sure the place could never be an hotel. You may need your American dollars, I said, but the Villa is a *family* home!'

Flora thought it was Edwige's turn to sound aggrieved. But surely *she* knew the reason for Xavier's obsession with violets. 'Please tell me what I need to know,' she said humbly.

'I could tell you about my life, and about Xavier's grandfather if you wanted.'

'I know it is not really my business . . . .' Flora said.

'I think it could have *something* to do with you. I suppose now I am old I too feel the need for confession. But I warn you – you will be shocked!'

Flora was thinking that she might not be a suitable recipient of an old woman's confessions; she was a little frightened at what she might be letting herself in for.

'You mean Ferdinando Leopardi's political beliefs would shock me? He wanted to be like that decadent poet he admired?' she asked brightly.

'The politics came later,' said Edwige and composed herself in her chair after pushing away her cup and saucer. 'I have never told anyone about when I first came here, and since Signor Leopardi died there has been nobody to remember.

The truth about him, I mean. Nobody knows . . . Josephine has never known. As for Ludovic, when he was older he took care not to understand . . . yet I feel the need to acquaint you with it.'

'Does Xavier know – about these matters?' Flora was intrigued.

Edwige looked up, and stared out of the window as she began to speak:

'If I tell you about part of my life, it is only to help you, Mademoiselle, so that perhaps one day you will be able to help Xavier. You seem determined to be part of his life!'

'I wish I could be.'

'Do not tell him what I tell you, unless he forces you to do so. Don't say anything to the family either – especially little Solange. She is fond of you, I know. I expect she has written to you?' She turned to Flora. Her face seemed somehow sadder, softer.

'Yes, she has.'

Edwige looked out of the window again as she continued in a low voice: 'Well, I met Ferdinando Leopardi for the first time in Paris in 1903 when I was eighteen years old. He was always a powerful man, Ferdinando, but when I was young I wasn't frightened of him. I'd worked for Eugénie Lesueur since I was fifteen – I'd gone there after my stepfather had put me out on the street for biting him when he tried to take advantage of me. "You'd bite the hand that feeds you," my stepfather said, and I suppose in a way he was right. But he wanted obedience too and I wasn't having that. I was sorry for my mother but she didn't believe me when I told her what her new man had been up to. Later, she did and we made it up, she and I. But that's another story . . . .

'As I said, I went to Paris and worked for Madame Lesueur. I knew when she took me in what kind of place hers was, but I didn't care. I remember thinking that I'd get paid for what they wanted me to do, *and* I'd get better food in my belly than my stepfather had ever provided. He'd have repaid me in blows too; he already treated *Maman* worse than a dog.'

Flora was hanging on her every word, shocked into silence but fascinated.

'One afternoon my Madame called me into her bureau. She had it really nice there – we were a posh establishment and I'd struck lucky, whatever strange things the men who visited *La Lune Argentée* wanted us to do.

' "Sit down," she said and she told me of a wonderful opportunity waiting for me in Italy with a client of hers, a young man called Signor Leopardi who needed a nanny for his son as he had an ailing wife.

'I didn't understand why she was wanting to get rid of me, and I was frightened. I thought, what if this Italian is a cruel man? I'm happy here, and I'm used to it now – and I know she likes me, so why does she want to send me away? Of course I found out later he'd offered her a good price. He was a rich man, you see, and it was slave money in a way – but I didn't know that then.

' "You'll have to do his bidding," she said, 'but there's nobody else I could recommend. He wants a young girl he can train up."

'I knew there was no refusing for she could always put me out on the street again and I'd never find such a good place as hers. She was an odd woman. Although she exploited them, she liked women better than men – if you get my meaning – and she liked me. What she added that afternoon was that, as I was clever, I might make something of myself, and she was doing it for my sake. I don't think she would have forced me but I felt I owed her something for taking me in.

' "You can meet him," she said. "He wants to see you first in any case before he decides." "What if he doesn't like me?" I asked. I'd grown bolder in the three years I'd worked for her

– I'd had to stick up for myself. "Oh, he'll like you," she said, "I know the type of girl he likes." "I thought you said he wanted a nanny?" I said. "Yes," she said, "but there might be other duties." She laughed. "He's a *chic type* – he won't harm you."

'He was to come to look at me the next morning. It was all arranged so quickly I'd hardly time to consider. But I was young, and ready for an adventure. She told me he spoke French and lived in a lovely part of Italy and that his wife was half Russian. "It will be *Le High Life*," she said.

'I was flattered, I suppose, that she thought I'd fit into all that. I didn't suppose she knew much about him really, except he was a good client.

' "His tastes are quite ordinary," she said to me in the drawing room that evening where we were all assembled as usual waiting for the clients to arrive. "He likes quality in girls and he's had a good few – but he's not mad." I knew what she meant by that.

'The other girls were really jealous but I don't think they'd have wanted to leave Paris. They were all town sparrows whereas I'd been born in the country, in Normandy. I'd lived there till I was ten when my father died and my stepfather Pépé had taken us all with him to live near St Denis – my mother and my brother Laurent and my sister Emma. That was before other babies arrived and he started to beat *Maman* – and then began to try other things on with me. All in all, I thought this was probably the chance of a lifetime – and so it turned out.

'That evening there was a group of army officers who came to us late – and drunk. We always took them to what Madame called the Pink Room. I was used to their kind but I didn't like having to pretend to be a bitch on heat for them. Excuse my language – I have to speak plainly. One of the men had a whip and a dog lead which he brought out when I was in the Pink

Room with him. Madame always made them pay first and so I knew I'd have to do whatever he wanted. He disgusted me. *She* knew of course what they got up to but she always said that if we were really frightened – and you never knew, some of the men wanted to hurt you, as well as you know what – we could ring the electric bell she had hidden behind the bed head in that room, and her servant Gustave would come and throw the client out. As far as I knew, no girl had ever rung that bell . . . .'

Flora was still listening, big-eyed, horrified rather than embarrassed.

Edwige spoke firmly but she was still looking through the window, her face averted.

'I did what the officer wanted that night and while we were doing it his friend watched – he'd paid extra for that – and then the friend did it though he only wanted it straight and they went away laughing.'

Flora stared at her, her face registering amazement as well as shock. Edwige did not turn to her as she continued:

'When I met Monsieur Leopardi for the first time the next morning I was surprised because he was younger than I'd expected and a handsome man. Not tall, but dark with black eyes and a presence. He had a loud voice too. I'd heard him talking to Madame in her private sanctum about the certificate from the police to say I was clean, so I guessed it was just as I'd thought – he didn't want me just for a nursemaid.

'But when I was introduced to him he was very polite and it turned out that he didn't want any other "services" then and there. I worried lest the night before she'd let him watch us through her special peep-hole when I was doing those things with the officer and I'd have been so ashamed.

'By the time I'd left my own country he still hadn't laid a hand on me, though he'd bought me a nurse's uniform and some new boots and a ticket for the train to Milan. He travelled on the same train. I was in the cheapest seats and he was in the best ones. When we got here he got a young maidservant called Angelica to take me to a room at the top of the house above the nursery. In the nursery there was just one little boy playing with a train and I told him I had to look after him as his mother was ill. I met his mother later that evening – Signora Leopardi – the first one, Feodora, that is. She was a pretty little woman, confined to bed because of a threatened miscarriage.'

Edwige stopped for a moment, obviously reliving that first sight of her new mistress. Flora, now the unpleasant part seemed to be over, managed to interrupt with:

'What was she like? Did you get on with her?'

'Oh, she was a quiet sort of person. I think she was in awe of her husband. He adored her – he wasn't faithful to her but he looked on her as a sort of angel. When she died – which was before she was thirty – he reformed for a time, but he'd always had women. When he was young they liked him. . . .'

'Did she die when the baby was born then? I suppose the baby was Josephine?'

'Yes, the next baby was Josephine – but after her birth Signora Feodora died. He was inconsolable.'

Flora waited, sure there was more to come.

'I was very young and I grew to admire him. I looked after little Ludo when she was ill – and then the baby fell to me after the mistress died. I was the nursemaid, but as you may have guessed he tried other things on me too. Not for long though – I was more use as a general factotum. That was all before the first war and it didn't last long. I wasn't the only one – there was Angelica the maid, poor girl, as well as all the women he brought in from I don't know where. Not women of the streets – not then. You might think that was what I was, but I wasn't. Once I came here I never went back to my old life – it was only with the master that I – what could I have done?

I was sorry for him, as well as admiring him. He used to say I had a better head on my shoulders than many men. I helped him with the accounts, and the other servants, as well as looking after the children. I became a sort of housekeeper. It all changed when he met the American woman, Paulina Vincent. But he didn't want to lose me – Oh, no!'

'He should have married *you*!' said Flora.

'I never expected that and it was a good thing I didn't because he changed after the first war. By then of course he'd married the Signora Paulina – she had a baby in the first year of their marriage . . . .

'Xavier's father Paul?'

'Yes, that's right – but Ferdinando carried on in much the same way! He expected her to stay at the Villa and entertain his friends – he was doing well in business after the war but he got in with a nasty crowd. You may think I have no right to call them that after what I've told you about myself but I didn't like it. His new wife liked it even less. She was angry with him – American women won't put up with what Italian women used to put up with. They only had the one child . . . . Well, she put up with Ferdinando – until she discovered with whom he'd been carrying on under her nose – as well as finding out about the "parties" he'd given when she was away. That was later though, when Paul was about fifteen. I refused to have anything to do with his goings-on. He could have sacked me, I don't know why he didn't, but I suppose he was used to me. His wife told him she'd go to America and he was welcome to go with her if he'd mend his ways. But he wouldn't – couldn't, I don't suppose, and in the end – only after a long time though – she upped and left!'

'Didn't she redecorate the villa? I think Delphine told me that?'

'Oh, she tried to please him now and then, I'll give her that – but she never fitted in. He should have stuck to his own sort.

She was too clever – rich too – she didn't need his money – had her own he couldn't get his hands on—'

'But how did this affect her grandson Xavier?'

'I'll come to that another day. I've talked too long, told you things I ought not to have done, I suppose. But you're another like her; she should never have married into the Leopardi family.'

'As you think I should not marry Xavier?'

'I don't think he would make you happy, Mademoiselle. Xavier might have seen things he should not have done – and if so it was all his grandfather's fault. If his father had stayed, it would have been different. I could do nothing. But whatever anyone says, I had nothing to do with what went on after the mistress left.'

'You mean the Fascisti?'

'That – and other things. You must go now – I'm tired.'

Flora got up and looked at the old lady who had sat telling her strange story, her hands folded in her lap as if she were recounting some pleasant matter-of-fact account to while away an afternoon. Edwige turned towards her.

'Thank you for confiding in me,' said Flora.

Now she knew what Edwige had once been she saw her in a different light. Had Edwige intended to shock her? And what could it have to do with Xavier? He had only been a little boy.

'You must come again,' said Edwige. She stood up, and for a moment Flora regarded her sombrely. After solemnly shaking hands with her, Edwige saw her out and shut the door quietly.

As Flora made her way back to the Villa, her mind full of fresh questions and speculation, the little black cat came up to her again. This time he allowed her to stroke him. She wished she could stay there, just talking to the cat, but eventually she told him to go home and walked along the path to the waterfall. She stood for a moment under a canopy of trees, the plashing of water and the distant barking of a dog the only sounds. She was almost frightened to return to Xavier.

She came slowly down to the gardens and decided to walk round to the front of the house to put off her return for a moment. On arriving at the great gate at the side of the tropical garden, she looked up at the white stuccoed building and imagined for a moment that it was a dolls' house and that its inhabitants had no more autonomy than puppets. She stared at the middle range of windows, at one end her own front window open as she had left it. Seen from the garden, the number of windows did not appear to correspond with the number of rooms . . . .

She came to with a start. Why should she be so concerned over Xavier's Violet Rooms? They were only rooms after all. Yet, in a curious way, she thought, the Villa was like Xavier. There were parts that were hidden, or that you thought you knew, but it turned out you did not.

Then, to her surprise she saw that the window of one of the Violet Rooms, the one on the right of the central window, was open. As she looked, someone closed the shutter and she thought she glimpsed a woman's arm, though it was hard to be sure from this distance. Who else did Xavier take there? Or was it just the maid, Mirella, shutting it? It had certainly been closed last night. Did Xavier, like his grandfather, make a habit of going to bed with his maids?

Flora waited a little longer, looking up at the Villa, before climbing the terraces where carpets of bougainvillaea flung themselves as carelessly as ever over walls and balustrades.

As she entered the house from the front nobody seemed to be around. She went up in the lift at the south end, feeling exhausted, wanting only to pull off her shoes and fall on the bed for a little doze. But when she had done that, and was lying down, sleep would not come. She got up and looked for a book, found the novel she was trying to read and then discovered it was less interesting than her conversation with Edwige.

She pulled her diary from the bedside table and flicked back to her entries of two years ago. Hadn't she written down questions concerning the Leopardis somewhere in her diary? She sat on the bed, with the warm air of early evening coming through the window, found the page and began to go through all her old queries and doubts.

Now she knew that Paulina Leopardi had left her husband because of his conduct and his politics, Paulina seemed quite an easy person to understand. Well, *she* did not disagree with Xavier's politics and she was quite sure he was not even right wing, never mind a Fascist, so she could not be compared with that first female outsider!

If he was in a good mood she would lead Xavier once more to the subject of his mother. He'd told her he was about four years old when she'd gone away. Perhaps there *were* no more mysteries, only the principal one of Edwige, an insight into whose life she had just been vouchsafed, although she still did not quite understand why Edwige had wanted to confess such things to her.

Xavier's father, Paul, had probably come to the same conclusions as his mother, and decided to make a clean break with his father. Why did he not go with his wife when she left? Did he send her away? That was still puzzling.

As for the Germans, and their occupation of the villa, and old Ferdinando's death, Edwige obviously knew more about all that. She had most likely looked after the place as long as she could?

There was still a mystery, things she didn't understand. Had Edwige known Mirella's mother, Cécile? She must ask Xavier again about her, since he'd mentioned her name himself. She might have told her daughter more about the set-up at the Villa in the old days?

But the last war had happened years and years after old Ferdinando and Madame Rouart had been lovers.... If Edwige had once loved him would she have betrayed him to the anti-Fascists? She might have grown to hate him? – become disgusted with his carryings-on? But she was a loyal person or she would not have stayed at all. *And* he'd left her that necklace! Ferdinando had probably been betrayed by some anti-Fascist villager.

She looked up, filled with the foreboding she had pushed away in the garden. Had that face at the window been Mirella's? She ought to have the courage to find out. She slid off the bed, put on her blue sandals and crept on to the silent corridor. This time there was a pervasive scent of violets. She passed the door in the middle opposite the stairs and the picture of the Violet Lady, and tiptoed to the door of the room she thought was the one she'd been in yesterday with Xavier. For a moment she stood irresolutely. Then she knocked. The door was opened by Xavier himself.

'Oh – it's you! you're back?' she said foolishly.

'Who else did you think would be here?' he asked.

'Nobody – I wanted to see you—'

'Come in. Have you seen Edwige?' he asked pleasantly.

'Yes – she gave me tea and talked about your grandfather.' She followed Xavier into the room. The window was open. It must have been Xavier himself at the window.

'I didn't think you'd come in here by yourself!' she said.

'Well, I'm not by myself, am I? Not now. You wanted me – so, you came.' He sounded pleased, quite his old self.

'Yes, I wanted to see you.'

Now that she was here and she was standing so close to him she felt only a desire to put her arms round him and to go back a few years to a more innocent friendship. But at the same time she wanted him to want her. She waited. He made no move at first. Then he went to a bookcase on the far wall that she had not noticed before, pulled it back and revealed a door in the wall. She gasped.

'This used to be a connecting room,' he explained. 'I had the wall put up to make two rooms. Here – take this—'

He handed her a little box from the shelf. She opened it, guessing what would be inside. It was. A phial of Parma violets scent with a garland of velvet flowers around the slim glass neck. She opened the stopper and sniffed.

'You know, Xavier, I'm awfully sorry but I don't think the scent of violets suits me!' she said.

He stood there, looking surprised and, she thought, rather foolish.

'Flora, I must smell that perfume on your skin!'

To how many others might he have said that? She complied reluctantly, patting the scent on to her wrists and behind her ears.

'There. But you don't *need* me to wear it, Xavier, do you? You didn't yesterday!'

'Yesterday I had to show you what to expect, Flora, when you come here. Didn't you enjoy it? It isn't much to ask that if you wear the ring you wear the scent too?'

'If it pleases you,' she replied, nervous now.

'Good – let me take the scent from you. There.' He looked excited and said: 'The secret room for a secret woman. Follow me!'

She followed him as he pulled back the bookcase and went into the next room. She gasped when she saw the opulence of this bedchamber. A great four-poster with swagged covers and hangings of violet silk, a chandelier hanging from a ceiling decorated with gilt cherubs, thick blue and violet rugs, an Empire sofa, a Chinese screen with a pattern of turquoise and mauve willow trees, and long curtains of silky violet damask. Xavier said: 'I shall not make love here to any woman but my wife!'

Paradoxically these words made Flora feel both rebellious and desirous. Suddenly she wanted him to make love to her then and there. What had he said last night? *If I want you it will be in* this *room – and you will come here whenever I do—'*

'Are you not allowed to make love to me *here* then?'

'No – only in the next room. This one is for later. Do you like it?' He spoke in a matter-of-fact way.

'Yes, it's in perfect taste.'

'You know it's for me to make the decisions about where we go – as I told you.'

She saw clearly now that he needed this play-acting to make him randy, had invented it all for himself.

'It has nothing to do with love,' she said, 'if I do as you wish.' She wished she were able to lose control, be – if only for half an hour – what he wanted her to be.

For answer he pulled her back silently into the next room, flung her on to the bed, and removed her clothes. Only in this way could he possess her.

She flinched, then felt she was melting away in the force of his desire as he slowly licked the scent from behind her ears and wrists.

Perhaps now it would be all right?

But in one sudden brutal movement he entered her even more violently than before, looking in her eyes until the very last moment when he shouted: *'Puttana!'* She felt nothing. Not even pain. Just an absence of pleasure. Her desire for him was immediately dissipated, not because of the name he had called her, but because she had loved someone who had gone away.

Her next coherent thought was: he ought to cover his own skin with essence of violets, not mine! It's not *me* he wants. It's not out of love for me that he makes love to me. Before, it was unsatisfactory, but I didn't mind. Now I do. Xavier has chosen the wrong woman.

Here in this room any woman but herself would do, especially a real *puttana* who would slake his passionate need!

Xavier was the man she had loved for so long – yet she had not understood him at all, and she was frightened. Despairingly, she recognized as she lay there that there was now an unbridgeable rift between the old and the new. What had happened to him to make him like this? Would it have happened if he had never left Paris?

She whispered, trying to understand: 'You must do all these things so you can possess me? With other women too? Or is it just for the sake of sensation?'

He was silent.

She got up, looked at him as he lay there now, satiated. Then he seemed to change character once again, for he said in a normal voice, as he watched her dress and smooth down her rumpled clothes:

'We must talk, Flora. I did not intend to – possess – you today. You caught me unawares. I told you yesterday, this room is for passion – when *I* want it. Do you understand?'

'I understand lust, Xavier. I believe I'm quite normal, but it's not me you are "loving". It could be any woman. Why me?'

'Because this way I can make you mine – as I could not before.'

'Any man might think that – for a short time. I *loved* you . . . . I always wanted you to want me . . . but not like this. Most women want to please men, but I've known you for too long, Xavier. You've haunted me. Now you want me only because you want sensation – not to receive it from me – nor to give me anything.'

'Then, Flora, marry me!'

'You want me as a "pure" wife – there is no connection between that and – sex – for you.'

'You are right. I had to see what you felt. It happened more quickly than I intended.'

'I know you better now, but I don't like to be used. Unless it is part of . . . .' She searched for the right words.

He supplied them for her: 'Part of what women call a "loving relationship"!'

'It is not only women who call it that, Xavier. I didn't want to lose you – or fall out of love with you.'

It had been like falling down a mountain. Falling out of love had already happened, leaving a residue of rubble . . . injured tenderness . . . .

'It would be different if you married me – we would forget – all this—' he said eagerly. He even smiled, but she sensed despair under the attempted jauntiness.

'You'd forget your Violet Rooms? Never!' She gathered her courage. 'I imagine that having installed me in the room with the four-poster next door you'd bring other women here? As perhaps you already do? Why would you – why do you – want *me*?' She needed to cry from misery and frustration but did not want him to see her weakness.

'Other women *have* come here from time to time.'

'Various "pensionnaires," you mean? The old Xavier would not have done that.'

'Come now, Flora, you are not a Puritan. If you do not want to be my *puttana* you can be my wife! It is for you to choose!'

I shall choose neither, she thought. I shall lose him now, but I must get out of this. Edwige was right. I should not have come. She said: 'Do you give *them* the violet scent too? All the others?'

'It helps, you see . . . .'

'What is it that has made you change? What is it that is different? We were friends. I want us to be friends still.'

'People change,' he said carelessly. 'You yourself told me to feel free. I'm happier now, Flora! And you can be happy too – I would make a good husband.'

'If you need these rooms for your love making it must be because of your past. Do you think I don't know about that? Some of it anyway.'

'Yes, I suppose I wanted the place as it was when my grandfather was alive. You know that.'

'Your grandfather was not a very admirable man, Xavier!'

'Oh, has Edwige been talking then? She has no room to speak – she knew what he was like.'

'Yes. She admired him fifty years ago, she told me. Why don't you ask her, Xavier, what he was like? You were only a child – what could you know?'

'Enough to make me want to return and create my own happiness here – where I was once happy,' he said.

'I think you are under a spell and that you could wake up from it,' said Flora.

'You want me to be like everyone else.'

'No, you will never be quite like everyone else, but you might be able to be happy away from here. As we were in France three years ago.'

'I had not carried out my dreams then. *I* was not happy in Menton, Flora.'

This hurt her more than anything he had done or said.

'This is your dream then? To have a wife who loves you but to whom you cannot make decent love? And women – very young women, I expect – waiting for you in these rooms? That's it, isn't it? But Edwige says your grandfather loved his wives as well as always having other women around him. He wasn't emotionally crippled as you are – he had children with his wives, didn't he?'

Xavier got up and began to walk round the room. He looked angry and disturbed.

'You are just jealous,' he said. 'I still offer you my hand in marriage, because you are an intelligent woman and you understand me a little, I suppose.'

'I'm like your grandmother who had to leave here when she couldn't stand it any longer. And your own mother who went too – I wonder why! And yet you persist in worshipping as well as hating that grandfather of yours.'

He sat down again in a chair by the bed. 'There were two compliments I offered you, Flora: either marriage – or an affair of passion. I think you will choose marriage. If you don't, I can continue to offer a "derangement of the senses" – remember Rimbaud? – a derangement not usually possible for young bourgeois Englishwomen. Francesca understands – you ought to talk to her – and I believe little Mirella would also be willing to go along with it.'

It is a sort of madness, she thought. What can I say or do? I am too sane for him. Aloud she said: 'You mean you'd want me to watch you make love to some other woman – here? No, I would never choose a life of passion in these rooms. I can't split myself in two – not for any man. As you seem able to do.'

'You are very desirable when you are angry,' he said.

She stood up. He was not going to start all over again. She'd rather he thought her a little English Puritan.

And he had never said he loved her. What was love if it had absolutely nothing to do with tenderness, never mind marriage? A romantic mirage you grew out of? Marriage – the taming of romance – she had seen as eventually inevitable. Physical passion for its own sake she had not denied, but sympathies had always been more important in the long run. 'I don't know what to do,' she muttered to herself.

He heard and said: 'If you really love me, Flora, you could rescue me. Marry me!'

How could she go down now and eat dinner, with the secretary staring at her, and the maid and that Mrs Dawson, whoever she was?

She tried once more to gather her thoughts and feelings together but it was impossible whilst he was in the room with her. The pull that Xavier had always exerted upon her had lost its power. It had vanished, whatever he did or said now.

Should she tell him that his mother was still alive? This might be the cure he needed. He stood, turned towards her and then fell on his knees. He was actually weeping.

'Rescue me, Flora! Marry me!'

Why did she feel so unmoved? A year ago she would have accepted his proposal.

'I don't think I want to be a married saint,' she replied. 'I want us to be equals, Xavier!'

Xavier got up and said in a completely different tone of voice: 'You are too independent. Let us go down to dinner – you have a long holiday in which to decide.' He put his arm round her and she felt unwelcome tears fill her eyes. They went out of the room together and he locked the door. Once on the corridor Flora said: 'I must wash my face and change.'

'Be in the dining room in twenty minutes,' he replied, looking at her sombrely. He walked away down the stairs.

Alone, she felt an immense relief. She could not rescue Xavier from himself, and she would have to leave him. That resolution must serve for the time being. Tomorrow she would go to talk to Edwige again, would ask her whether she thought Ferdinando Leopardi's grandson had inherited his grandfather's temperament. But she really must acquaint Xavier with the astonishing news that his mother was still alive.

Flora thought Signorina Vitelli looked rather critically at her when she entered the room; well, the Signorina could think what she liked.

'Mrs Dawson is taking her supper in her room on a tray and is to go on holiday tomorrow,' she said to Flora. She took the opportunity then to discuss some of his investments with her employer during the meal. Flora felt she might as well not have been there. Xavier appeared quite cool and collected. Whilst they were drinking their coffee, served by Mirella, the secretary spoke of her own forthcoming holiday in Stresa. 'So you will have Xavier all to yourself,' she added sweetly.

'I am rather tired,' said Flora at about ten o'clock. 'Will you excuse me? I shall go to bed.'

'You walked to Madame Rouart's this afternoon?' asked Francesca.

'Yes.' Flora supposed Mirella had told her.

'She is a most interesting lady, isn't she?' said the secretary.

Xavier did not seek her out that night and Flora fell into a heavy sleep in spite of her mingled apprehension and agitation.

She decided she need not be afraid of Xavier even if he had more or less raped her, for she was certain that it could now happen only in one of his Violet Rooms.

At breakfast he said: 'I have to go to Como, there are complications. Ludo is to return next week.'

Flora decided to walk up to Edwige's house immediately. She passed the kitchen where Mirella and a village girl were washing up.

'I may be late for lunch,' she called in the window. 'I shall be at Madame Rouart's.'

'Yes, Signorina Flora.'

Did Mirella look at her then with a sort of slightly cheeky complicity? Or was it her imagination? On an impulse she said: 'I believe your mother once worked here for Madame Rouart?'

Mirella looked surprised but said nothing at first.

'She was called Cécile, was she not?'

'Cecilia, Signorina. She didn't work for Madame Rouart – she worked for Signor Leopardi's grandfather,' said Mirella with a sort of pride.

And what sort of work was that, wondered Flora, but she smiled, saying: 'How nice that you should return to work for the same family!'

'Oh I shan't be long at the Villa,' said the girl. 'I want to manage a restaurant. The Signor is going to buy me one.' Something you didn't know, said her look.

'Really?' said Flora. 'How kind of him.' She walked on.

How she missed Delphine, and what had seemed to be normality. She even missed Uncle Ludo. As for Tante Jo – had Xavier warned her off a visit or had she preferred not to come? She might not stay away for ever.

Xavier might appear to know what he was doing, but she had grave doubts, and hoped his finances – obviously now looked after by Francesca Vitelli – were in a healthy state.

As Edwige opened the door to her, Flora's composure broke.

'I'm sorry to come again so soon but I had to see you, Madame Rouart!'

Edwige looked at her quizzically, saying: 'It's always a pleasure to have a visitor. I don't get very many – come along in.'

Flora followed her into the kitchen where she had been preparing a meal; there was the lingering smell of onions and garlic.

'Will you have a grappa – or is it too early in the day?'

'Thank you – I will.'

The woman took a tightly-stoppered bottle from the cupboard and poured them both a drink which she placed on a tray. 'There – you can take them into the sitting room.'

How could this dignified woman once have been a young prostitute in Paris, Flora wondered. Yet for that very reason it might be that she was the only person who could help her to understand Xavier, whose tastes – she now felt – must tend toward the same direction as his grandfather's.

Edwige said nothing to help her begin, but sat down at the table and lifted her glass. *'Santé!'*

After gulping a mouthful of the fiery stuff, Flora said slowly: 'I think that I shall have to go away – it is so awful. Madame, will you help me?'

'How can I do that? Remember what I told you yesterday. I don't have a respectable background.'

Was she teasing her?

'I don't think I am all that respectable either,' said Flora. 'But I do know the difference between someone who can love and someone who can't.'

'Has he asked you to marry him then? Yesterday?'

'I am given a choice. I am invited to stay with him as his wife, or become his mistress. I think I should say; one of his mistresses.'

'Poor boy. I would not have thought he had the stomach for that,' was all Edwige said as she continued to regard Flora pensively.

'What I must know – since you knew him as a child and have known him since he came back here – is whether you think he is really like his grandfather – that he can't help it, it's something hereditary?'

'In what way?'

'A womanizer with a large sex-drive!'

'Those would not be the words I would use to describe Xavier,' replied Edwige dryly.

'I think his difficulties with women – and I don't really understand completely what they are – exist because his mother left him. I really ought to tell him what you told me – that she is still alive. But—'

'You believe me then?' interrupted Edwige mockingly.

'I believe that you know where she is. I don't know how you know, but I believe you.'

There was a pause. Then: 'It would not be a good idea to

tell him now,' Edwige said flatly.

'I thought it might help him. She probably left because her husband was unfaithful to her? But why didn't she take the child with her – and why did she never contact him?'

'Oh, Paul was never unfaithful. He was an upright man. She had to go – she might even have been paid off. I can tell you that.'

'It was Ferdinando who paid her to go away?'

Edwige only raised an eyebrow.

'Why?'

'There are some matters about which an old woman can only hazard a guess, Mademoiselle. But there are other things I *know* and do not need to guess.'

'Please tell me what you know – that might help Xavier—'

'His mother trusted me, but I don't think she told me the whole truth when she wrote to me after the war. Everyone in the village around here thought that it was I who had betrayed my old employer—'

'Yes, I think even Xavier believes that—'

'Well, he is wrong. Victoire would not have cared about that – she hated Ferdinando – but she might have imagined that I had something to do with her husband denouncing her in '35. I had not.'

'Denouncing her!'

'Yes. He said she was no better than a prostitute – that she slept with the Fascisti. It was not true.'

'Then why did she go?'

'Because she loved Paul – and Ferdinando took away her self-respect. Whatever happened to her later was because of that. Ferdinando may have had some hold on her. I believe he knew her family . . . maybe she was threatened with something. I don't know. She knew that Xavier would be well looked after. She never imagined that Paul would go away too, which he did a year or two later. She did come back once to see her child, though Xavier never knew. Nobody did, except me.'

Flora felt her head spinning, though whether from the strong grappa or these revelations she was not sure.

'She came again in the autumn of '39 and begged me to help her find her husband, said she had something new to tell him. But by then it was too late. Josephine had taken Xavier with her and Edouard to France. There was only the master and myself and a few servants left at first, till he began to fill the place up with his political friends and then with army officers. Ludo had been conscripted – he was in Rome. I never heard from Josephine once the war had begun. Not until it was over.'

'Why didn't you go with her and Xavier to France?'

'I often ask myself why. I suppose I didn't want to depend on their charity. I knew it would all end badly here, but Ferdinando persuaded me he needed me. I hated the Republichini – even more so by '43. As I was French I'd have been interned, but he got papers to prove I was Italian. They were faked. I've always been French!' She drew herself up proudly. Flora felt sure the woman had still been in love with old Leopardi whatever she might say.

'You said Signor Leopardi knew Victoire's family. Are any of them still alive?'

'Oh, her mother was an old alcoholic – she's dead now. She lived with her daughter for a time – they moved to Parma after the war. I only know Victoire is still alive because, as I told you, when the war was over she wrote to me. But by then she refused to visit the Villa.'

'Even though she knew Ferdinando was dead?'

'Oh, she knew Ferdy was dead – everyone knew that. I told her the family was coming back.'

'Didn't she want to see her son again?'

'No – she said she'd been no good to him and that it

was better he should regard her as dead.'

'I'm sure he'd want to see her now.'

'He might, but it wouldn't help him. It's when we are children that the damage is done, Mademoiselle!'

'But he *loved* the Villa and his childhood! That's what I can't understand. He comes back here and works for years to make it beautiful again – after all it was left to him, not Ludo! Then he gets these ideas about women – and "Violet Rooms", and – oh, I don't know. I just feel I'm not the right woman for him.'

'Who do you think he should marry then?'

'I don't think he should marry *anyone* – he wouldn't make a woman happy. I used to think he would – and I loved him – he wasn't like anyone else I knew. But then it all went wrong – and I don't know *why*.'

'He is the victim of his grandfather's life – as I told you yesterday—'

'But what exactly do you mean by that?'

Edwige put down her glass. 'If I describe to you what I think has happened, you can tell me if I am right, *n'est-ce pas*?'

Flora waited apprehensively.

'His grandfather had many women around, you know. I can only think that Xavier saw more than he should have and, as he was an impressionable boy, connected some of the women with his mother.'

'He told me once this his mother smelled of *violettes de Parme*! I think that's why he has this fixation, this *fetish*, for a certain scent. But I'm sure there's something else . . . .'

'I suppose memory can be powerful . . . .'

'I don't understand why this should make him divide women up into two kinds—'

'The wives and the mistresses?'

'Yes – or the women you *desire*, and those you respect and *love*.'

'Which are *you* then, Flora?'

'Xavier doesn't seem to know.' She was thinking, what an odd conversation.

'Well, some women are born mistresses! I don't think you are exactly one of them. On the other hand—'

'What has *love* to do with all this, Madame?'

'I have never read or heard an adequate definition of that word, Mademoiselle.' Edwige looked as if she had actually considered the matter.

'From what you've told me, Signor Leopardi's second wife, Paulina, would have been a victim of her husband if she had stayed. And you said I was a bit like her – an outsider—'

'She was a good wife to *him* but I imagine she could have been something else for another man. She put herself first, even before her own son. I don't think you are like her – and Xavier is not at all like his grandfather. Xavier was a good little boy who found it hard to grow up.'

'I feel that something – it sounds silly, I know – but that *something* has gone underground in him. If only I could find the key, it would all come gushing back!' Her own words made her want to cry.

'But this love you had for Xavier, the love you talk about – was it nearer to the love of a wife or of a mistress?'

'Neither, I think. In England we don't make that distinction. I loved him as a friend, and then as an ideal. I missed him when I went back home the first time, and when I saw him again I wanted to get close to him. I wanted him at a time when he was not really interested in me in that way – and then I took your advice and stayed away. Now that I've come back, he's changed – made me feel he is some sort of emotional cripple. I confess I did sometimes almost want him to be vulnerable so that he would need me. I thought I could help him. I wasn't very sensible, was I?'

'You sound to me as if you mothered him, Flora.'

'Yes, but I wanted him to be strong for *me* in the end, and now he *is* stronger but it's as if he's acting a part—'

'For you, sex – *le désir* – is not the end of the quest but only one way of pleasure, of getting closer to a person? You are not one of those *grandes horizontales* who want to devote their lives to men. Most men adore them – how could they not?'

'But there must exist timider men – or men for whom the mind is as important as the body?'

But Edwige went on: 'In my experience, the men who make the most fuss about love are usually the ones who do not feel all they should! Take Signor Leopardi's hero – that poet d'Annunzio. He was brave, and some women were flattered to be adored by him, but other women I met told me he was not a natural seducer. He ended up with village girls who had to tickle his senses all night for him to achieve *la jouissance*! Xavier is more like *him*. His grandfather was a more rough and ready type as far as women were concerned.'

Flora realized that the old woman had guessed the truth. After a pause, she said: 'I do think he ought to know his mother is still alive. It might make all the difference to his happiness.'

'To know that she is and does not care to see him?'

'But there must have been some reason!'

'Tell him then. He can ask *me* where she is. Still near Parma, as a matter of fact.'

'He even went to Parma not long ago!'

'Are you going to tell him?'

'I don't know. If I feel the right moment comes along, I think I will.'

'Then it will be your responsibility. Do you think you could bear that?'

'I should have to. He's grown up, so he must decide for himself what to do about it. I'll have to go now. I've kept you too long.'

Then she remembered there was something else she had

wanted to ask the old woman. 'Did you know Mirella's mother well? Cécile, I believe she was called. Mirella is about seventeen, and very pretty. I have the queer feeling that Xavier somehow connects her with his past.'

'Yes, I knew a Cécile. She died in the war. She was about ten years younger than Victoire. They may have known each other.'

'Would Cécile have told Mirella what she knew about Xavier's mother?'

'I doubt it. Some things are better not discussed.'

'You're tired – I must go. I'm very grateful for your telling me what you have.' Flora rose to her feet. 'It's out of your hands now. Leave it to me.'

'So long as you are determined to tell him his mother is alive?'

'He could write to her?'

'If he insisted, I could even take him to her – but he had much better write first. Of course she may deny it – or never reply. I am still against it.'

Flora still begged inwardly to differ, and they parted, each thinking their own thoughts about Xavier Leopardi.

After Flora had gone Edwige sat down heavily and remained in her chair motionless for several minutes. At last, with a sigh, she got up, put on her second best black straw hat and went into the village to shop.

There were so many unanswered questions. Flora had the strong impression that Edwige was still withholding something; perhaps more than one thing. She decided to go back the long way through the village, to give her more time to consider how and when she was going to approach Xavier.

When she arrived at the Villa, she saw a car waiting at the bottom of the steps and for a moment imagined it was Xavier going away for good. But it was Mrs Dawson, leaving with a large suitcase that Enrico was heaving on to the top of the car. Flora did not especially want to say good-bye to her, so she waited under the trees until the car had left, then toiled up the woodland path through the tropical garden.

Xavier was sitting alone on the top terrace at the front, gazing at the lake. He hardly acknowledged her presence except to turn his head, look at her and then turn back again.

She sat down beside him in silence. After five minutes he said: 'You went to see Edwige Rouart?'

'Yes.'

'And?'

Suddenly she decided. She must get this over with.

'I have something to tell you. Edwige did not think I should, but I think you ought to know . . . .'

He waited, staring at her.

Everything seemed to stop; even the birds were not singing.

'Your mother. She's still alive,' she said in a flat voice.

He continued to stare at her but said nothing. Then suddenly he banged his fist on the table before him.

'Do you want to know where she is?' Flora asked quietly.

He turned towards her. 'You believe the old woman?'

'Yes, I do.'

'Why didn't she honour me with this information? How long does she say she has known?'

'Since the end of the war. Do you want to know where she is?'

'I don't believe her!' Flora waited, and he added, trying to keep his dignity, but sounding like a hurt child: 'I only want to know why she went away.'

'Edwige has her last address. She says you could write to her in Parma.'

'Parma! Why did she never tell me?'

He stood up, very angry. He believed Edwige all right.

'You could go to her – if you wrote first. Or ask her to come here—'

'I write a letter to some Anastasia-like impostor? You've been spending too much time talking to Edwige.'

'Edwige understands you, I think—'

'So you've discussed me?'

'I think she is a wise person. I don't understand why you don't like her.'

He was fiddling with the large crystal ash-tray on the iron table.

'She says that your mother did come back to see you once. You were asleep. Please, please, Xavier, don't be angry. It's worth a try – I only want you to be happy – truly.'

'Yes, I know.' The muscles in his face sagged. 'Don't you think it's a bit late for that?'

He turned on his heel and went in through one of the French windows.

Late that night he knocked at Flora's bedroom door. She was already in bed and half asleep.

'No – don't get up – I come only to say I have sent to Edwige for the address and I *will* write to Parma.'

'Oh, Xavier, I am so glad!'

He remained standing at the door. 'I shall not disturb your sleep. I want to say this, Flora, then I'd like you not to mention it again.' He leaned against the door, and she thought, how handsome – and how remote – he is. 'I shall go to this address in Parma, though I expect nothing will come of it. Remember, whether I find my mother or not, I shall still not be able to offer you the love you think you deserve. But as long as you are prepared of your own free will to put up with my – needs – we can marry. I should like us to have children. Accept me as I am – or leave me for ever. I can't change – whether Parma disgorges some woman who turns out to be Victoire Leopardi or not.'

She thought, I can't accept him as he is. But she said nothing, only stared at him as she sat up in bed, feeling nervous. She ventured: 'I am certain that your mother will make all the difference to your life.'

He gestured a parody of a bow, saying: 'I shall tell you when I have a reply from Parma.'

He added nothing further over the next few days. She knew Edwige had sent him the address for she saw the envelope with its curly French writing on the breakfast table. All she could do was wait.

One morning, after Flora had been at the Villa Violetta for almost three weeks, she came down to breakfast to find that Xavier was not there, though his secretary was. The immaculate Francesca looked a little upset.

'Has Xavier been down?' asked Flora.

'Yes – and he went straight back up to his room with his mail – without even staying for a cup of coffee!'

Flora knew immediately that he must have heard from his mother. She did not know to what extent Francesca Vitelli was in his confidence so she said nothing more to her but resolved to go up to Xavier's room. She finished her coffee and made her way in the lift up to the top floor. She had never yet during this visit been up to Xavier's room, but she had to know what Victoire had written. Had she agreed to come to the Villa? Or perhaps she had refused to acknowledge her son? She felt she had a right to know. Without her, Xavier would never have known of his mother's continued existence, for Edwige would never have told him. She knocked at the closed door at the end of the corridor. There was no reply. She knocked again, louder this time.

'Go away, Flora!'

'Open the door, Xavier – please tell me what she said.'

The door was opened so suddenly she almost fell back.

'How do you know she has written to me? What is it to do with you anyway?'

'I guessed. I'm sorry. I wanted to make sure you were all right.'

'Why should I not be? Yes, she has written to me. She says I can visit her. She won't come here.'

'You will go then – to Parma?'

'Yes, to Parma. You are so *romantic*, Flora! Don't expect me to make a fuss after all these years. I shall go there this very afternoon – by myself.'

If Flora had thought he might want her to accompany him she suppressed the thought.

Xavier was as good as his word. He left that afternoon and there was nothing to do but wait.

Whilst waiting, Flora wondered about Edwige and why she had not wanted Xavier to know his mother was alive. She was sure that in spite of everything Edwige did want her old charge to be happy.

At dinner that night Francesca surprisingly opened the conversation with: 'Do you think he will find what he is looking for?'

'You know then – about his mother?'

'I could hardly not! Last year he never stopped talking about her disappearance when he was a child. I gathered he connected her with his passion for the house – his worship of the past. I nearly asked him if *she* had always dressed in mauve, but I thought that might be a bit rude!'

Flora was surprised at the flippant tone. Had this woman really had an affair with Xavier? If she had, was it over? She sounded so dismissive, almost – Flora searched for the right word and came up with irreverent.

'I wouldn't expect *you* to agree,' Francesca went on. 'Xavier always said you were the only person who understood the effect of the past upon a person. I got the impression you always took him seriously?'

'Well, of course I did! He was abandoned in childhood by *both* his parents, caught up in a war as a sort of refugee, and then discovered his grandfather had been killed. No wonder he wanted to find out what had happened to his mother!'

'I can see you were hopelessly in love with both him and his family.' The secretary buttered a piece of croissant and then said in a different tone of voice: 'But he was never actually told she'd died, was he? I tried to worm that out of him, but he shied away. Well, I've had enough, I can tell you. He'll miss a good accountant, but I find the whole place too gloomy. Don't you? You're young – you shouldn't bury yourself here, you know.'

'I thought you liked him! He gave you jewellery and—' She didn't want to say: and shared his bed with you, so she stopped. Francesca however finished the sentence for her.

'Oh, he's attractive, I'll grant you that – but not much fun in bed, is he?'

Flora was tongue-tied.

'I'm sorry – I've shocked you. As I said – you love him – and English girls are so romantic, aren't they?'

'I'm not a ninny,' said Flora with spirit.

'Take care then! He likes young easy girls best and you are not easy, though you are still quite young! How long have you known him?'

'Since I was eighteen.'

'*Dio mio!* you'd better marry him quick then! Unless his Mama sends him crazy!'

Flora was angry, but did not wish to appear naïve, so she did not reply. Mirella came in with the dessert then and they finished their meal in silence.

She went alone then into the big sitting-room to look for the old phonograph and the records of Gigli singing Tosti and Puccini. She wound up the machine, having found the song she had loved, the song Edwige too had enjoyed. It now seemed so long ago. It brought back the old Xavier, and was unbearable.

Two days later, early in the evening, Xavier returned. Flora was sitting in the courtyard at the back of the house, wondering whether to go to Edwige to see if she had heard anything from Victoire, when she heard a car engine stop at the bottom of the terrace.

She got up and ran along the path at the side round to the front of the villa and hid in the tropical garden. It was green and hot and smelt like an English conservatory. From here she glimpsed Xavier as he slowly climbed the terrace steps and came in to view at each level. Finally he reached the top terrace, stopped for a moment, looked back, then went in through the porch and the great door. What should she do? It was hard to tell whether he was excited, jubilant, or weary.

She came out on to the path again and turned to look back over the lake. The highest nearby mountain, San Primo, showed its peak clear today. Was that a good omen? As she looked at it she remembered that someone in Paris had once told her the meaning of the name Xavier, that it was a Basque name, meaning New House.

Oh, if only there could be a New House, she thought, if only we could start again far from here . . . .

She was full of apprehension as she went back into the Villa by a side door. It was only seven o'clock. Where should she go? Would he come to find her? She took her courage in both hands, went up the stairs to the middle corridor past the portrait of the Violet Lady and advanced towards the Violet Rooms. She was sure he would be there.

She knocked at the door. No answer. She tried the door.

Locked. She waited for a time. If Xavier did not want to speak to her there was nothing she could do for the present.

Downstairs not even Francesca was in the sitting-room. Flora went through to the kitchens where Mirella was at the sink.

'Has Signor Leopardi told you he is back? I suppose he will want his dinner tonight. And Signorina Vitelli?'

'She has gone, Signorina Flora!' said Mirella. 'She said to tell you she is starting her holiday sooner than she had planned. She took the boat at three.'

It looked as though she and Xavier and Mirella were to be the only inhabitants of the Villa tonight. She felt uneasy.

Mirella went on: 'I did not know he was back. There was no message.'

Flora felt she ought to go to Edwige Rouart to tell her that Xavier was back. 'I am going for a short walk,' she said. 'Tell him if he comes down that I will be in the dining room at eight.'

'Very well, Signorina.'

But she did not need to walk far, for as she toiled up the slope by the torrent she saw Edwige in the distance walking down through the wood. She stopped and waited for her.

'He's back – but he won't answer – I know he's in one of those rooms,' she gasped, out of breath.

'I knew he'd be back – his mother telephoned me from Parma! I thought I'd come down to see you were all right.'

A telephone? From Parma? That this woman Victoire who to Flora was a figure of myth and legend should possess a telephone – and use it – seemed outlandish, weird.

'Please come up to the Villa with me – he must talk. What happened – did she tell you?'

'She said he was in a strange state as soon as he arrived—'

'Because at last he'd met her – I should not be able to bear it myself—'

'*He* didn't say very much to *her* – I believe the conversation was more on her side—'

They spoke disjointedly as they walked back, Flora trying to go more slowly for the old lady, but in an agony of impatience. When they were half-way there Edwige stopped and said: 'I told you I did not think it a good idea. You see, she would have something to tell him – something she would have to tell him if she ever saw him. She has told him. That is all. But he will not be very pleased to have heard it.'

'Do you know what she had to tell him?'

'I think so. Look, Mademoiselle, I think I shall rest a moment or two on this bench. Go and see if he will talk to you, and if he won't, then come down to find me. I'll be waiting in the vestibule.'

'I'll ask Mirella to give you some supper – and I'll try to bring Xavier down to see you.'

Flora ran back into the house and went up in the lift to the Violet Rooms. She did not knock this time but tried the doors to all three of the rooms at the far end of the corridor. They were all locked. She chose the one where he had made brutal love to her and then tapped softly.

'Xavier? Are you coming down to dinner? Edwige is here.' She waited. After a long pause she heard footsteps and suddenly the door was flung open. Xavier stood there, hair dishevelled, a cigarette between his fingers.

'Flora, would you please go away,' he said in a cold voice.

'Not until you tell me what happened in Parma. I have a right to know. Was it not a happy meeting then?'

After another long pause, during which he stood at the open door contemplating her, he said: 'I am not who I thought I was. That is all.'

'What did your mother tell you?'

His eyes were red-rimmed and she was sure he had been weeping. Never had she wished so much to take him in her arms and soothe him.

'I don't need to come down to tell Madame Rouart,' he said, 'since I feel sure that she already knows what I was told yesterday.'

'Please come down Xavier. I'll send Edwige away if you wish.' She tried to take his hand but he pulled away from her.

'I am even less worthy of your love now,' he said. 'Leave me be, Flora.'

'Why should whatever you've heard change my feelings?' she cried. 'Even if she turned out not to be your mother – that was what she told you, was it?'

'You are wrong! Victoire Verrani, as she calls herself now, is certainly my mother – I even recognized her, though it's over twenty years since I saw her, and now she's middle-aged. I look rather like her, I think.'

'Come and tell me in the sitting-room – no, don't tell me now – I shall wait for you downstairs with Edwige.'

'*You* will not like what I shall tell you,' he said quietly. 'But I have a few other matters to settle with Madame Rouart. Tell her to wait for me.'

He shut the door and Flora walked back to her room where for a moment she looked unseeingly out of the window. Involuntarily, and with no idea why she was doing it she began to fold her clothes into her suitcase along with the few books she had brought with her. Once she realized what she was doing she decided to leave her journal under the mattress. It contained all her thoughts and feelings.

She took the lift down to the ground floor, half expecting Edwige would have left. But when she went into the room there she was, waiting, hands folded on her lap as though she was waiting for an exceptionally demanding dental appointment for which she had taken a bromide in advance.

'There was a draught in the vestibule, so I came in here,' she said.

'He wants to talk to you,' said Flora. 'I'll pour us a drink. Mirella is cooking in the kitchen. The secretary has gone on holiday.'

'No, thank you. I don't want anything.'

Flora felt more in need of a drink than did Edwige and her hand trembled as she poured herself a glass of grappa.

'He says he has discovered he is not who he thought he was,' she said, 'but when I told him I'd sometimes wondered if Victoire really was his mother he said, of course she was. So there is something else I don't know—'

'It is his father, not his mother he is worrying about,' said Edwige. 'Victoire said she would tell him.'

'You never said anything about that to me.'

'No, I left it to Fate. But I did tell you that for him to know Victoire was alive might not be a good idea, didn't I?'

'What has he to know about Paul? Surely you're not going to tell me *he* is not dead either?'

Edwige did not reply, was looking towards the door.

'My father was the man I thought was my grandfather!' said a cold voice, Xavier's voice. He had stolen silently into the room whilst Flora was staring at Edwige. He took a glass from the cupboard and poured himself a large grappa.

'Now you know, it need not worry you,' said Edwige quietly.

'Worry me? At least I know now why my father left home – I mean my *presumed* father.'

Flora was remembering all Edwige had told her about Ferdinando, how he brought his women to the Villa. Had Victoire been one of those! Had she been a servant? She looked at Xavier who was now seated next to Edwige on the sofa staring into his glass. His face was pale but composed as he said:

'Ferdinando wanted her to go on having an affair with him, even after she was married! She was frightened of him, terrified that my father – I mean Paul – would discover what had been going on before her marriage. He did find out, didn't he? That's why he left. Someone must have told him. And that was why he left *me*.'

Edwige stood up and looked out of the long window. 'Paul went to find his mother, to find Paulina,' she said. 'He suspected that she had put up with a lot from Ferdinando, but he was fond of you, Xavier, when you were a little boy. It was only that after he discovered the truth he couldn't bear to see you – you reminded him too much of your mother—'

'But it was not *her* fault!' interjected Flora, looking from one to the other of them. 'You really believe that your father was Ferdinando, Xavier?'

'I have just told you,' replied Xavier coldly. 'There was no reason for my mother to lie to me.'

'But she didn't ask to be seduced! It was your grandfather's – I mean your father's – fault.'

'Yes, my *father's*! Now you see why I am as I am—' He stopped abruptly.

'That's nonsense, Xavier. It needn't *always* happen that someone inherits a characteristic – even if you had something in common your upbringing would be different.' Why had she wanted him to know his mother was still alive? She had made things worse.

'Do not blame yourself, Flora,' said Xavier. 'You were not to know – and I am glad that I do know the truth now – though not feeling especially thrilled to have seen her at last.'

'How was she?' asked Edwige. 'I think I *will* take just half a glass of that—'

'*You* must know what she was!' Xavier hissed the words savagely as he turned to Edwige.

Flora, who was pouring the glass of grappa, hesitated in mid-stream for a moment, shocked at his tone of voice. What could he mean? She handed the glass to Edwige, who took a large sip. Then she said: 'Victoire refused to stay here, and Paul didn't know where she was. If she had to look after herself after she left, what else could she do? In the war women managed as best as they could. She had her mother to look after as well!'

'She told me her mother was an alcoholic,' said Xavier. 'She told me everything. There was no light in her eyes – it was as if she had lost her soul. She wasn't unhappy, she said, and she was glad to have seen me at last. She didn't think I would ever want to see her when I knew the truth, but of course I didn't know the truth, did I? That was why, like a fool, I went to look for her!' He put his head in his hands. Then he looked up. 'She said there was nothing I could do for her. I was going to offer her a home here – until I met her.'

'You would be right to do so,' said Flora. 'It's not too late to make reparations—' Even as she spoke, something was nagging at her. She could not bring it to the surface of her mind. But Xavier was continuing to speak, not looking at her but at Edwige.

'*You* knew. You knew everything, didn't you? Why didn't you tell me she was alive when I came back here after the war? And Tante Jo? Ludo? Didn't they have any idea why my mother was forced to leave the Villa? Didn't Paul tell them *anything*? Did *they* know she had not died?'

'Ludo may have known why your mother left – but Josephine – never!' answered Edwige, looking at him steadily.

'But that she was alive? Did they know?'

'I believe Josephine was not curious,' replied Edwige. 'She'd never liked her little stepbrother's choice of wife! One of the servants, you see. Josephine was quite happy to bring you up. As for Ludo – if he knew, he never said. Ludo always preferred not to enquire too closely into people's private lives – so that nobody pried into his.' Edwige looked quite calm, thought Flora, and yet some blame must surely attach to her?

She turned to Xavier and asked: 'But what did you feel when you saw her?' She did not really expect a reply, for he looked so drained.

'Very little, if truth be told. She was much as I'd remembered her. Coarser I suppose – she hasn't had an easy life.' He turned to Edwige again. 'Will you stay for supper?' he asked politely. 'I assume Mirella will have prepared something.'

'I'll go and see,' Flora said and escaped out of the room wishing that she could be alone with him. Now at last she might help him to bear the truth. She might even feel happier about him . . . .

Mirella was in the kitchen and seemed not at all surprised to hear that the master was back and that Madame Rouart would be staying for supper. Flora went back to the others and was at the door to hear Xavier say:

'I could forgive her, but not him.'

Edwige looked up as Flora came into the room.

'It's all past history!' she said. Flora thought she sounded unusually nervous.

'What else?' said Xavier. 'I have been doing a few calculations, Flora. Do you realize that with a new-found father, I am also given a half-sister – my so-called Aunt Josephine – and two half-brothers, though one of them is unfortunately dead: my "uncle" Ludo and my "father" Paul? That is, if I can believe that my also newly-found mother was telling me the truth—'

'Yes, she was,' said Edwige, '—yet I'm told everybody wants me to be happy – but you see there are other things I remember – I have memories not conducive to adult bliss – quite apart from being a bastard.'

'You were born within wedlock,' said Edwige. 'Paul loved your mother and she loved him. You might just as well have been Paul's. In any case it would have been impossible to prove you were not.'

'Except that she was sure!' he replied.

Mirella's appearance with their dinner brought this conversation to a close. Flora hoped there would be nothing more to be said, but feared there would.

As the coffee arrived, Edwige said: 'I shall have to go soon, I have to fetch my tabby cat back from the vet early tomorrow.'

'I didn't know you had a tabby as well!' exclaimed Flora.

'No? Minou has been with him for a week recovering from eating some poison a village woman laid down in her cellar against rats. I did not think she would pull through.'

'You have a maternal instinct,' said Xavier. Flora detected a sneer in his voice. He went on, speaking to Edwige: 'Flora will have to leave the Villa.'

Her heart began to jump irregularly. Was he going to explain why?

'She understands why,' he went on, still turned to Edwige.

'Yes, I know,' said Edwige. 'I'm sure she does not wish to stay with a stranger. But Flora does not care who your father was!'

Flora felt a surge of gratitude to her. 'Of course not,' she said to Xavier in a strangled voice. She touched his hand. 'Why should I care that your mother lied to everyone about your parentage – except in so far as it affects you, Xavier?'

'Edwige knows that last year I tried to revive my grandfather's way of doing things – I must now say my *father's* way, I suppose,' said Xavier, not looking at her. 'She even tried to dissuade you from coming, Flora, so sure was she that you would not approve.'

'You knew that I would not help you with your plans,' said Edwige. 'If your desire to take up Ferdinando's habits was in order to purge yourself of your memories, well, I could understand that but not excuse it.'

'Flora knows that it helped me – made a man of me I think they say!'

'Stop, Xavier – there is no need to torture yourself!' interjected Flora. 'I did hope that seeing your mother would make things better for you.'

'Like magic? – Well, I suppose I *am* glad that I've found her at last, but it hasn't made things better.'

'I really must go,' said Edwige, and stood up. Xavier made no move so Flora accompanied her out of the room and to the door at the back of the house. They stood for a moment in the courtyard.

'Mademoiselle Flora, he's in a strange state of mind. If he demands that you leave immediately, Ludovic is in Milano, I could ask him to—' She was upset. Flora laid a hand gently on her arm.

'Things are no worse for me though, are they? I wanted to leave a few days ago. I felt I ought to, he was so strange and peculiar, but I'd like to stay on a bit to try and help him adjust to what his mother told him.'

'There may be other things bothering him,' said Edwige.

'What else has he to worry about? Surely this has been enough?'

Edwige did not answer this, but went on: 'It would have been better for you not to have come at all, but since you are here do what you can. I will keep in touch. I am fond of him, you know – and of you too—' She leaned towards Flora and kissed her cheek. 'It is not your fault,' she said.

'I hope your little cat will have recovered,' said Flora, returning her kiss.

'It was all – *all* of it Signor Ferdinando Leopardi's fault,' stated Edwige, and turned away. Then she looked back again and said: 'Victoire was *innocent* – whatever he thinks. Go in now.'

'I wish you were still living here. You are good for him,' said Flora, but Edwige shrugged her shoulders and walked away with her usual erect bearing.

Flora hurried back to the sitting-room, noticing that the

lights in the kitchen were out. Mirella must have gone to bed. She might as well take the bull by the horns.

'What *exactly* did you do last year?' she asked Xavier as soon as she entered the room. He had extinguished the lights, except for one little lamp on the table at which he was sitting, his head in his hands.

'I had various women around – you know that—'

'Up in your Violet Rooms?'

'Of course.'

She realized now that he had tried to treat her as he had treated any of the women who had been there last year. Such relationships had worked for him so long as he did not love the woman.

She sat down, trying to order her thoughts. I still love him in a way, she told herself. Loving and being in love were different. He *had* asked her to marry him, after all.

'You must not love me – I can't love you,' he said.

'Are there other things I ought to know?' she asked.

He looked away from her as he spoke: 'I wanted my mother. All through my childhood I thought about her,' he replied. 'Once, when I was a little boy – I think it was a few years after she had gone away but I'm not sure – what are years to children? – I thought I had a terrible nightmare. Now I think it was not a nightmare and that I did see my mother—'

'Edwige told me that she did come once to see you at night, but you were asleep—'

'This could not have been that time. She was – she was—' He swallowed and then stood up and looked out of the window. 'It was in the room upstairs with the violet scent. There were women there and then in another room beyond I saw a woman being attacked by a man – I mean I thought she was being attacked by a man. I was terrified. Of course she was not being attacked – she was a prostitute, one of the many whom Ferdinando – *my father* – brought to the Villa, I expect.

She had her legs up in the air, and there were animal noises – and I screamed. Do you think it was my father standing there? No, no – it could not have been. They said my Grandpapa was not there that night – but I think it was her – Victoire!'

'Stop torturing yourself, Xavier. I do not think it could have been your mother – she would not come back to your grandfather's – your father's house.'

He did not listen to her. 'My mother the whore? There was another man standing there . . . .'

'You may have dreamed it. How could it make things worse for you now? Was that the memory that was pursuing you?'

'I saw that woman, I saw that woman,' he repeated. 'She was not a good woman . . . there were men and it was horrible . . . my mother was not with me any more by then, but when I knew her she smelled of violets, *violettes de Parme* . . . . Not yesterday though – she did not remember them when I asked her! – but if it was my mother that time – I tell you I feel now as if it were – then you see I could never love a woman with the love I had for her. I can only lust after her – oh yes! – and it will never change, never change . . . .'

She looked over at him despairingly.

'Go to bed now, Flora. You need not leave till tomorrow,' he said flatly.

'Will you sleep, Xavier? I will sit up with you if you like.' He seemed calmer now, no longer spiteful.

'No, it doesn't matter. Look – before you go up, she gave me a photograph – one taken years ago—' He took a leather wallet from the pocket of his crumpled linen suit and extracted a small snapshot. Flora took it from him and as their hands touched she had to stop herself from taking him in her arms. She wanted to comfort him so much, and there was nothing she could do, nothing.

The photo had been taken in winter by the lake. It was of a

THE VILLA VIOLETTA ·

woman in a long coat, wearing a cloche hat. The face was very
young, the hair dark, the eyes like her son's. But there was
something else. Flora struggled to grasp a fugitive impression
but it eluded her.

'She is very pretty – she looks a nice young woman,' she
said quietly.

'Don't you think they could at least have given me a photograph when I was small? They never did – my family were
not very psychologically acute, were they?'

He gave a wry smile and she gave him back the picture,
touched his hand, and went out into the high dark entrance
hall. She walked up the long stairs past the woman with the
violets, and then on and along the corridor to her room.

She could not sleep.

Some memory was dogging her. She tried the pillows one
way and then another, lay on her right side, then on her left,
then on her back. Sleep did not come.

Something Edwige had said, something she had seen
before, something – was it about Victoire or about Xavier or
Paul? In the end she counted sheep, tried slow breathing,
saying the two syllables of the name Vic-toire over and over
again with each breath, and still sleep did not come.

Suddenly she knew what her mind had been groping after,
and knew it for the truth. She got out of bed, pulled her journal from under the mattress, and began to write in the semi-
darkness. Afterwards, she wrapped it in her scarf and put it
at the bottom of her suitcase. Xavier must never read that!

She must leave him now, for what she had guessed would
destroy him, and she dared not trust herself to say nothing to
him of it.

She woke with a queer sort of headache and finished her
packing. It was eight o'clock. She went down to the ground

floor in the lift. Xavier was already in the dining room. She saw that he had not been to bed.

'I shall take the boat at eleven,' she said.

'No! No, wait till this afternoon,' he exclaimed. He sounded surprised. Had he thought he would have to persuade her, force her, to leave him?

She weakened. 'All right, I'll go to Como this afternoon. I have a return air ticket from Milan.'

Whatever happened she must not let slip what she had realized in the night. They must part on good terms even if not happily. They had been *friends* for eight years, a long time. But she thought her heart would break. She ought to have managed things better. She had been too young, too unworldly.

'You must go. You pity me, Flora,' he said flatly.

'I wanted to help you,' she said, her face averted. 'You know that.'

'Am I allowed no pride?' he asked.

'It's too late to talk about it all again.'

One part of her still longed to try; even if she were no longer in love with him, she was still fond of him. But fondness could not help him, never had and never would. Xavier had to work out his destiny alone. If only they could abolish the past, a past which even now he did not fully comprehend, and which she believed she did.

'Don't live in the past Xavier. Forget it!' she said quietly. He looked at her as though he were a stranger, with a curious expression of sly petulance.

'I suppose you say such a thing for *my* sake, not yours?'

'Yes, of course I do.'

'I don't think I ever loved you, Flora. I thought I did. But how can I love anybody if I so hate myself?'

'There is no reason for love,' she said, staring at her coffee cup as though salvation was to be found there. Her conclusions of the night were going round and round in her head, and she was afraid they might appear on her face, that he would read them and see even further reasons for his despair.

'We need not see each other again after today. It was all a mistake,' he said.

'You did love me,' she said in a low voice. 'But it doesn't matter – it's much more important that you love yourself.'

'Quite the psychiatrist!' he said ironically.

'Don't, Xavier. There's no need to make things worse by mocking me.' She tried to eat but managed only a little coffee.

He said more kindly: 'As it is your last morning, Flora, we can walk in the gardens together if you like?'

She was so relieved that he had changed the subject that she said quite brightly: 'I forgot to tell you – Signorina Vitelli has gone – well you must have realized. She said it was her holiday. I don't think she will return though.'

He shrugged his shoulders.

Walking on the terrace, his mood changed again. He said: 'In spite of my problematical nature, I can still ask you whether – knowing what you do – and seeing that unlike me you want neither passion nor a respectable marriage, you would reconsider just being my friend, Flora?'

Her eyes full of tears, she stopped by an urn of geraniums; their pungent scent filled the warm air. She *was* still tempted, still wished she could accept him, but not just as a friend. In spite of everything, one part of her wanted to stay, and one part of her own nature wanted to be his wife. You did not need sexual passion to love a lost soul . . . . But before she could answer he gripped her arm.

'You know I cannot love you in the way you want, but I think I could love you enough to make a few babies . . . .'

She found herself saying: 'I *will* always be your friend, Xavier, but your idea of marriage is not mine. In any case I couldn't become a Catholic, and I couldn't watch you fall into the wretched excesses of – of lust – with other women.'

'No, I did not think you could,' he said dully. 'You'll marry a nice Englishman, Flora. One who knows who his mother and father were. You never loved me!'

She wanted to say: when I loved you most, the rest of my life receded. Now, I think I need my life back. That's what it is . . . . Instead, she said: 'I used to think if I lost you I'd lose everything. But now I begin to see it differently, and to feel that less.'

'You are no longer in love with me Flora! You see, you are a *failed* Romantic.'

He was right. But unfortunately she also pitied him now and he would not want her support if it were mixed up with her pity. Nor even her friendship?

'Will you come just once more to look at the Violet Rooms and the portrait? Then I will bring down your bags. We can have an early lunch – I've already spoken to Mirella – she is preparing your favourite salad.' He had known she would leave. He spoke lightly but her eyes were moist. She felt guilty as well as miserable, knowing that underneath his changeable moods and mixed emotions what he felt was despair, and that she could not help him. Probably nobody could. Certainly not his poor mother.

They stood by the portrait of the Violet Lady.

'She does look a little like the snapshot of your – of Victoire,' said Flora carefully. Her throat was dry with suppressed emotion and with the fear that by some small word she might hint at that secret she felt sure she'd unlocked, of which, thank God, he had no inkling and of which, she prayed, he never would.

But Xavier was apparently now returned to his old self. He put his arm round her. 'I shall miss my English girl,' he said.

He sounded middle-aged now, world-weary.

'Let's look in your "Palace Apartment",' she said. Hand in hand they walked down the corridor to the Violet Rooms.

'See,' he said. 'Only three doors on this side of the staircase, but many more than three rooms! You've seen the bedroom with the grand furnishings, and the room with the bed and the mirror, and the Empire sitting-room, and their intercommunicating rooms, but there is one room you have never seen.'

'Then show me that one now.'

He walked to a door almost at the end of the corridor and put the key in the lock. 'The others have inner doors,' he said, 'but this one has none. I sleep here sometimes – always alone.'

She followed him inside. A narrow divan covered in a plain blue spread; a crucifix on the wall, a small table with a statue of the Madonna. A rug. A neat shelf of books on the wall; a window with a plain blue blind. Nothing purple or violet or mauve.

'It is furnished like my boyhood room,' he said. 'No violets here. As you know, upstairs I have a study in the room I used to sleep in, but here I have made my childhood anew. Look at the books!'

She went to the shelf and found *Alice in Wonderland* and *Treasure Island* in translation, and in English *The Secret Garden*. Nothing French. No philosophy. She took out a book called *Some Poems for Children*. Inside was written: 'to dear little Xavier from his grandmother Paulina Leopardi November 1934.'

'Except she was not my grandmother,' he said, and it was said with real bitterness. He was not resigned to his new knowledge. Until yesterday he had at least had a proper father in Paul.

'Did your grandfather never give you anything?' asked Flora. 'I mean, your father—'

'I cannot get used to the idea that Papa was not my father,' he said softly. 'I was a little afraid of Ferdinando Leopardi when I was a child – and now I *hate* him!' He said this with a peculiar ferocity. The man was, after all, dead – had been dead for twelve years.

Flora said hurriedly: 'I can send you some more English books for your shelves. I'll send you Keats, who died in Rome, and Shelley, who died in Lerici—' She stopped, her throat tight with sorrow.

'Don't cry, Flora.'

'Why do you have the crucifix here?' she managed to ask.

'It was mine as a child. I used to talk to it and to the Madonna – not prayers, you know – more a conversation between equals. I suppose, like my *father*, I didn't like feeling inferior to statues.'

After they had gone out of the room she sensed his mood had changed once more. Brusquely he said: 'Leave me now. Come down to the dining room at noon.'

Was he angry because she had not accepted his strangely half-hearted proposal? His rapid changes of mood frightened her. Did they presage real mental disturbance?

Over lunch he said: 'I don't suppose women like you *should* marry, Flora. We men don't like strong women who don't need us, you know!' This was so unfair that her breath was taken away. He added: 'You are going away because you pity me. I know that.'

'I know I have my own problems, everybody does,' she said soothingly. 'But I wouldn't mind if *you* were sorry for me!'

'Men are different,' he said briefly and his expression became withdrawn.

'Flora persisted, saying: 'I don't care who your father was!'

'But I do,' was his reply. 'I know we shall not see each other again.'

'Don't say that!'

'Why not? Why should you wish to see me, Flora?'

'Because we are friends – apart from everything else – you said so yourself—'

'But it cannot be apart from everything else. You can't help me – you never could – it has all been a mistake.'

She got up from the table. 'I don't want to leave you feeling so unhappy!'

'Don't worry about me, Flora. You will leave here in half an hour. You could stay if you were minded to become what I want you to become, the way I want you to be!'

She wondered whether he really did want her to stay. Was it just his pride that was hurt?

'You make me feel so wretched – so guilty,' she said and felt as though she could weep for days. But no tears came.

She said again as she moved towards the door to go upstairs for her suitcase: 'Please Xavier – whatever happens – do not live in the past. Make a future for yourself.' If he only knew what further revelations might come upon him . . . .

' "Whatever happens" – you sound as if my life were about to change. You know it cannot change now. I shall not see my mother again.'

Flora left the room but found that he had followed her to the lift.

'I shall see to your bags,' he said. He took her case down for her and said nothing further.

As he put her on the boat from the landing stage, she thought, how handsome he is . . . and how I did truly love him. Maybe I still do, even if I don't know what love is any more . . . and my love is not what he needs or wants. He put out his hand, and she took it.

He did not kiss her good-bye. She tried to kiss him, a last tender kiss in recognition of their past, but he pushed her gently away.

There was an emptiness in her head and heart as the boat moved away. He did not wave to her but stood stock still, hands at his side, staring at the boat for a moment.

Then he turned, to walk out of her life.

The steamer took her past the boathouse where his father had died, before it went into the middle of the lake and headed south. When she looked back she saw the Villa Violetta shining distantly, white in the sun.

It was only later that afternoon when the boat had arrived in beautiful Como that things began to seem to slip away out of her head and she wondered where she was. But she managed to find a taxi to take her to the station for the train to Milan. She had apparently just missed one so she had to wait on the platform with her suitcase for the next. The case was terribly heavy and her head felt even heavier so that when the train came and she found a seat, she slept, to waken only in a panic.

It was dark, and raining.

Where was she? When the train stopped she realized she must alight, for she had a plane ticket in her pocket, hadn't she?

Alerted by Edwige Rouart who had telephoned Xavier to see if Flora had gone, and to discover at what time she might arrive in Milan from Como, Ludovic Leopardi had been waiting for two hours at the end of the platform for Flora. When he saw her he was shocked. The child was in no state to take the plane tonight. She was pale, hardly spoke, seemed bemused, said, when pressed, that she felt a little sick.

He decided to book her a room in a hotel and to book another for himself.

'I'll see you safely on the plane tomorrow,' he said. 'You need a good sleep, my dear.'

Inwardly he cursed his nephew, whom he supposed he must now regard as half-brother. Not that he hadn't nursed his suspicions for years; Edwige had only confirmed them. Thank God he'd never had anything to do with that messy mixture of sex and love men and women went in for together!

Flora accepted his help as though she was in a dream or a trance. She accompanied him in a taxi to a hotel he knew well. She even forgot to take her handbag from him when he deposited her at her bedroom door. He was too absent-minded himself to give it to her when he said:

'Good-night. We'll see how you feel in the morning, then.'

As he undressed in his own room, he thought that something more than the recent revelations from Victoire must account for Flora's state. Xavier's telling her to leave must have given her a body blow – unless she'd freely chosen to go? He hoped she was not pregnant. Xavier would have to marry her if she were, and he didn't think Xavier Leopardi should marry anybody.

FOUR

London

1957-8

She heard it over the Tannoy at Heathrow: Will Miss Flora Russell on BEA flight no 2464 from Milan Malpensa arrived nineteen thirty hours please contact Mr Thornton in the BEA office on level 4.

Why on earth had she allowed Ludo Leopardi to telephone John Thornton? She recalled that in the taxi going to the hotel the night before she'd actually given him the number, even handed him the address book, saying she felt too tired to ring him herself.

Well, it couldn't be helped; she'd have to invent some reason which didn't involve her in long complicated explanations about Xavier. She didn't want to talk about Xavier to anybody. The whole idea of him was like a lump of misery stuck somewhere in her gullet and guts.

Losing her memory had perhaps been nature's way of giving her an emotional rest. It hadn't lasted very long; she still felt a bit wobbly but fortunately no longer had a headache.

She thought, might I even tell John I did actually forget who I was for one whole morning and part of an afternoon? I needn't mention Xavier!

As she stood waiting for her luggage while the carousel trundled round she had another sudden mental jolt, with the visualization of a kind of empty space filled for so long with thoughts of Xavier, love for Xavier.

Was it falling out of love with him that had done the trick, so that her memory had been taken away for a day to spare her grief?

Grief would arrive, she knew, but not yet, and when it came it would be grief for having lost her own feelings of love as much as for losing Xavier.

John Thornton knew she'd been having some sort of affair in Italy for years, so he *might* suspect her return was something to do with it. But all she'd need to do would be tell him she wasn't going to marry anybody. It was over.

She found John where the message had said he would be. He'd come all the way out to Heathrow after receiving Ludo's call the night before.

'Flora – what's been going on? This Mr Leopardi sounded really worried!'

'Don't worry, John, he thought I didn't look very well, and that someone had better meet me. But I'm all right now, truly. I could do with a cup of coffee though. We can take the airport bus back to Gloucester Road – that's not far from the flat—' He took her case. She was longing to read the diary that lay at the bottom of it. Otherwise it would all seem a dream.

They went for a coffee and he made her drink a brandy with it, saying she looked pale. Over the drink she considered telling him that she appeared to have had a bout of amnesia, but decided against it. He would be too worried. Anyway, it had come most likely from not sleeping too well for ages.

'Ludovic Leopardi knew I'd had to leave rather suddenly,' she said carefully. John did not ask any questions of her. He knew she would tell him eventually. Flora had never been one for keeping things to herself. 'I'm all right now,' she repeated, determined to convince him. 'I began to feel much better on the plane—' Was it only that very morning she'd woken up and not known who she was? It seemed aeons ago.

John however was not stupid, though he might be tactful. 'I hope you won't regret curtailing your holiday!' he said.

'Oh well, I suppose – once I'd decided not to marry Xavier Leopardi – it was all a bit fraught—'

'I see.' Though he didn't really, how could he? She saw him looking at her surreptitiously when he thought she was unaware. 'Will you go back to work soon? You told me in your last letter you were going to continue at your 'coaching establishment'. Do you really want to go on with it?'

'Term won't start till September,' she replied. Talking about work was the last thing she wanted to do just now, so she put him off, saying there was plenty of time before she needed to contact the tutors. Still, they might have some holiday work for her. She'd have to earn some more money soon. She could go home for a week or two, she supposed. She needed a few days at least to think about what had just happened. A whole long chapter of her life had closed.

John accompanied her into London on the airport bus, then, after urging her to see a doctor if she went on feeling fuzzy, he left her at the flat in Pimlico she shared with Clare Goodwin, who was often away. 'Be sure to give me a ring if you feel depressed,' he said when they parted. She promised she would.

She unpacked like an automaton when he'd gone, had a bath, sorted through her mail and made a list of all the things she had to do: boring things like going to the launderette and putting a note out for the milkman.

Puritan morality satisfied, she made a cup of tea and then unwrapped the precious journal from its silk wrappings in the bottom of her suitcase. She sat down to read what she had written two nights ago. She might find it all now belonged to a kind of dream, or a night-time fantasy. She had been holding off all thoughts of Xavier, but once she had read her journal she would know whether she would be able to put them off for ever. The leather binding said: **Journal F M Russell. Private.**

She turned to the date she had inscribed at the beginning of her holiday: July 1957, and then to a few pages further on.

She had not written as much this year as on her previous visits, yet what she now read filled her with foreboding.

She wrapped it all up again, resolving to reread it only when she had had more time to compose herself.

She had resolved not to write to Italy, except to Ludo to say she had arrived back safely, but she could not stop herself from sending a short letter to Xavier, feeling that in some curious way she must absolve him from any further anxiety he might feel for her. She also wanted to add her thanks for their long friendship, and to hope for his future happiness (little as she really entertained that hope.) Even as she penned the words of her letter, they rang false, sounded as if she were congratulating him on his forthcoming marriage to someone else.

She knew herself for a sentimental creature; she had always been one. Doubtless it was another of those English qualities Xavier had once teased her about. Would she have gone on hoping for so long that things might go right between the two of them if she had been less sentimental?

She had a short reply from Ludo, then – nothing. She left her journal safely entombed in her handkerchief drawer, and tried not to think about it. From time to time she was still a little afraid of losing part of herself as she seemed to have done in Milan, but when she went back to work she was determined to ignore her own misery, if not to forget Xavier's.

*

One morning in early November, three months after she had returned to London, Flora was rushing out to work, late as usual, when she found on the mat a letter with an Italian stamp, addressed to her in Xavier's handwriting. She had no time even to scan it then. She stuffed it in her handbag as she ran for the bus to Sloane Square.

In the square she bought a paper and arrived just in time at the tutorial establishment where she was working, hoping to read the letter before her pupils arrived. Like herself, they were bad at getting up in the morning and were often late. But this morning two girls arrived on time and she was busy going through their French proses with them until the coffee-break. The staff common room was crowded, so she took her cup of coffee to the basement where they kept an ancient cyclostyle copier and pretended she was preparing something for it. She had only ten minutes, then she'd be required upstairs again to coach a young public school drop-out.

The letter was dated the Tuesday before. Considering the vagaries of the Italian mail, the letter had not taken too long to arrive. Her hand trembled as she drew the paper out of its envelope. **Xavier Bruno Leopardi** was printed at the head of the first page: He began in Italian and then continued in French:

'Flora, carissima,
This is to say thank you for all you have meant to me. Also to say good-bye.

I received your letter but could not reply. What was there to say? I was relieved that you had arrived home safely. Ludovic told me you had looked ill when he saw you in Milan. I ought to have gone with you. I ought perhaps to have abandoned everything and tried to make a new life far away from this house of unhappiness, but I could not, even though they gave me the name Xavier which means "New House", as you once pointed out to me.

Once you had gone, thoughts of my past and of my child-hood and of the pasts of all my family obsessed me completely and would not leave me alone. I spent three months of agony here, alone for the first six weeks until Ludo returned at the end of September. He made me see a doctor but there was nothing a doctor could give me to assuage my pain, which is of the mind and the spirit.

My 'brother' Ludovic would say nothing except that he did not wish to discuss our father *ever*. All that was past, and if I had any sense I would start afresh, return to my studies, leave the Villa – he was quite capable of making money for us both, and so on . . . .

I decided for my peace of mind – what irony lies in that phrase – that I would have to speak to Edwige once again. She had been avoiding us, would not come up here. Finally, on Sunday, I went to her. I had to talk to someone and I felt there were yet things I did not know which she might explain to me. I had not written to my mother – I *could* not. It was better that she should forget me.

Edwige received me gently, as if I were indeed ill. I challenged her to tell me more of my 'grandfather' and what kind of man he was. Oh how I hate him – my *father* – Ferdinando Leopardi. I always hated his politics. Yet I thought, if I could understand him I might understand why I am as I am, and why I felt compelled to try to recreate his ambience.

Edwige made me sit down and told me at first some extra-ordinary things about herself and about him. She said "Flora knows some of this." But I could see she was holding some-thing back.

Oh Flora! a demon came into me then! I kept shaking her and saying: "You are lying! You are lying!" I asked her why my mother had not wanted to see me even after she knew that the old devil Ferdinando – and poor Paul Leopardi, the pre-wedding cuckold – were dead. There had to be something more. I could understand that I was the result of a liaison or even of a rape. I did not blame my poor mother, but there was no reason after the war why she could not have come to me. I would have been so happy, even if I had suspected she was a light woman who was not averse to doing what her employer wanted.

Edwige went quite white. Then she said: "You have asked me, so I will tell you."

And then she told me.

Oh Flora, such a terrible thing! I cannot write it down, cannot speak of it to you. I do not know what to do. I now realize that I was spoilt from the very first day of my life. The Germans have a word – *verdorben* – which expresses it exactly. I can *never* be normal and *never* be happy.

I had lost my 'good' father, Paul, all over again but I still idolized the memory of my young mother. I now know it was not her I saw as a child in my Violet Rooms.

Yet she – no, I cannot write it.... Victoire was tainted too ... and now I feel I have lost her all over again. I have been handed down a cruel dose of heredity. From it comes my incapacity to love – I can never enjoy possessing a woman unless I can humiliate her – and then I cannot love her.

I am shattered and can never again put the pieces of myself together. How could you possibly understand? You could not have been and could never be what I wanted you to be, except by surrendering your true self. I suppose we could have loved each other spiritually, as soul mates: love each other, as Dante is supposed to have loved Beatrice. But you deserve a real man. Also, it was only when Beatrice was dead that the Ideal could never perish, and *you* must not die.

I lied when I said I did not love you. At least I *wanted* to love you.

I have no desire to live. I came back here after Edwige had spoken to me and I have not slept for three nights. Yesterday I resolved to write to you to ask for forgiveness.

Ludo is away again and Mirella avoids me except when she

brings me my dinner. Francesca Vitelli has also written to me and she will not be coming back.

I went up this morning to the clock tower and thought to hurl myself down from it, but at the last moment my nerve failed . . . .

Flora turned the page and in a shakier hand was written:

By the time you receive this, the die will be cast. The Leopardi line must not go on. Only Solange will be left and she is only the grandchild of Ferdinando, and in any case a woman, and that does not count in the same way. She resembles her French father.

You cannot help me, Flora. I see now that it has been my fate from the beginning of my life.

I should never have been born.

That is the stark truth.

Do not blame Edwige, and above all do not blame yourself. You gave me the only truly happy days I ever had since I was a child. I shall never be able to reconcile the two parts of my nature – even less so now that I know who I am. Edwige will explain.

Forgive me, Flora. Find a decent man one day but remember me sometimes.

You can listen to Beniamino Gigli singing Tosti's *Chanson d'Adieu* and think then also of your

Xavier.'

Her throat dry and her eyes pricking with unshed tears, Flora put the letter back into its envelope. The bell for the next lesson was ringing. What should she do? She could not go into her next class. She found her coat and bag and went upstairs to the secretary's office.

'I'm sorry, I don't feel very well. I ought to be in room 3. Could you find someone to take the lesson? It must be something I ate—' She dashed away as if to vomit, leaving the secretary staring after her. But Miss Lawrence had suffered more peculiar tutors than Flora, some of whom took their lessons when they were completely drunk, so she shrugged her shoulders and went up to the staffroom to find a substitute or send the class home.

Flora sat in one of the new coffee bars on Sloane Square, where she often went for what was supposed to be a *cappuccino*.

Xavier's letter lay open before her. Did he mean to kill himself? His nature was so changeable that it must have been on the impulse of the moment that he had written to her as he had?

A good-bye to their love, not to his life?

She had not underestimated his anguish, nor his conviction that he was doomed. If only she could have persuaded him – could even now persuade him – that adults owed more to their childhood environment than to the casual assortment of genes they had been handed. But a childhood trauma might count for more than genes.

Xavier had lost his 'good' father – Paul, but had it not assuaged his sorrow to know that it was not Victoire he'd seen in that room with the two men, one trauma at least he could now lay to rest? His despair might have expanded into *thoughts* of suicide – yet he had not jumped from the clock tower . . . .

*

She reread the letter: the die will be cast . . . .

She must find a way of telephoning Edwige, or perhaps Ludo? But he might be in Como.

She got up, her coffee untouched and cold. Her only coherent thought was that she must go straight home and telephone *somebody*.

She went down into the Underground.

When the Circle line train came in she found a seat next to a middle aged man who was reading the morning paper. She shut her eyes, trying for a few moments to forget everything . . . . After two stops she opened her eyes again in preparation for alighting at the next one.

She glanced vaguely over the man's shoulder at the newspaper, remembering that she had not yet opened her own copy of the *Manchester Guardian*. Suddenly, under Foreign News, she saw the headline: LEGACY OF FASCISM? YOUNG ITALIAN FOUND DEAD IN COMO BOATHOUSE.

She stumbled out of the tube and bought the same paper from a newsagent at the corner of her square. But she knew already. Xavier Leopardi had hanged himself.

Like father, like son. Hanged in his own boat house. Xavier, Xavier. . . . Because she had meddled in his life. . .? Because she had told him his mother was still alive. . .? Because she had not loved him enough. . .? It was her fault.

On 2 December Flora wrote to Solange Duvallier and Uncle Ludo. Their replies were not long in coming. Both their replies were typical of them:

12th December 1957

Dear Flora

I write in reply to your letter. I am sorry that you had to read of Xavier's death in the English newspapers for I understand the shock you must have had.

I believe Madame Rouart, who attended the funeral, will be writing to you.

If my sister or I had thought you should attend his funeral mass we would have written to you, but we thought it best, all things considered, to have only a small family funeral prior to interment in the cemetery in Como.

There is little more I can say except that you are innocent of any blame. Please believe this. Xavier is now at peace and we can take up our lives once more.

We are hopeful that the Villa will eventually receive the status of Ancient Monument. An application to this effect has already been drafted but these things take a long time in our country.

My niece Solange has asked me most particularly to send you her kind regards. I have given her your address in London, which she told me she had lost.

I am, dear Flora, always your sincere friend,

Ludovic Leopardi.

Paris, 14th December 1957

Dear Flora

I wish you had been there when Xavier was buried. His death was gruesome, *n'est-ce pas?* I wish I understood why he did it – I don't think Maman knows any more than I do. I need to know why – I mean apart from life being on the whole a sad affair – and I intend to find out. Uncle Ludo and Madame Rouart spend hours whispering together. I am sure he did not kill himself because you would not marry him – that was what Maman hinted – but I am sure it is not true.

I was furious that they did not invite you to the funeral – after all, you loved him, and it was unfair not to invite you. Maman had a wonderful time saying masses. On account of my poor cousin's suicide, the Church kicked up a fuss about burying him in hallowed ground, and Maman had to twist the arm of the priest and his bishop to be allowed to do so.

I hope to come to England one day soon to improve my English and when I do I shall let you know. In the meantime, will you write to me just now and then? I liked it when we were at the Villa together.

We left Madame Rouart looking after Uncle Ludo since the maid Mirella had given notice. Uncle has some plan to get rid of the place to the administration of Lombardy or something. He says it is far too expensive to keep up properly and there

will be death duties as well. Maman says she will never go again to what she now calls the Villa Carolina. But I shall go!
  With love from
  Your friend Solange.

A week later, when the streets of London were already looking Christmassy, Flora took out her journal and reread the entry for that last night at the Villa. Then she wrote to Edwige.

In the New Year, on Twelfth Night, a cold miserable Monday, a letter with an Italian stamp was waiting for Flora on the mat when she returned from her work. It was Edwige's reply.

Before she slit it open Flora unwrapped her journal again from the silk scarf and held it in her lap. Then she sat down to read the letter, which was in French.

New Year's Day
1958

Ma chère Flora
It is in the midst of much sorrow that I finally write to you. I am sorry you had such a painful shock when you read the paper but the discovery was also a great shock for us here. Monsieur Ludovic found him and was very upset, though he does not show his feelings.

  You say that Xavier wrote to you, though he gave no proper explanation. The last time but one I saw him, when I had no suspicion that he had guessed anything further, he said to me 'One day, Edwige, you will tell Flora everything you know'. That was all. He did not know that you had already guessed the truth – as I see from your long letter to me.

  I write not to burden you with further unpleasant details. I wish to forget them as I tried to forget his so-called grandfather's death in '45, though I never forgot *him*. Xavier was not at all like him, though he feared he was.

  I have to tell you that you were right in all you wrote to me in your letter.

You have guessed those further secrets which Xavier also discovered, though he did not wish to mention them in his letter to you. These were the secrets that led to what our doctor called 'suicidal depression'. I should rather have called it despair. You can now imagine why I wanted to keep these things hidden. But it was not your fault, and you must not feel guilty that you suggested he met his mother. I knew it was not a good idea – but I also knew that I ought to have told him years before. At whatever time he came across her – for he was bound to find out sooner or later that she was alive – he would not be able to rest until he had discovered the whole *truth*.

When Paul fell in love with Victoire, I knew what would happen. I tried to warn him, but he wouldn't listen. I knew how much he loved her. They ran away to marry. I did try to warn Paulina too, without being able to tell her why exactly her son should not marry Victoire – I just hinted that her husband had had an affair with her. I didn't dare add he might still want to go on with it even after she was married to his son! Victoire, who was a remarkably pretty woman, was frightened of Ferdinando, and she had no power to refuse him.. Even if Paul didn't know for a long time that Victoire's pregnancy was not due to him, Victoire knew.

Some years later, when Xavier was about four years old, I believe Paul discovered from his mother-in-law, who was probably drunk at the time, that Xavier was not his. I don't know how *she* knew – perhaps Victoire had confessed to her. Paul told *his* mother and she confronted Ferdy with it. Then Paul told Victoire to go away and leave the child at the Villa with his father and 'grandparents' and to stay away. But it was the last straw for Paulina to discover little Xavier was not even her own grandchild.

Flora looked up, remembering the inscription in Xavier's childhood book: *From his loving grandmother.*

How it must have hurt Paulina Leopardi to realize that she was not. Would a greater-hearted woman have stayed? Xavier

was, after all, as far as she knew, at least her husband's grandson.

She returned to Edwige's long letter. The old woman was
using her as a sort of *confidante* and it made her feel a little
uncomfortable, even though she already knew the gist of the
confidences.

I must tell you, as I have told you before, that the behaviour
of Signor Ferdinando Leopardi was the cause of all the sorrow
and grief that filled the Villa, which has ended only with the
death of our little Xavier. If I still think of him as a child you
must forgive me.

I think Ferdy even blackmailed his first wife's family into
allowing him to marry her! Feodora's mother was Russian, her
name was Tatiana Lermontova but her father, Adolphe
Moirier, was Swiss-French. Ferdinando once told me he was
not rich at the time of his marriage. His mother Henrietta
Arnaud was half French – they were all of mixed nationalities
who came for the holidays round the lake. There were your
countrymen too – he thought the English very dull and
worthy. He probably had something on the Moiriers – I don't
know what exactly – but to do with money, I expect. There was
always something not quite above-board about his relations
with women, and that made him attractive to them when they
were very young. Of course I didn't know what he was really
like when I fell in love with him myself in my early twenties.
He had been kind to me and taken me away from a terrible
life, and I was grateful.

But I must come to the point, and it is hard.

As I have said, Xavier was not at all like him. Ferdy had
started having women around the Villa, giving big parties to
which the Fascisti were invited, long before Paulina upped
and left. Paul did not stay long after both his wife and his
mother had gone away, and by the time Paul left us, Ferdy was
getting more and more embroiled with the Fascisti. He'd
invite them to the Villa to enjoy the women he could provide

for them there. Just as during the first war he had officers
coming to the Villa to enjoy poules de luxe. He'd have had me
entertain them too in 1915, but I refused.

Well, Josephine and I looked after little Xavier when he was
deserted by everybody. Ferdinando showed no particular
interest in him. Once though, before the others went off to
Paris, I saw him looking at him and I guessed he realized it
was his son for sure. He preferred him to poor Ludo who had
always been a great disappointment. As you know, he left the
Villa to Xavier, so he must have known. He had no time for
Josephine either. She was not beautiful and he encouraged her
to marry the pederast Duvallier. I tried to dissuade her, but
perhaps I should have encouraged her. After all what good are
red-blooded men to women? Forgive me if I speak rudely . . . .

Flora turned over a page of the flowery script. Someone had
once taught Edwige Rouart to write a fair hand and write it
well, although in her matter she rambled and could not seem
to come to the point.

This has been a kind of unburdening for me – there was so
much only I knew. I have had many years to think over all this,
all these secrets – old sorrows and old misery – and all the evil
– I can call it that now I am an old woman. That was the result
of one man's lust. Signor Ferdinando Leopardi was still, even
at the end of his life, trying to imitate the poet we talked about
– except he never took cocaine, as I know for a fact the other
did. Like him, he had scores of women – the ones from the
family were only part of it all. He had young women – usually
part-time prostitutes – brought from all over the place. Even
the police knew all about them and were often implicated
themselves. At first, during the week-ends when the rest of the
family were in Como, he would have women brought to the
Villa and put into the shuttered rooms where he had sofas and
cushions and candles. He fancied himself talking to them as he
imagined the poet had done, but he hadn't much to say to

them and the girls were a poor lot. Later he just invited them for sex. But even when he wasn't there, other men would come – until Ferdy found out about that and stopped them. The women needed the money. I knew some of them, but couldn't do anything about it unless I faced up to Ferdy and lost my job. I know that was wrong of me. That goose of a Josephine knew nothing whatever about it. There were officers around whom she assumed were connected with her father's 'business'! Ludo just shut his eyes to it all.

I knew when Mussolini was caught that Ferdy would be killed and I was right. He'd known Musso in '43 when the Fascisti regrouped around Lake Garda. Musso's lady-friend, Clara, lived there. I could have given Ferdy up to the new Liberation Committee but I did not, and I didn't tell them where he was. I left him to atone for all he had done, but they got to him in the boathouse before he could kill himself – as his innocent son eventually did.

I blame myself for telling you about his mother, and for revealing the whole truth to Xavier, but I swear he insisted I did, the second time he came to me after you had gone. When I told him, he said he had already guessed – just as you had.

I had to write to you. You must not think you were in any way to blame for Xavier's death, Mademoiselle. I feel sure he did love you, as far as he could love any good woman. None of the guilt is yours. But I did try to tell you not to come here again after the first time, didn't I? Yet whether he had known you or not, he would have indulged himself with another sort of woman – as so many men prefer to do. I know all about that.

Whoever he had loved, it would have ended in the same way, even though what he saw when he was a little boy – that woman *in flagrante* – was not, as he thought later, his mother.

They gave Angelica money for keeping quiet about what had happened years before. Angelica told me everything before she died. I knew her quite well. Before she became an alcoholic she was a pleasant woman, if rather stupid.

I do not see any point in our writing to each other in future but, believe me, I wish you well.

Sincerely,

Edwige Rouart

Flora looked up. All she had guessed was true. All she had written down that awful last night at the Villa Violetta and then in her letter to Edwige was confirmed now by the old woman's reply. And even now Edwige had not wanted to write it!

She put the letter down and opened her own journal, turning to the pages she had written on her last night at the Villa. She read:

I am writing this in the dark. I feel I must write what I guessed tonight. Writing it down may help me to come to terms with it in my own mind. That sounds mad, I know, but it is too awful, and tomorrow my mind may refuse to believe it. I shall never, never tell Xavier, even though I am convinced it is the truth.

It was Edwige mentioning during one of our conversations that Victoire's mother used to work here at the Villa and then on another occasion giving me the name of a maid with whom old Ferdinando – though he wasn't old then – was having a sexual relationship. Not an 'affair' – just one of the women he exploited, I think. The maid was called Angelica and I calculate that it must have been when Ludovic and Josephine were still very small – after their mother had died – around 1908 to 1910 – before the first war, anyway. Perhaps Angelica became a prostitute later. Certainly she became an alcoholic, because Edwige told me so.

How can I write it?

I am sure Angelica was Victoire's mother.

There, I have said it. Nothing much in that?

No, not quite all.

261

Ferdinando was Victoire's father.

If I am right – and I am sure I am, Ferdinando had relations with his own daughter. And she had a son – and that son was Xavier.

I remember now who Xavier's mother looked like on that photograph he showed me. I'm surprised Xavier didn't see it himself. She looked like Ferdinando Leopardi when he was a young man! – I remember his showing me that photograph of Ferdinando taken years before in Paris, when he was very young. Xavier has, so to speak, a double dose of Ferdinando in his blood and bones and genes. I can easily imagine what that knowledge would do to any man, never mind such a sensitive one as my Xavier.

Yes, Xavier's father was Ferdinando and his mother Victoire. Victoire confessed to Xavier yesterday that Paul was not his father. But would she ever dare tell him who she was herself, who her own father was? that she was Ferdinando's own daughter by Angelica Rienzi?

Xavier is the child of father daughter incest, a terrible thing!

All the other relationships fall into place now. Victoire could not have known about her own parentage when she was seduced by Ferdinando, or when she fell in love with Paul and agreed to marry him. Like Ludo and Josephine, Paul was her half-brother. And her own son – Xavier – was her half brother too! If Xavier had been Paul's own son – as might have been possible – he would still have been the result of half-brother-half-sister incest, but that's not quite as awful as being the result of a man seducing his own daughter.

Xavier has always been worried that his mother was some-how connected with the scent of violets and the goings-on of the middle corridor, which he didn't understand when he was a child. But his adult subconscious did. He never quite spelt it out to me and I think until tonight he'd never remembered that when he was a little boy he had thought his mother might be

262

the woman he'd seen <u>in flagrante delicto</u> with a 'client' in one of the Violet Rooms. But she wasn't – I'm sure of that. She wouldn't come here to the Villa again, except to try to see her son. I feel sure Mirella's mother – Cécile – knew her and I'm sure Delphine too had her suspicions, probably from gossip from her own mother who was also a maid here.

The child Xavier did get it right in a way: If the woman he saw was not Victoire and the man was not his grandfather, it was still true that his mother and his grandfather had once been involved in such a scene. His subconscious knew, and that is why he has been tormented and why he became fixated on the violet perfume, and why he still cannot love the woman he goes to bed with – and cannot desire the woman he loves.

But if he is the result of the copulation – I will not say love-making – of his father Ferdinando and his own daughter, he had a grandfather who was also his own father. Strange that Ferdinando <u>was</u> his grandfather – as he had always assumed – but his maternal grandfather, not his paternal one!

Edwige keeps on saying It was all Ferdinando's fault. I am certain she is thinking of all the ramifications of the truth. It all arose from the lust of that one man.

Edwige must be the only person in the world now – apart from Victoire herself – who does know that truth. No wonder Edwige wanted to keep Victoire under wraps! Yet she must have thought, when she first told me Victoire was still alive, that it would be enough for Xavier just to know that. But once the cat is let out of the bag everything else follows.

Will Xavier ever guess the whole truth of his parentage? If he does, he will go to Edwige, I know, and it will finally upset the balance of his mind. I shall never tell him that Ferdinando Leopardi possessed Victoire as he had once possessed her mother Angelica when she was working at the Villa before the first war, when she was about seventeen. It would be the time his wife Paulina was pregnant with their son Paul. I'm sure that when she began to work at the Villa, Victoire had no idea who her father was. Her mother would not have revealed to her that particular liaison. Did Edwige know? Angelica should have told her daughter, but it wasn't Edwige's business – till she discovered Paul wanted to marry the young woman who was his half-sister. When Paulina was told that her husband had already seduced Victoire she could have had no idea that Victoire might be her husband's own daughter! Until Edwige told her – and then she immediately left the Villa. Did Paulina ever confront her husband? And what about Paul? Did she or Edwige tell him?

Did Ferdinando himself ever realize he had seduced his own daughter? Nobody will ever know that for sure. But I am absolutely certain that I am right about Victoire being Ferdy's daughter. Victoire didn't know that she and Paul were half-siblings. She ran away without even knowing that, just because she felt she had let down her beloved Paul, something that wasn't her fault at all.

I shall say nothing to Xavier tomorrow. I shall be as normal as it is within my power to be, but I must leave as soon as I can. Such knowledge is too much of a burden.

Even if Xavier could love and desire the same woman, he would never want to marry me if he knew the truth. He would not be able to bear the weight of such knowledge himself, would believe it accounted for all his problems.

I would be glad to be told I am wrong, that my perceptions are skewed, but I have no way of finding out. I cannot ask Edwige such a thing; it's better not to speak of it at all, than to look for evidence.

I even feel sometimes that my own personality is under threat here from an unseen enemy. Not from Xavier, who is also a victim, but from that old man whose presence I have often felt even though he died twelve years ago. How many more women did he seduce? Such terrible things have

happened here in such a lovely place. When people think of
seduction or rape they think of blood and noise and violence
but I feel it all happened over the years almost in silence.

It must be nearly morning. I can see more light coming in
now through the window where I left the outside shutters open.
I wish I did not know what I know. I shall try to go to sleep
now. I just wish I were not myself. I can never save Xavier.
That was a child's silly dream. Everything was stacked against
him from the beginning . . . I shall close this diary, wrap it in
the scarf he gave me in Menton, and put it in the bottom of my
suitcase, where nobody will find it.

I wish I could forget what I've discovered. There are other
pages in this diary that recall happier times and I don't want
to lose them, so I can't destroy the book. One day, when I am
old and grey, I might read it all again and it will bring back
Xavier and his beautiful Villa Violetta.

Flora folded Edwige's letter and placed it on the last page of
her journal. She would stop writing a diary. Living was
enough – too much. 1958 could not possibly bring anything to
alleviate her sorrow at Xavier Leopardi's death.

During the spring of the following year, 1958, Flora dreamed
often of Ferdinando Leopardi's death and of Xavier
Leopardi's death, and one mingled into the other. Repeatedly
she would dream of walking down in bright sunshine to the
boathouse and peering into its darkness from the steps. Then
she would see them both, father and son, dangling there.

But Xavier had not needed to die; his young, strong, and
healthy body had been swung and wrenched into death by an
obsessed imagination.

In these dreams she fervently believed that she could save
him so that his body was allowed to go on living, and she

planned to cut him down and revive him. The truth when she awoke was all the starker and more terrible, for then she knew that she could not have saved his imagination.

She comforted herself by thinking she had been right to go away from him that last afternoon after she had guessed the truth. Nothing she could have said would have made any difference; his own new-found knowledge would have taken him out of the world for ever. But then she would lie awake after such dreams and such thoughts, wondering whether if she had consented to marry him she might have saved his life.

Somehow she managed to go on living herself, managed to get up, to dress, to work, to sleep – even if that sleep was populated with dreams of what might have been. At first, nothing seemed to matter very much; other people were ghost-like; her favourite food and drink had lost their savour, and there was nothing whatever to look forward to.

Then, as time went on, she tried to make a virtue of stoicism, of accepting this nothingness as positive suffering. Her solace was to be able, just occasionally, to concentrate for long enough to listen to the music that brought back Xavier and her old feelings for him.

Later, she began to feel that there might be a future for her that was not full of anguish; that she might remember her own past happiness as part of her own youth that would never return.

John Thornton, now a professional economist, had gone to work in the States a few months after Flora had returned distraught from Italy that summer of 1957. Two years later, after his return to England, he sought her out again and their friendship blossomed into something deeper. Just before the Christmas of 1960 they were married.

On the day before her wedding, Flora placed several items

in a box, and sealed it up: letters, picture postcards, diaries, photographs, maps . . . . Her marriage was to be a new beginning.

For their honeymoon she and her husband did not go to Italy, or even France, but to the United States.

When he married her, John knew that Flora had been in love, in Italy, with Xavier Leopardi, but he never pressed her to tell him the details. He supposed that the Italian boy had never made Flora happy and he knew she felt it was partly her own fault for interfering. She would tell him more in her own good time. All she said before they were married was that Xavier had been the child of an unhappy family.

By the end of 1965 she and John were the parents of two children, Richard and Catherine, and her energies were devoted to a new generation.

FIVE

i

Como

1975

In the summer of 1975 Flora saw the Villa once more.

She and John had gone to Lake Como for ten days' holiday, for once without their children, now aged twelve and ten, who were being well looked after by Flora's parents. At last, eighteen years after she had left Italy with Ludovic's words in her ears: *Don't ever come back!* she had thought it time she did. Apart from anything else she wanted to see the Villa again. She had begun to allow herself to remember her old love. In the past she had always avoided talking about him; now she wanted to set the record straight, to tell her husband more.

On the afternoon of the third day of their holiday they went over in a boat from their little holiday village on the eastern peninsula to the further shore, where, only a mile away across the water, stood the Villa, now owned, as Flora knew very well, by Italian 'Heritage', or *Patrimonia* as they called it. Its name had reverted back to Carolina.

From the boat Flora looked across at the distant white building on the further shore. As far as she could see, the windows of the middle floor were still shuttered.

'Let's just go and look at the gardens,' she suggested. John was intrigued. He had never pressed her for further details about those long-ago summers she had spent in Italy. All he really knew even now, after over fourteen years of marriage, was that she had loved the man Xavier Leopardi, and that he had killed himself. Could she, after all these years still believe that it had been her fault?

They alighted from the little paddle steamer and John followed his wife as she climbed up to a narrow road that wound above the lake until a fork descended precipitously, and they arrived at a pair of tall wrought-iron open gates. A large notice was fixed to them:

VILLA CAROLINA
OPEN TO THE PUBLIC on TUESDAY THURSDAY
and SATURDAY
10 am to NOON & 2 pm to 6 pm.
At other times by appointment.

'Fortunately, it is a Tuesday,' said John.

'You see, the middle floor is still not open to visitors,' whispered Flora as they peered up at the beautiful building standing on a rise behind its terraces and gardens.

John looked at her curiously. 'Do you want to go in? The place is obviously visited a good deal . . .' There were groups of tourists with cameras wandering in the gardens. Several of them were looking out from various heights of terrace.

'I don't know. I'm beginning to imagine it already as somewhere different, somewhere I never knew,' said Flora.

'Don't go in if it's too painful,' he said. He was a kind man.

They had not come by way of the lake side, and now she said: 'I don't think I could bear to see if the boathouse is still there, but the house – it was here long before Xavier – and it will be here long after we are all gone.'

After her marriage she had from time to time corresponded with and occasionally seen Solange Duvallier. The last time she had seen her had been when Solange had visited England in the early 1960s when Flora was expecting her first baby. She and the French girl had not talked about Xavier then, and afterwards their exchanges had been only on the level of Christmas or New Year messages. Solange was not in any way present to her mind as they stood looking at the notice and as a long black car passed them, making them draw in further to the space in front of the gate.

Flora turned to look at the road as another black car with black streamers came slowly by. The two cars in procession seemed to be winding round the lake to the cemetery. At the window of the second car was a young woman, and for a split second Flora saw someone she knew who yet also seemed to be someone else, quite who that other was she could not have said. She clutched John's arm as this second car disappeared in a stately manner along the shore towards the village and its lakeside cemetery.

'It was Solange, I'm sure it was Solange!' She was agitated. 'I wonder whose funeral it is?'

'I expect the locals will know,' replied her husband, pointing to a gardener working on a flower bed just inside the gate. Flora looked at the man. The gardener! Enrico had been his name, hadn't it? Eighteen years ago he had been a young man of about thirty, and this man looked as though he were in his late forties.

'Shall we go in?' asked John patiently. For answer, Flora took his arm and walked to the part of the great gate where a little door was open at the side. Beside it was a booth with a woman selling tickets. Flora bought two. 'Expensive!' she said as they walked up the path. As they passed the gardener she went up to him and said in her best Italian that now seemed strange on her lips: 'Excuse me – could you please tell us whose the funeral is? We have just seen two cars pass.'

The gardener stood up and mopped his forehead. 'Why, the Signora Rouart's. She was ninety—'

'Edwige Rouart?'

'You knew her, Signora?'

'Yes – many years ago – you won't remember me – I stayed here in the summer—'

'Oh yes? Sorry, I don't remember . . . .'

'There have been many changes here?' Flora asked cautiously.

'Everything changed when the government bought us all up!' he replied.

'Is Signor Ludovic still alive?'

'Sure – He lives in Milano now. Excuse me, Signora – I must get on with my replanting.' He bent down once more to his spade and Flora rejoined her husband.

'It is Edwige Rouart's funeral!' she said breathlessly.

'She was the *éminence grise*, wasn't she?' said John who had gathered a few crumbs of information from Flora over the years and remembered that the French girl, Solange, had mentioned her. 'Shall we go in the house?' he asked her now. 'Of course, only if you really want to.'

Flora took a deep breath. 'Yes – I want to look round. Don't worry – I feel nothing at all – it might have all happened to someone else. You'll like it – it's mostly French Empire style,' she added.

For answer he took her arm. He had never been a jealous man and was interested in his wife's past only in so far as it affected her present. Flora was obviously ready now, and willing, to come to terms at last with that past.

'It's a sign,' she said. 'Just imagine! that Edwige Rouart should have died and be having her funeral the very day I come back!' They walked past the fountain and began to climb up the terraces, which were less overgrown now than she remembered. 'I never really belonged here,' she said as they went in at the tall door. A guide was stationed at a table in the hall selling booklets and postcards and an arrow pointed to the left next to a notice with the word *Ascensore*.

'Let's look at the ground floor first,' Flora suggested.

The hall was enormous. There were several statues sculpted in white marble which she could not remember having seen before. Twenty or thirty German tourists were peering at them.

'Don't people usually say when they go back to a place that it looks smaller? Well, this seems a lot bigger than I remember!' she murmured to her husband.

'Perhaps you just didn't notice?' he suggested. 'You were young and probably thinking of something else.'

'Yes, thinking about the family – and Xavier,' she said.

Once more she had said his name. But Xavier's spirit was not there among the tapestries and the pictures and the polished furniture. Only when they got into the small lift cage in order to ascend to see what were billed as maps, souvenirs of the gardens, and the pictorial history of the eighteenth-century Villa, did she feel the hairs rising at the back of her neck. She was sure it was the same cage, the new one Xavier had put in, in 1955. The lift did not pause at the middle floor but went straight up to the top.

Flora approached one of the guides who, as is usual in such places, was sitting on a small chair with his eyes shut. 'Excuse me, but what is there on the floor beneath us?' she said in halting Italian. The guide opened his eyes, looking bewildered. Flora repeated her query.

'Nothing – there is nothing. The rooms are not open to the public,' he replied when he had finally understood her question.

'Shall we go down by the back stairs?' whispered Flora. 'I want to see if the picture of the Violet Lady is still there.' But although John agreed to follow her they found the staircase blocked at the end of the corridor. An inquisitive woman in a long overall approached them. She was probably a cleaner.

'You can only go up and down in the lift,' she stated.

'It must be difficult with so many visitors,' murmured Flora.

'They probably restrict access that way. Not too many people at once,' said John as they moved away. 'Shall I ask permission for you to see the picture?'

'No, no, I've had enough. I feel it may have been removed. Perhaps I'm not meant to see it? I've had enough for today, John. I don't want to see any more. I keep thinking of Edwige. I wonder if she died in her little house? It was up there beyond the waterfall,' she said, pointing in that direction as they came out of the Villa.

They walked through the great gates after a quick look at the tropical gardens, which were much the same as she remembered, and saw one of the big black cars, which had stopped by the lakeside. Flora pulled at her husband's hand saying: 'It's Solange – it must be!'

They crossed the road and saw a man in a uniform at the wheel. For one wild moment Flora thought he looked like a Fascist policeman. The boathouse had been situated down there under the road but the road looked wider now.

'Excuse me – but is Signorina Duvallier with you?' she asked the man politely. John stood by. Flora had better get on with whatever she intended to do.

The man answered just as politely: 'They have gone on to Como, Signora.'

'Then the burial has taken place?'

'Surely. Are you a friend of the family?'

'Yes – I am sorry to have missed the funeral.'

'You can go to the cimeterio tomorrow,' said the man. 'I'm off home now. I was just getting a breeze from the lake.'

'Thank you,' said Flora. She turned to John: 'We could look tomorrow – I must write to Solange,' she said.

After dinner that evening, eaten at a table on the roof terrace of their hotel, they had gone to sit in a café by the lakeside with a coffee each.

'You can just see the Villa from here in daylight,' Flora observed.

'Tell me more now about the whole Villa family,' said John.

Flora considered. 'There's a lot I still don't understand,' she said. 'But I suppose it all began with Ferdinando Leopardi.'

'When was he born?' asked John. 'Always a good idea to get your dates right!'

'I worked it out as being about 1875,' replied Flora, and then she told him all the rest of the story, especially impressing upon him all she knew of Edwige Rouart, whose funeral car they had just seen. The woman's life now seemed to her like something she had read in a book.

'What about the lady you told me they called the Villa after? I noticed it's gone back to being the Villa Carolina,' asked her husband.

'She was a rich American, rather intellectual and artistic. But her husband wasn't faithful to her – or to anyone.'

'I imagine there must have been a sort of *droit de seigneur* atmosphere around the place?'

They sipped their coffee. Then Flora said: 'You know, I don't believe Xavier's childhood was all that unhappy. I can remember feeling rather more sorry for Uncle Ludo the first time I stayed at the Villa. The whole family was messed up by Ferdinando Leopardi.'

'Xavier was a sensitive sort of fellow?'

'Yes.'

'And he loved you. And you loved him. What a sad state of affairs.'

'Yes, it was hopeless. That wasn't *exactly* the reason he

killed himself though. When you find out that you're not the
child of a Resistance hero – or the grandson of a refined
American – but the grandson of an alcoholic prostitute and
the result of the forced union of an ageing roué with his own
daughter, well, it must be quite devastating.'

'The aunt you knew in Paris – Josephine – knew nothing of
the truth whilst Xavier was growing up?'

'I think she was more upset about accepting an American
stepmother. Tante Jo seemed to be a very unworldly woman.
She took to religion. Now I come to think of it though,
perhaps she wasn't as ignorant as we thought – maybe that
was why she became a "font frog" – as the French say.' She
sighed. The moon was now shining over the lake, the scene as
peaceful and unthreatening as Flora could imagine.

'I think I'll have a cognac. I hope I sleep tonight. Being here
brings it all back.'

John beckoned the waiter to their table and ordered two
brandies. As they waited for them to arrive Flora said: 'When
I first met Xavier he didn't seem a disturbed kind of person.
As I said, I'm sure if he'd gone on living in France it would all
have been different. It was the Villa that became the symbol
for him of everything he'd lost – and everything forbidden
and exciting too . . . .'

John said: 'I suppose sex *is* responsible for a lot of suffering.'

'The times have changed though,' said Flora. 'Xavier has
been dead for eighteen years – I can't believe it's so long—'

'He lives on in you – he always has – a bit.'

'We remember our failures much more keenly than our
successes. I felt for a long time that I'd failed him – failed to
love him enough, you know. If only I'd been a little older—'

'It seems to me from what you've told me that he must
always have been impossible, darling. The whole of your
Villa story is one of failure all round, I'd say.'

278

'Edwige once said to me that Paulina was the only woman who didn't go on being a victim of Ferdinando – because she put herself first and scarpered. I suppose I put myself first in the end too.'

'You never felt you really belonged there, did you?'

'No, but if I could have got Xavier away from the place he could have been happy.'

She remembered that she had tried that in Menton, and it hadn't altered Xavier's priorities. Even now the recollection was painful.

'The family story sounds like a late nineteenth-century Italian opera – the one where someone smells violets and dies – didn't that piece have something to do with Gabriele d'Annunzio?'

'I never knew of an opera where violets killed the person who smelled them! – you still think the whole psychological mess could have been tidied up by everyone using a little more common sense? Poor Xavier might have been quite normal and happy if people hadn't behaved in such an operatic fashion? But melodrama is a fact of life – especially in Italy, not only in opera—'

'Strange that we English have always carried on a love affair with the place.'

'*We* ought to take more holidays here soon, once the children are off on their own devices,' said Flora. 'I want to visit Mantua and Cremona – even Parma!'

'Padua and Bologna and Ferrara . . .?' added John.

'You're not jealous of my past, are you?' she asked after a pause.

'One of my rules is not to be jealous of the dead because the dead always win,' he said, and she knew he was only half joking.

Shortly after that, they went up to bed.

ii

Paris

1979

Flora did write to Solange and sent the letter to the last address in Paris she had known for her. If there was no reply, she would write to the Villa. Surely they would know where Ludovic Leopardi lived, and he would know his niece's whereabouts.

This was not in the end necessary for she received a reply to her letter about a month later.

Dear Flora,
I write in English so you can see how well it has come along! It is ages since you last wrote to me but I apologize that I did not reply then. It was a difficult time for me. I was studying hard for my law exams and had problems with my love life. All that is now settled!

I am so pleased you wrote to me and sorry that you missed seeing us in Como. How strange that you were there the very day of Madame Rouart's funeral! I would love to see you in Paris – and the children too one day – but I have no plans at present for coming to England since Mother is not well and I have to look after her.

The funeral was a quiet affair though several of her neighbours came and I hired two cars so we should look respectable. Her house is up for sale and I often wonder whether to buy it. Mother does not care for Italy though and prefers to stay here where the hospitals and the pension schemes are better. I am now a partner in a law firm and am enjoying the work. Since you ask, no, I am not married nor ever likely to be.

Please keep in touch and when you do come to Paris next, promise to come and see us.

Your sincere friend,
Solange Duvallier

The two were to correspond quite enthusiastically for a year or two but it was not until Flora's son Richard was sixteen, in 1979, that Flora managed to get away alone. For various reasons she had been obliged to put off the visit. The children had wanted to go ski-ing and then John had a sabbatical and they went to the States, and her own work, which she had taken up again once the children were at school, was more and more time-consuming. She had retrained in the teaching of English as a foreign language (shades of her tutoring Solange years ago), and enjoyed her work, which was ever more in demand. Everybody wanted – or needed – to speak English now.

She decided to see Paris again by herself. It would be thirty years since her student days there, when Xavier Leopardi had first burst upon her horizon.

The visit was settled by a letter from Solange telling her of Tante Jo's death. She had been ill for a long time, Flora knew, her illness being one of the reasons for Solange's delay in coming to London, but Solange now wanted her to come to

Paris, though Flora insisted she wanted to stay in an hotel, not be given hospitality. Solange was a busy woman.

Dear Flora,
I am delighted you are coming at last. I have something very interesting to tell you. Come at your 'half-term' as you say. Telephone as soon as you are ready to come round to me. Amitiés affectueuses – Solange.

Flora chose deliberately not to stay too close to her old haunts in Paris, yet still in the sixième and near enough to them to know her way round. It had snowed the day before her arrival and from her little hotel near the Luxembourg Gardens she looked out on the familiar park, covered at present in white icing. It was very cold. She did not remember ever having been in Paris when it was snowing. When she heard the familiar bells of Saint Sulpice ring the angelus, all seemed familiar, as if at any moment now she might meet Xavier on a bench in the snowy gardens or in one of the brightly lit cafés on the Boulevard St Germain.

Before meeting Solange on this short solitary holiday, she would begin by going to the places she remembered from long ago. She'd be ready then, would have had time to practise short conversations in French with waiters and hotel staff and shopkeepers, for she feared her idiomatic French was a little rusty.

With no Xavier, and no husband for the time being, and as yet no Solange, Flora felt strangely liberated. The feeling wouldn't last for ever but she would savour it for as long as it lasted.

She walked the next morning in narrow quiet streets, whose pavements were now host to illegally parked cars, half on, half off the street. Many of the Parisian friends whom she had kept up with at different times during the last thirty years no longer lived here. Before she arrived at the new apartment block where once had stood the *Foyer Accueil*, she had known that she would not see the high black *porte cochère* nor the little extra door in the wall, and that the courtyard and the tree and the seventeenth-century house would have gone. But the rest of the street had changed little and she half expected to see the blue-robed nuns approaching her. She walked back to the noisy boulevard where now the tall Montparnasse Tower brooded over the ghost of the former station forecourt.

She would retrace from here her walk to the lycée; it wouldn't take more than twenty minutes.

She could not at first understand what it was that had changed, but then she realized that the noise of constant traffic in her ears was there to remind her that here as in London the car had taken over. The walk of long ago had been peaceful and almost silent.

Were the trees the same ones she used to pass? Were even some of the passers-by the same? Those in early middle age who scurried by now would have been children younger than herself then. The shabby old café at the corner where the men had downed their *marcs* had received a face lift; the *Impasse* had gained an ivy-covered wall at its dead end.

On the other side of the road, just before the Boulevard des Invalides became grander and broader, the great church of François Xavier came into sight and she stood stock still for a moment. Silly that its very name brought Xavier back more than all she had seen up till now.

But Paris was changed, even if they still called it Paris.

Was she still the same Flora?

She thought: Love, Time, Change, Death and Loss. All realities, except for time, which was true only subjectively? . . . they had talked about those things in the philo class at the lycée. They hadn't analyzed the power of the past over the present though.

The lycée buildings appeared to be just the same, though the great door for pupils that led into the paved courtyard was shut and she could not see whether the inside had changed. It was half-term; she would not go in today. A few flakes of snow began to fall and she pulled up her collar and waited a moment – for what? – before she turned and began to walk back, a little more quickly this time.

On the rue de Sèvres she went into a café for a pot of tea, sat down at a table and took out an old copy of a magazine she used to read when she was eighteen and which she had bought at a second hand book shop on the rue du Cherche-Midi.

She read:

The past we truly remember is the past that ran like a hidden river underneath the days we lived, a river whose reflections we may catch sight of for a few magical moments, many years after the waters on which they were carried have ceased to flow . . . .

Must she now add memory to those other realities? The memory of a love that might suddenly annihilate time? But you could not retrieve a memory just when you wanted. A memory that had nothing to do with words could not even be expressed in them: the sudden sighting of the angle of a chin, a wrist; the inflection of a long-gone voice . . . . Her memory of Xavier could not now be changed, but he was more present to her here in Paris than he had been in the place where he had met death.

She ate her dinner alone in a small, pleasant, new-fangled restaurant near her hotel. There seemed a good many of these small restaurants in the district now, most with fancy chi-chi names.

As she ate, she thought again about change. Paris was still changing, had changed more in the last ten years than during the first twenty that had followed her student life here. It was more American now, with new fast-food cafés and young students eating their dinners on the hoof. The smells were less distinctive too: fewer whiffs of garlic or eau-de-cologne on the Métro. Gauloises were still around, but somehow less pungent. The old loves – Edith Piaf and Colette and *Les Enfants du Paradis* – had become history.

She would telephone Solange next morning. After that, there might be still time for a visit to the Comédie Française or to a new film before she had to go home. She remembered Xavier's love of the cinema. He should have stayed here, in Paris, she thought again.

It was no longer painful, though it was sad, to think of him. She no longer needed to forget him, and no longer felt she had failed him.

Her husband was a rationalist and a down-to-earth sort of man. He loved her and she loved him, with a different kind of love from the love she had once felt for Xavier Leopardi. She might not always be ecstatically happy but she thought she was as happy as any married romantic might ever be, with just enough of what John called common sense to keep her head above water.

She remembered how on that boat journey to Como, on the afternoon she had seen Xavier for the last time, she had been suddenly visited with an urge to jump overboard, to let herself be pulled down into the depths of the deepest lake in Italy. That memory had been repressed ever since but now rose to the surface. She greeted it, knowing that when, long ago, something had made her decide not to jump, she had already chosen life. The hard part had been afterwards.

An American at a table opposite smiled at her and she smiled back at him.

*

She woke in the night in the unfamiliar room, thinking about her children. They might not necessarily have inherited their nature from either of their parents: in any case the experiences of their childhood would already have been decisive. In these matters, she had done her best. Xavier had not necessarily inherited his nature either; it was only his childhood mixed with his heredity that had led him towards the problematic nature of his relations with women.

In the morning when she awoke again to ordinary existence and breakfast, the soft, white covering of snow was deadening all sounds, allowing people if they wished to inhabit a temporal and possibly spiritual No Man's Land.

Her first feelings for Xavier, released from the past, were now sharply present. As she ate her croissants and drank her coffee and prepared what she was going to say to Solange, she was overcome by those strong feelings from the past. Now that she was back here, in Paris, alone, she didn't need music or perfume to remember them.

She would take a bus part of the way to Solange's flat, which was not far away from where Tante Josephine had lived with Xavier and Solange thirty years ago. She could always take a taxi back the whole way. She put on her new boots and her long black coat, and in case it snowed again took an umbrella.

The bus deposited her on the Boulevard du Montparnasse and she walked the rest of the way, although it was not a part of Paris she was very fond of. The boulevard still drew a firm line in her mind between home ground and foreign parts just as it had thirty years earlier. The only time she remembered coming in this direction before she met Xavier was on one foggy night when she had tried to find the boys' lycée, where it was reported there was to be a party at which girl students would be welcome. She had never found the party, but remembered stopping at a news-stand where a jolly man had laughed when she had asked for *Le Monde*. 'Not going to read *that* are you?' he had said.

Today she walked in the whiteness and the cold. The pavements were sepia-coloured only where they were well-trodden. Women were walking past quickly from their marketing, heads down, a longing for home urgent in their demeanour. She soon found the apartment block, built quite recently, with an un-French appearance, on a featureless street that was much wider than those of the sixième. There had been more development here, she supposed, after the building of the Montparnasse Folly – or rather Tower. But not far away there was the faithful old rue Vaugirard, the longest street in Paris, that started near the Luxembourg Gardens and ended up even further along in the fifteenth arondissement.

Solange's voice, a little deeper than Flora remembered, answered the apartment phone in the lobby and she went up in a rapidly ascending lift to the fourth floor.

Solange looked a little shy, though her welcome was warm.

'I'm so pleased you could come – I've been wanting to see you for so long!' she said, and led Flora into a pleasant modern sitting-room leading straight off from the hall. It had a high bookshelf covering one whole wall, some etchings of the Left Bank on the opposite side. The smell of cooking was wafting through from the kitchen, though the door was shut. The bedroom where Flora left her coat and boots had a double bed on which a small cat was snoozing.

Solange provided slippers, settled her in a comfortable chair in the sitting-room and then offered either whisky or an aperitif. Flora chose a vermouth and soda. It was warm in the flat; a cold pewter-grey sky could be seen through the high modern plate-glass window.

It was all very domestic and a far cry from the Villa, she

thought. Perhaps they would not talk about the past at all. Solange busied herself in the kitchen and then came back to Flora, a whisky in her own hand. But, after lifting her glass with an *a ta santé!* Solange said immediately:

'I can't tell you now pleasant it is to see someone from the old days. Since Mother died and I moved here I seem to have been living in a different time as well as a different place. Work's hectic of course – I'm enjoying my first break since Christmas – since the end of December I've even been working week-ends.'

'I never imagined you'd become an *avocat*, Solange!'

'No – if we'd had one in the family a bit earlier it might have done some good!'

'I don't suppose you could have changed anything though.'

'No, I don't imagine it was a lack of knowledge of the law that killed my poor cousin.'

'Rather it was matters which laws were made to prevent,' said Flora. 'Do you deal with family cases?'

'Not so much now, but one hears of all kinds of awful things that happen in families – especially to women, you know, that's what I meant.'

'Laws couldn't have prevented whatever Xavier saw as a child.'

'Did you feel guilty when he died?'

'I blamed myself for insisting he met his mother, once Edwige had told me she was still alive.'

'I know most of what happened, I think. We've had cases where a child has been badly abused when it was young, and loved the abuser. Not surprisingly when he or she grows up he finds intense pleasure is available to him or her only in a certain way. Not that that was exactly what happened to Xavier – but he was a sensitive person and saw things he should not have seen. Desire is irrational,' said Solange.

'You understand the background then. I'm relieved.' Flora
wondered how Solange had guessed the rest.

'I'm glad you say that,' said Solange, 'because as a matter
of fact – I wasn't sure whether to tell you – but I don't myself
find men sexually desirable. I'm a Lesbian, or whatever they
call us now. I didn't choose to be one. I didn't even know I
was one until I was about twenty-five, and I'm thirty-eight
now. I shall never marry, so the curse of the Leopardis won't
be carried on by me!'

'Don't you ever think – when we know that some people
can achieve sexual pleasure only in a certain way or with a
certain kind of person – that God – or Nature – made sexual
pleasure too overwhelming?'

'Yes, I do. Think how terrible for a person to find he – it's
usually a "he" isn't it? – can't get pleasure except by killing
someone or seducing a child . . . then we are told we have free
will! But child molesters are often, not always, molested
themselves as children. Not all abused children go on to
molest of course. My poor cousin – or should I say uncle –
Xavier's problems were not quite as bad as that, I assume.
Uncle Ludo was never very specific, but I take it that sex for
Xavier was a destructive force?'

Flora had never heard Solange talk so much. It was odd talking so intimately about Xavier with a member of his family.

'Did Xavier ever tell you that my father was gay?' asked
Solange.

'Yes, he did as a matter of fact. Did you know that your
uncle Ludovic was that way inclined too?'

'I guessed so. My goodness, the whole family had problems! I don't think *Maman* did though – she was quite well-
balanced, I think.'

'Religion helped her, didn't it?'

'True. My poor mother! I think she suffered from not being
beautiful.'

'She was always kind to me, you know.'

'She was a kind woman. I wish I were more like her in that way.'

'You know,' ventured Flora, 'after I caught sight of you near the Villa the summer Edwige Rouart died, something kept niggling at me. At first when I saw you at the car window – it was only a glimpse – you seemed like someone else – I wondered whether I was seeing Xavier in you – you were his niece, if not his cousin!'

'I think I must tell you a long story,' said Solange. 'You'll stay for a light lunch – just some salad and fish?'

'That would be lovely, but I hope it's what you were going to eat yourself anyway? I didn't want to make work for you!'

'Oh you English! I always make a decent lunch – I don't eat so much in the evening. Will you have another vermouth? Bring it in to the kitchen while I cook. It won't take a minute – everything's prepared.'

Flora accepted another aperitif and followed Solange in to her small but well-ordered kitchen.

Some time later, after they had eaten a delicious lunch of grilled trout and tiny carrots glazed with butter, salad tossed in a light herby dressing and generous slices of a fragrant *tarte aux abricots* they went back to the sitting-room with cups of strong black coffee. Solange produced a packet of Gauloises and offered one to Flora.

'Absolutely forbidden!' said Flora with a guilty smile, taking one nevertheless. She plumped down in an armchair and stretched out, relaxed, her feet on a footstool, and puffed at the pungent weed.

'You know,' said Solange, 'I've something else important to tell you today.'

She paused and cleared her throat, lit a cigarette nervously and sat down opposite Flora in the other armchair. Flora waited.

Solange looked very serious. Flora hoped she was not going to say that as a potential Lesbian, she'd been in love with her when she was fourteen – which on reflection, might have been so, but was obviously not so any longer.

No, it was to be something quite other.

'You remember when Madame Rouart died in 1975?'

'Yes?'

'Well, after she died, Mother had a – surprise. More than that. A shock, I suppose.'

Flora waited, her heart jumping up and down. Solange was now looking into the distance, not at her. Then she turned to Flora again.

'She left a will, you see. I wasn't allowed to see it at the time. Mother read it and told me she'd been left the precious necklace – you know – the one old Leopardi left Edwige?'

'Yes, I remember.'

'But mother was very secretive about the whole thing. Finally – to shut me up, I think, she said that the necklace would be mine when she died herself. I really didn't care for it. I don't wear much jewellery, as you know.'

Flora waited, sure there was more to come.

There was. Solange turned to her and said: 'Edwige Rouart told her something else in a letter attached to the will. Mother showed the letter to me only just before she died last year . . . .'

'Yes? What?'

But Solange was musing again, seemed to find it hard to come to the point. 'She still loved him, you see. I'm sure she did – so she wouldn't leave him. She'd help him as far as she could.'

'You mean during the war? I'd guessed Edwige always loved Ferdinando. I'm sure *she'd* never betray him, though

Xavier told me she hated the Republichini – Mussolini's Fascists. Some of them even lived in the Villa in 1943.'

'Of course she didn't betray him – but I think she colluded with him in his end. She knew that if it came to it Ferdinando would kill himself – and she wouldn't try to stop him. But what if Victoire had betrayed where he was to the socialists? She could have done! In revenge.'

'You don't *know* – you're only guessing?'

'True.'

'Victoire did go with German officers before she went out with GIs. I believe she was a "hostess" in 1945 with the Allies. So was Cécile Agostini. I have a feeling about *her* child, Mirella, that her father was a Nazi. But Edwige wouldn't collude with anyone but old Ferdy.'

'I think she decided she wouldn't try to save him, wouldn't try to hide him. She may still have loved him – but she'd have hardened her heart years before if she'd found out he had known Victoire was his daughter, or even known that his son Paul was in love with Victoire, and that he'd gone ahead anyway and seduced her! When she spoke to me about Ferdinando I knew she must once have loved him passionately. Even though she didn't approve of what he did – and was probably jealous. She stayed with him, didn't she? When she could have gone back to France in 1939 with your mother?'

'She told you about his rescuing her from the brothel?'

'Yes, how did *you* know about that?'

'All in this long missive along with the will. Mother never mentioned it until she knew she was dying herself. It was when she handed over the necklace to me that she gave me the letter to read and told me she'd thought of burning it, but Edwige had made her promise she would tell me the truth. I think she thought of it as a sacred promise. It was highly embarrassing for her, you may imagine. When I tell you . . . .' She stopped.

Flora said gently: 'I think Edwige told me most of the facts about her love and life with Ferdinando. But there's something else, isn't there?'

'Do you still not understand? Can't you guess?' Solange sounded quite impatient but she was half smiling. 'I'm not talking about the war or the family in general but about something much, much further away in time.' Suddenly Solange stood up. Flora stared at her and then cried: 'You! It was Edwige you looked like in the car!'

Solange went to the window and said in a quiet voice without turning round:

'It was all in the letter with the will. Mother knew for three years before she died without telling me. When she told me last year, it was a shock, of course. Edwige Rouart had always wanted to keep my mother ignorant and innocent – she knew how to keep her so—'

'Ignorant of what?'

'That she – Edwige Rouart – was her mother! Edwige Rouart was my grandmother, Flora! Your Xavier's Tante Jo was the child of Edwige and Ferdinando, not of his first wife Feodora – who conveniently died around the time my mother was born. And Ferdy swore her to secrecy.'

Flora looked at Solange open-mouthed. Then she said: 'When you say "conveniently" you mean she didn't die after having a baby? Or of a "galloping consumption"?'

'We shall never know. The dates were all in the will – and all the circumstances – if we are to believe her.'

'I do believe her about her being Josephine's – your mother's mother – I see that now. How blind I was! You even look like her! And Josephine was always more French than Italian, I always thought. But how did Edwige keep up the deception all those years?'

'We ought to ask ourselves: why did she need to keep it up?'

'Because there may have been something fishy about Feodora's death?'

'Edwige – the nanny – knew all that had happened, whatever it was. She could hold it over Ferdinando's head in exchange for allowing everyone to think that Josephine was the child of his dead wife.' Solange turned round and came back to her chair, adding, 'Have I given you a shock?'

'A surprise, but not a shock, now I come to think about it. I thought I knew all the secrets of the Villa – but I didn't! Tell me what you think really happened.'

'Well, what she wrote in the letter was quite clear-cut. She said she had succumbed – she used that word – to her employer at the Villa when she was twenty years old. In the first year of her working there he left her alone and she got on well with Feodora who, she said, had just had a miscarriage. She became pregnant again pretty quickly. I think this was just at the time when my grandfather began to make up to Edwige, I suppose because he'd been told not to make love to his wife when she was pregnant in case she miscarried again. She was always said to be delicate and she'd been told not to have another baby. Edwige must have become pregnant not long after Feodora's third pregnancy. Well, Edwige said that Feodora's baby was a still-born girl, and Feodora died two months later, apparently of complications to do with the birth. But in the meantime Edwige had given birth to her own baby! You know how isolated from the village the Villa was even in our day? I think they bribed the servants – who must have known the live baby, Josephine, was Edwige's baby – to say that she was Feodora's baby who had not been still-born at all but whose mother had then died soon after.'

'I don't suppose we'll ever know for sure? What more did she say in the letter?'

'She said—' and Solange looked up and quoted something she seemed almost to know by heart: "I loved Ferdinando

Leopardi and bore his child in the summer of 1906 when I was twenty-one. Feodora Leopardi died the same week as my baby was born. She had already given birth to a dead baby, a girl. Ferdinando was terrified his in-laws would cut off his allowance if they discovered he'd been carrying on with me, the nursemaid – they were Russian Orthodox and very religious – so I agreed to say that her baby had not died and to pretend that my baby was hers."

'So he had five women pregnant with his children, not four – you knew about Angelica?'

'Yes, but I expect there may have been more, you know. I was never sure about Victoire's mother, but my grandmother – I suppose I may call her that now – mentioned it again in this letter. Mother made me burn it when I'd read it.'

'It must have shocked your mother. Poor Tante Jo! Not the daughter of a Russian aristocrat but of a French ex-poule!'

'Grandmother wanted my mother kept ignorant, as I said – and Mother was by nature a very innocent sort of person.'

'I know—'

'So Edwige was pleased when Mother caught religion. I think it was a shame that my grandfather never liked Mother, but I suppose she reminded him all too forcibly of his past sins. Edwige stayed on, I think, because he relied on her.'

'Do you think she procured women for him? I mean – I didn't want to believe it, but it seems likely?'

'I don't know, Flora. She certainly must have had a hold on him. She wrote: "I would have been a good wife to him but he didn't want to marry me. He decided to marry the American woman when my daughter was two years old. I wanted domestic love. Strange for a *poule*, I know, but that was what I wanted. Being a housekeeper was the next best thing. I was able to help Angelica Rienzi when the same thing happened to her that happened to me. It was the year after Paul was born to Paulina that Angelica became pregnant and I got her away to another job. I never knew what happened to the child until after Victoire came looking for work and I took her on". Then she confessed that her mother had once worked for the old man.'

'So Edwige didn't know at first who Victoire was?'

'I think she didn't realize at first, but she'd warned her against Ferdinando in any case, not realizing the new servant was his own daughter! If she'd known that at first I feel sure she'd have sent her packing. It must have been a thunderbolt when she discovered who Victoire was. She was horrified when she discovered that Paul loved the girl, and she was determined that Paul should not marry his half-sister. She was jealous of Paulina, as you might imagine, but she tried to persuade her to intervene to prevent her son from marrying Victoire. Paulina didn't believe at first that her husband had been carrying on with Victoire. She thought Edwige was just jealous of Victoire as yet another of his mistresses and because she had always wanted to marry Ferdinando herself, which was true. But Edwige didn't tell Paulina that the servant he'd already seduced – and made pregnant – was his own daughter. Paulina must have been told just that Paul wanted to marry his father's mistress. She might have thought at first that Edwige was just getting her own back on a rival – I'm sure she did know that my grandmother had been her husband's mistress. But in the end she must have realized it was the truth.'

'And Paulina would have told her son later who would then confront his wife and *then* she'd break down and tell him their son Xavier wasn't his – still not knowing herself that Ferdy was her own father? Her mother only told her years later. What else did Edwige say?'

Flora was looking at Solange intently as she spoke. It was so obvious when you knew that she was like her grandmother. She possibly resembled her more in character too. Josephine had not been at all like her mother.

'Well, she ended: "You were the child of love, Josephine. I loved Ferdinando when he was a young man. You must solemnly promise to tell your daughter Solange that she is my granddaughter and tell her she has my blessing".'

'How sad that she couldn't tell you before.'

'I suppose that as she'd kept her secret so long she could not face my mother with it directly. I did see her once or twice looking at me rather carefully at the Villa.'

'Yes, I remember her saying you were a polite child, more French than Italian!'

'She had a high opinion of the French.'

'So it's true what you said – she really was another of his victims.'

'Only in the sense that she fell in love with him, but I think he must have respected her in the end.'

'She certainly appeared to be in charge when I first went to the Villa. I still wonder how much of the goings-on before the war she aided and abetted him with.'

'We'll never know now. What would she have thought of me, Flora, if she'd known I couldn't feel attracted to men?' Solange looked troubled.

'I think she might have been relieved, knowing how one man ruined so many lives. She saved her daughter from her past. I couldn't save Xavier from his.'

'When I once said to you I'd like to have a child it's because I'd like to carry on Edwige, not the Leopardis, for it all not to come to an end. It's a great pity, isn't it?'

'Yes, but the whole mess was the old man's doing – I wonder what I'd have thought of him if I'd ever met him.'

'I'd have shot him, I think!' exclaimed Solange. 'Serve him right what happened to him after the war.'

'He wouldn't have liked either you or me,' said Flora, 'I've never been attracted to that sort of *macho* man—'

'You found Xavier physically attractive though?'

'Xavier was a sensitive person – he had to wrench his personality around when he decided to be more "brutal".'

'You might have been like other women and found Ferdinando attractive, *quand même*? He caught lots of women in his net.'

'I suppose I might – thank God I never met him. Your grandfather got the women he wanted through seduction – what nowadays one might call rape! Oh, I'd have married Xavier if I'd thought I could make him happy – but—'

'My cousin saw women either as virtuous wives or wicked ladies?'

'Yes – either he felt degraded, or saw himself as the instrument of someone else's degradation.'

'Yet you could have stayed with him – by altering your own needs – I suspect many women do.'

'I couldn't rescue him from himself. He couldn't change. His life had become static.'

'Would you have wanted his child?'

'Yes – he had so many good qualities – he was very intelligent for one thing, but he might have found it difficult to deal with a son – and he'd have wanted him brought up at the Villa. Also, I suppose I was scared that things would eventually go wrong – and that's no way to begin a marriage.'

'I'm thirsty,' said Solange after a pause – 'Let us have a cup of your English tea that cheers.'

'Yes,' agreed Flora. 'I think we need a calming beverage.' She got up and followed her hostess into the kitchen. 'You know what I think your grandmother Edwige would have done in the matter of Xavier's father if she'd been able to?'

'Poor Grandma couldn't work miracles!'

'No, but I think she would have told him what his duty was.'

'If Paul had been more of a man he would have stayed and had it out with his father – and loved the child anyway. But he was too shocked and hurt. Italy wasn't the place for him.'

'Nor for Xavier – even if a false memory of his mother hadn't come surging up out of the past—'

'Paul made up for any moral cowardice in the war,' said Solange.

They stayed in the kitchen, sipping the Earl Grey that Solange had bought specially for Flora. Then Flora asked permission to take a few photographs of her old friend. Solange complied and brought in a neighbour from the flat next door to take a picture of them both.

'For the record!' she said. 'All women together!'

'I forgot to give you my little presents,' said Flora before she left in a taxi. It was late by then, and snowing.

'One present is in memory of the Villa, and another in memory of Edwige – though I didn't know exactly why I'd brought it,' she said.

Solange unwrapped a Lalique bottle full of extract of essence of Parma violets, and a photograph taken in 1955 of herself on the Villa terrace with, clearly visible behind her, the figure of Edwige Rouart pausing at a door.

Flora had also brought *The Life and Lyrics of Gabriele d'Annunzio* with her to Paris but decided not to give it to Solange. As she did not want to keep the book she sold it to a second-hand bookshop near her hotel for a goodly sum.

Paris,
Thursday

Dearest John,
You will have received yesterday's letter by now, I hope, with Solange's amazing revelation.

Last week you asked me whether the past still exercised its power over me. Yes, I suppose so, but only in my imagination, and we can't live permanently in our imaginations, can we? To exorcise the past I think some people have to recreate it imaginatively – I mean write about it, or paint it.

We can never go back to what we were when we were young, but we are what we are because of choices we made then. A solemn thought. A good thing the young don't realize how much hangs on their early decisions. We never stay in one place unless we say good-bye to ourselves, as poor Xavier did. I remember Xavier now without too much pain or grief or guilt. Strangely, as I spoke to Solange I felt the ravages of future time, future loss.

If I had stayed with Xavier – and at one time the temptation was great to throw caution and common-sense to the winds – I'd have become a fossilized toy.

Like Humpty Dumpty, nobody could have put Xavier together again. He was spoiled perhaps from the day he was born, but his heredity wouldn't have mattered if he had not become fixated on his memory of the Violet Rooms.

Solange was saying that all the people who once lived or worked at the Villa Violetta are dead now except for Enrico the gardener, and perhaps Delphine, though nobody has heard from her for years. She told me that Uncle Ludo died last year. He was always kind to me.

Solange, who never belonged at the Villa, is apparently quite well-known as a feminist over here! She's grown into a strong woman, not unlike her grandmother. She agreed with me that life must be a compromise if it is to continue at all. I never thought I would be able to write that with any conviction!

Memory is always subjective, and I remember my feelings better than I remember their object. My feelings were all mixed up with being young, and with what I saw as the glamour of Paris – and then of Italy. I suppose they were feelings shared by many other young people after the war. Xavier was my growing-up. It's strange to write that, and to know that neither he nor my youth will ever come back, though the Villa – and

Paris – remain.

Time, death, loss. Is that what all our lives are about? I wish I believed in an after-life and could pray for departed shades in a church that believes they still exist somewhere. But that might be another self-indulgence.

I have been enjoying myself here in my old haunts! These sudden sharp involuntary memories keep returning, and then the years roll away. But only for a few moments – and only so long as I don't try too hard to recall them. Thank you for bearing with my introspection.

I shall return to London on Friday as I promised.

Look after yourself till then!

Lots of love to Dickie and Kate,
Your loving
Flora

EPILOGUE
1992

In summer, the deep lake usually lies dark blue, calm and unruffled.

The Villa still stands by the lake and is visited regularly by tourists of all nationalities.

In the spring, gardeners both amateur and professional come to gape at the great plantations that have been much improved and even extended. Slopes of profusely blossoming azaleas and rhododendrons blaze away, and there are mysterious green paths by giant ferns, leading one knows not where.

There are many acres of trees: cedars of Lebanon, pines of many varieties, oaks, willows, beeches, cacti, palms, orange trees, lemon trees, grapefruit trees and kumquats, pomegranates, bananas . . . . Even trees from Australia, eucalyptus and casuarinas. There are tea-plants too, and camellias, magnolias, hibiscus, myrtle, jasmine and orchids . . .

The gardening tourists and the ordinary ones lean over the balustrades to gaze down on the great fountain. They are all looking forward to returning to their hotels for meals of lake fish and local wine.

Later in the year they will enjoy wild strawberries and

myrtle berries, will pour litres of San Pellegrino down their
thirsty throats and take lumps of *grana* home to grate over
food they will try to cook in the Italian way.

Naturally, they will have taken many photographs of the
lake, and the gardens – and of themselves – standing in front
of 'that heavenly Villa Carolina'.

The pictures are for their future delectation, and also,
perhaps, to help along the processes of Memory.